"As you'd expect with Marianne, the writing is full of twists and turns, the characters jump out of the pages and you can see each combative maneuver in your mind's eye with amazing HD clarity."
Falcata Times

"There is a definite power to Marianne's prose, an underlying current that draws you in while you enjoy the story. These are skills to place her in the leagues of Williams and even Zahn and Brin."
Aurealis Express

"Compelling, intriguing, and utterly fantastic, if you haven't read it I highly suggest you do. One of my favourite books this year."
Cotton Candy Reviews

"Gorgeous twists… dazzling set pieces that leave you breathless for more…"
Terra Incognita

"This is terrific stuff: beautifully written, majestic, cunning, disquieting."
Orb Magazine

"You're in for an engaging read."
Mysterious Galaxy

"An action-packed, roller coaster ride… and a lot of fun."
The Australian

BY THE SAME AUTHOR

MARIANNE DE PIERRES

PEACEMAKER

ANGRY
ROBOT

ANGRY ROBOT
A member of the Osprey Group

Lace Market House,
54-56 High Pavement,
Nottingham
NG1 1HW
UK

Angry Robot/Osprey Publishing
PO Box 3985
New York
NY 10185-3985
USA

www.angryrobotbooks.com
Park life

An Angry Robot paperback original 2014

Copyright © Marianne de Pierres 2014

Cover by Joey HiFi
Set in Meridien and Press Style Serif by Argh! Oxford

Distributed in the United States by Random House, Inc., New York.

ISBN 978 0 85766 418 1
Ebook ISBN 978 0 85766 419 8

Printed in the United States of America

9 8 7 6 5 4 3 2 1

To Dad. Thanks for your love of pulp westerns and all those conversations about the stars. I miss you.

To Mum. Thanks for your sense of fun. I miss you.

To Ros Petelin for being the best mentor and friend when things got tough.

ONE

Gold faded to purple and then a dying red. Sunset from the butte.

In my mind it was called a tabletop, but the company insisted on butte because the tourists liked the name. It fitted with the Wild West park theme.

Visit the Wild West in the heart of a Southern Hemisphere super-city. Just plain weird.

But the park wall, the haze of city pollution floating in, and the glare of the dying sun hid the city skyline. Right at this moment I could believe that my beloved piece of outback was more than a mere oasis in a sprawling conurbation.

Conurbation. I'd learnt that word from Dad.

He liked to use words that others had forgotten, remind us all of the old ways. That's why he raised me to love the land and hate the wankers who ruined it. Dad was the reason I preferred sunsets alone in the park to the city bars. The reason I was a ranger and not a corporate hellcat.

Dad was the reason for everything, really.

If I could, I'd *live* in the park, but the company scientists deemed it too environmentally fragile to handle the impact of permanent residents. Tourists did enough damage.

And we had to have tourists.

So instead, at the end of each work day, I got to go home to my one-bedroom in the Cloisters multi-rise and stare at the 3D spinifex and iron-red rock photos that hung on my wall. Dad had taken them when he was young, before the city had devoured most all of our countryside.

He spent ten years out there – the real outback – learning to live dry, letting the iron leach into his blood. When he came back, he started the park lobby. He could see the way things were going, knew that we'd already gone further than we should.

And he brought me up to continue the fight.

That was OK. That was good. I believed. And I could handle the indifference of politicians, the political maneuvering of my colleagues, and the crap pay. What I couldn't deal with was being considered not good enough at what I did.

I slid down from my rocky perch and trod carefully, avoiding the fragile desert grass clinging to the foot of the butte.

It was half an hour until dark, and another half hour until I picked up my new co-worker from the airport. Time to shift arse.

My phone rang as I climbed into the saddle and nudged Benny's sides. She loped in the direction of home without guidance from the bridle – we'd done this many times.

"Virgin Jackson," I said into the mouthpiece.

"It's Hunt."

"Yeah, boss?" Bull Hunt hated it when I was casual, which was most always.

"You haven't forgotten have you, Virgin?"

I sighed. "Gate 65, Terminal 21. Tall guy wearing a uniform. His name's Nate."

"Not just Nate, Virgin. *Marshal* Nate Sixkiller. Great fricking grandson of Johnny Sixkiller, the–"

"–greatest Native American lawman in history. Yeah, Bull, I know."

"And don't you go all defensive on me. Nate Sixkiller's good. Maybe the best."

Well, that sure prickled me. "Good for him. But I still don't see why you're spending all this money on bringing him here. Why now? Is there something I don't know?"

Bull hesitated. "Don't push me on this, alright?"

"I just don't get it. One tiny amphetamine bust in the park a week ago and suddenly I'm being lumbered with a hotshot cowboy from the other side of the world. I know my own territory, Bull. Been doing a good job of looking after it. So, what the hell's going on?"

"Something's been flagged at the top levels. I can't talk about it yet but I need you to make him welcome and help him in anyway you can. Am I clear on that?"

I gritted my teeth. "Like a glacier."

Bull Hunt was Superintendent of Park Ecology and an expert fence-sitter. If there was a person alive who could balance the tightrope between politicians, greenies and the tourist and resource industry, it was my boss. But I'd never known him to jump so high over a park arrest, especially one that didn't involve land damage. The two guys I'd stumbled on out by Salt Springs over a week ago had been exchanging a parcel of drugs. It happens. There's lots of space out here. So why the fuss?

"Virgin."

"Yeah, boss."

"Don't talk like that around Sixkiller. You sound like you've never even been to school."

My three university degrees would argue. "Yeah, boss."

I hung up, slipped the phone into my coat pocket and slumped in the saddle. Benny slowed to a trot and I didn't bother to raise for it, letting myself bump around like a sack.

Soon, we were at the windmill and the outcrop of desert palms that hid the water trough and the gate to the stables.

I let Benny drink from the trough, while I slid down and buried my head in her neck. My horse was the most grounding thing in my life, the warmth of her skin and the faint tang of hay that clung to her.

I paid for the real thing, had bales of it flown in from New Zealand every month. It was freaking expensive, but the Land of the Long White Cloud produced a good part of the raw produce that sustained the Southern Hemisphere these days.

When Benny finished drinking, I led her through to the Interchange– several interlocking gates, identity-protected and monitored. Red dirt became cement and a wall rose unexpectedly out of the desert in colours that graded from golden yellow up to sky blue. From this angle, the top of it blocked the sight of even the highest downtown skyscrapers.

I slapped the DNA sampler so the gate would open and led Benny through into the stables.

Totes, the techie, was waiting there, sitting on a stool in front of his monitors, eyes closed, earbuds in his ears, foot tapping, sucking on a USB stick.

I yanked the buds out as I walked past, and he fell off the stool in fright.

"Jeez, Virgin. Don't do that. How many times…"He jumped up, smoothed down his suit and patted his cornrows, searching for stray, out-of-place hairs.

"There's dandruff on your shoulder," I lied, and walked off.

I could hear him fussing behind me, dusting his jacket. Could picture without looking his angular pale face, lips pursed up like a prune.

"Virg-in!" he bitched.

"Just jokin', Totes," I called back.

He chased me down to Benny's stall, where I slipped her bridle off and un-cinched the saddle.

"You're the last one in."He didn't say any more. He didn't have to. I was always the last.

"Sunset's not the same from city. You know that."

"I know that you're spending too long in the desert and not enough time in the real world. Besides, I've got places to go."

I pulled a face at him. "Liar!"Totes had less social life than me.

"Well, you could have at least rung me. I was getting worried," he grumbled.

I slipped my hand in my coat at the mention of my phone. It wasn't there.

I groaned. "Crap. I must've dropped it near the trough. I'll be back in a minute. Get Leecey to rub her down, will you?"

"Leecey's gone home. And you can't go back in there now that it's dark."

"Keep your undies on," I said as I headed to the gate and tickled the ID pad again.

As I stepped back through, the locks clunked closed behind me and I found myself back in the park in near dark and almost dead quiet.

Even though I'd been ranger here for a few years, I was suddenly a little nervous. The sand and rock and palms that I knew so well during the day had taken on an eerie quality.

The company didn't like us "on board" (their expression for being in the park) after dark – something to do with insurance. I always pushed that directive to the limit because I like to see the sunset.

The sun was gone now, though, and I could hear, rather than see, the trickling of the water into the trough.

A dozen or so steps and I'd be close enough to the trough to start feeling around on the ground for my lost phone. Nervousness was replaced by exhilaration. I never got to be on board completely alone. My horse, Benny, was imbedded with recording equipment that sent information back to Totes and then onto the company storage and processing centre, aka the Black Hole.

But right now, I stood alone and unobserved, even by the satellite spies, for the first time.

A desire to disappear and lose myself in the

thousands of hectares gripped me. I knew the land, could maybe survive on the food and water the park would throw up.

But…knowledge of the penalty if I was caught sobered my fantasy. The Federal government hadn't spent billions of dollars on creating the park to suffer squatters. Last I heard, it was a lifetime jail sentence.

Shaking those thoughts down, I stepped toward the sound of trickling water. The damn ball valve was leaking again!

As I bent to fumble with the pump, I felt my phone underfoot. Then another sound attracted my attention – muffled voices from the other side of the semicircle of palms that skirted the Interchange area.

Voices? *Impossible!* I was the last person out of the south-east sector every day. Park scanners and satellite imaging confirmed it, as well as my own visual sweep.

I picked up my phone and crept towards the sound, my boots silent on the sand. There were two of them, arguing, but I couldn't get a handle on the thread.

"…the next wet moon," said one.

"How could you know that?" said the other.

There was a moment of silence. Then one figure raised an object. A strangled cry got me running toward them, hauling my pistol free from my holster.

I barrelled through the line of palms and bellowed, "Stop!"

But the pair had fallen down onto the sand.

I flicked my phone light on and shone it at them. Only one person was there. Blood trickled from a small, deep wound on his neck.

Impossible! There were two!

Keeping the gun cocked, I stepped over, knelt and felt the man's pulse with my phone hand.

Dead. *Shit!*

TWO

Still kneeling, I shone the light around. The other guy couldn't have escaped. I was watching them the whole time.

Nothing.

As I glanced back at the dead guy, a shadow seemed to detach from his neck, and a bird's cry cut through the night, chilling enough to make my muscles clench. Wings beat close to my ear, feathers scraped across my cheek and pain knifed across my neck below my ear.

I clawed at the shadow, or whatever it was and hauled my pistol up. Four shots at point-blank range sent it spinning, but rather than fall to the ground, it seemed to *dissolve*.

I was left staring at empty space.

What the…?

The sting from the wound brought me back. I fumbled in my pocket for a handkerchief and pressed it against the already-slick wound. Involuntary shivers started over me, as if the warm desert air had plummeted in temperature. I shoved my gun in my pocket and rechecked the man for life signs.

Nada.

I knew I should call this in – the Park would want to investigate – but my wound was seeping and I had an overpowering urge to get the hell out of there. The carcass crew would be in before me tomorrow, though, removing any dead fauna, so Totes needed to warn them.

I got to my feet and ran back past the trough to the Interchange gate.

Totes was waiting for me on the other side.

"Jeez, Virgin. Where the hell've you... Oh, crap. What happened?"

"Not sure," I said, pushing him away and heading for the wash station.

He hovered over me as I sloshed my face and neck and examined my neck wound in the mirror. It was small but deep, and hurt as bad as a dozen wasp stings.

"What did it?"

"I don't know. It kinda looked like a crow, but it was dark, and crows don't attack people, especially at night. But I found a dead guy out there past the trough. I'll tell Hunt. Search the sat feed and let the carcass crew not to touch anything."

"What do you mean, a dead g–"

"What's the time? Crap." I cut him off because now I was running late to meet the famous lawman. "I'll call the cops on the way to the airport and I'll tell you about it in the morning. Gotta go."

I ran down the corridor to my office, grabbed a Band-Aid from the first aid kit hanging by its strap from one of the upturned horseshoes adorning my only shelf and left the Interchange station at a run.

• • •

The transition into the city was like a face slap. Red rock, sand, desert palms and space left behind; noise, people and buildings in their place.

Nighttime on the Park Esplanade was fast. The road ringed the entire park circumference and a city eco-chain had birthed to service it. Motels for the tourists, plazas that sandwiched never-closing restaurants, travel agents, net cafe rubbed alongside each other.

The Park had saved our country's tourism industry and the people were grateful. They were also hungry to benefit. We knew how to make a buck Down Under, despite what the international community thought.

Getting a taxi to pull over on the Esplanade was hard; none of them wanted to leave the dense traffic stream and then have to try and reenter it.

I gave up trying to flag one and took the pedestrian underpass to the nearest plaza. The rank there was full of empty cabs, so I jumped in the lead car and told him I had to be at the airport ten minutes ago. Hunt was going to carve me to pieces over this.

Being a Park Road cabby, he didn't spare the juice, but the flyover to the airport was at crawl pace and I got to the International a half hour after Nate Sixkiller's scheduled arrival time.

There was no one at the gate, so I sprinted down to the baggage lounge and found the right conveyer. I would have known him right away despite the fact that he was standing alone by the rent-a-car kiosk, looking pissed.

His hair was seriously straight and dark, dipping below his shoulders and crowned with a Stetson you could tip upside down and take a bath in. He wore jeans and a white-collared, buttoned-up shirt; his build was muscled, heavy and gave the impression of power. I knew some hand-to-hand moves, but Nate Sixkiller had me wondering if I could handle him.

He had a presence, no denying it, and His Presence wasn't happy.

"Marshal Sixkiller?" I said, striding up with my hand outstretched.

We were almost on the same eye level, and he narrowed his without responding to my handshake.

I let my hand drop. "Apologies for being late. I had a… er… problem in the park."

His glance flicked over me, then up to the plaster on my neck. "Thet yer problem?" he asked in a slow drawl.

My hand slipped automatically to the wound. Then I glanced down at my shirt. Blood flecks across my breast. "Sure. Maybe. Look, let's get you back to your apartment first. You must be tired."

His expression stayed stony. "I don't get tired."

"Good for you. But you need to drop your bags off." I turned on my heel and didn't to bother to see if he followed.

The taxi ride back home was quicker. Hunt had rented Sixkiller an apartment in the Cloisters, a floor down from me. I wasn't happy about it, but it made sense if I was going to be his babysitter.

I already had the key and handed it to him when we got to his room. He stood for a moment or so, staring at the door.

"Problem?" I asked after the silent scrutiny started to get uncomfortable.

He exhaled and shook his head, then passed the key over the lock.

I didn't follow him in. "My room is the floor above, number 20-20. Come up when you're settled, or call me, and I'll come down. I'll take you out for a bite."I was hoping to hell he'd say no, but his brow creased.

"Bite? What's thet?"

"Food. It's dinnertime here."

He nodded slowly. "I could do with *a bite*. I'll be in the foyer in thirty minutes."

Damn. Not only had he accepted, but he was calling the order of things. I'd cut him some slack tonight; tomorrow would be a different story.

Nodding curtly, I turned on my heel and left.

Once in my apartment, I stripped off, removed the band-aid on my neck and stepped into the shower, running the water hot as I could stand it, letting it beat against the wound. Trails of blood swirled to the floor tiles. The wound still oozed, like the thing that attacked me had somehow injected some anticoagulant.

What the hell had I seen out there in the park tonight? It couldn't have been a bird. Could it?

I shivered despite the scalding water and kept on shivering until the delayed reaction finally subsided. Then I towelled off. I should report it to the cops now, but no one went into the park after dark, not even them, so what was the point? Tomorrow morning would be fine. I'd just have to fib a little, say it happened just before dusk.

Totes would back me up. He didn't want any extra attention. Anyone checking too closely on his personal life might flag his obsession with buying dolls and stripping them naked. That might be awkward for a highly regarded, upwardly mobile tech guy. Totes earned three times as much as I did for sitting on his butt all day.

Sound like sour grapes? Not really. I loved what I did. And I didn't mind Totes most of the time. But Dad had bought me up not to trust anyone, least of all the people close to you. It probably explained why I lived alone and preferred it that way.

That circle of thoughts brought me back to Marshal Sixkiller. I wanted to be down in the foyer before him, so I grabbed fresh jeans and a collared shirt. As a concession to going out to eat with someone else, I pulled on my casual narrow-toed dress boots and took a moment to comb my hair in front of the mirror.

The face that looked back should have pleased me. Honestly, I was reasonably good to look at – brunette all the way with thick, arched eyebrows and a straight nose. I didn't carry any extra weight, on account of my lifestyle, and my jaw is defined and (I liked to think) strong. Not the kind of face you'd find on a commercial but not one you'd run away from, either.

I usually only thought about my appearance once a year, when I had to frock up for the company ball, and I wasn't changing that routine for a visiting cowboy. So I pulled a face at the mirror, grabbed my wallet and phone and headed for the lift.

My girl, Caro, called me just after I hit the lobby button.

"I'm getting in the lift; signal is crap," I said.

"Hi, Ginny." She was the only person in the world who could call me that. "You want to go for a drink?"

"Can't. Working tonight. New guy in town and I have to look after him."

"*Him?*"

I sighed. Caro had been obsessing over my single status since I turned twenty-nine a few months ago. I would have preferred that she worry about her own, but she maintained it was because she didn't want to be stuck with me in old age.

"Work," I said.

She let it pass, though I could sense her storing it away for a future conversation. She was an investigative journalist. Her kind never let anything go. "Tomorrow, then?"

"Yeah."

"Ginny?"

"Yeah?"

"At least be nice to him."

I was still smiling over her plea as I entered the lobby.

"Something funny?" asked Sixkiller. He was leaning against the wall mirror, dressed in a thin T-shirt and denims. He could have been a local except for the narrow, high-heeled, embroidered boots and the Stetson. The local boys favoured RM Williams, and Akubras were the only hat to wear.

"Yeah," I said noncommittally.

He studied my face for a moment and then straightened, leaving faint smudges of his body heat on the mirror.

I blinked, uncomfortable under his scrutiny. "So... I can show you a place where the steak is so big it comes on a tray."

"I prefer vegetarian."Suddenly, the cowboy drawl had gone and he was all New York urbane.

"Oh?" Shit. "Sure."

I led the way to the food hall, in the building adjacent to the Cloisters, figuring that would cover all food bases.

Sixkiller stopped at the soup and salad stall while I went for All You Can Eat Meat & Noodles.

We reconvened at a slightly sticky Formica table overlooking the elevator well.

Sixkiller swept his gaze across the table surface and picked up the soup bowl, taking slow sips from a plastic spoon. The eatery was busy, even for a Friday night, people brushing past us, leaving the waft of their body scent. In most cases, it was tolerable, but I noticed my visitor tensing from time to time as if he didn't find it always so.

Neither of us seemed to know where to kick the conversation off, so silence went on longer than it should.

"How did you get your neck wound?" he asked eventually. Not a man for small talk, it seemed, which was a small tick in his favour.

"You don't start until tomorrow – you want to wait until then to talk about work?"

"Wait for what?"He gave me that steady stare again. His eyes were dark enough to be black, though his personnel file described them as dark brown. "What's the point of that?"

I shrugged. "I dunno. Maybe you're not ready to get into all that tonight; new country, jet lag – all that."

He put his soup plate down and leaned back, folding his arms. "I'm here to work, ma'am. Not socialize."

Well, kick a girl for being considerate! "Fine."

I shovelled the last forkful of noodles into my mouth and pushed the plate away. "The park has an evening curfew. I'm usually the last person out. Tonight, I was leaving just on dark and I heard two people near the Interchange gate – arguing."

"So, you weren't the last person to leave."

"Well, I'd done my sweep and the scans verified the south-east sector was empty. I should have been the last person there," I said patiently.

"Your scans don't sound reliable."

"Our scans are perfectly reliable. Something strange happened there tonight. As I said, I heard them arguing and snuck up to have a look."

"They didn't see you? My understanding is the park is quite barren."

I hesitated; he was being kind of irritating and I wasn't going to tell him I'd stayed there after dark. "It was close to sunset. The shadows were long and they were standing beyond a ring of palm trees. I planned to listen in first, but one of them drew a pistol so I had to intervene…"I had his full attention but I didn't know how to tell the rest of it, so I glanced out into the crowded plaza.

Something on the escalator barrier made me freeze. Perched only a few feet away was a large wedge-tailed eagle.

My hands became instantly clammy. Occasionally, we still got snakes in suburbia, and there were plenty of rats and seagulls near the coast, but wedge-tails had been extinct for fifty years.

Besides, this one was different. And the way everyone was going about their eating confirmed it. The eagle was Aquila. At least, that's the name I'd given her when she first appeared to me. I hadn't seen her since I was fifteen, long enough for me to think her presence was just a manifestation of my angsty adolescence.

Seeing her now in the food plaza, under the glaring fluorescent lights, I didn't know what to think.

"Ma'am?"

I bit my lip and sprayed Sixkiller with belligerence. "*My name* is Virgin Jackson. Or Ranger Jackson, if you prefer. But if you call me ma'am again, I'm likely to break your face."

An over-the-top reaction, considering how polite I'd been acting, but Aquila's appearance kinda tore the ring top off my goodwill. I wiped my damp palms on my jeans and wrenched my gaze back to my companion.

He glanced over his shoulder to where I'd been staring and then back to me. His face was quite expressionless. "Then please call me Nate. Or Sixkiller. Or…"

He let it hang, and I didn't want to know what he'd left unfinished. I gulped down my lemon soda and felt the rush of sweet fluid fuel my edginess.

"Virgin, what attacked you in the park?" he asked carefully.

"A… A bird." I glanced briefly at Aquila again. Her eyes were gleaming and she stretched her wings as if ready to fly. "A crow, I thought at the time. But I couldn't see it. It… was… getting dark," I finished with a whisper.

"A crow?" His brow creased. "You mean a raven?"

"If that's what you call it," I said. "Look, I'm going to have to go. Been a long day. Can you find your way back to the apartment?"

He nodded. "I'll escort you, ma… Virgin."

Aquila lifted from her perch and alighted right next to us. There was a trace of bloody meat trapped and hanging from the corner of her beak.

"No!" I jumped up from the table. "I'm fine. See you in the morning. I'll come by around seven."

I turned and ran down the escalator, not really caring how weird my behaviour seemed.

By the time I reached the lobby of the Cloisters, I was drenched in sweat and shivering. The mirrors showed me the disturbed expression on my face, and that my hair was plastered to my head, so I took some deep breaths before stepping into the lift.

Aquila hadn't reappeared and I began to calm, but when the lift door opened on my floor, she was back, perched on the light shade outside my room.

"What do you want?" I said aloud.

The wedge-tail stared at me as solemnly as she used to when I was a teen.

"What?" I said, a little louder.

A door opened as I walked the corridor, and a neighbour ventured out. I nodded congenially, forcing my mouth into the shape of a smile. I knew the guy by sight but we'd never spoken. We didn't break our habit. After a quick acknowledgement he passed on, head down.

Aquila stayed on the light fitting as I keyed the lock and pushed the door open. But as I stepped inside, the eagle left her perch and swooped, talons first. I ducked on instinct and felt the movement of air.

Then bird screams exploded in my head. I hit the light switch as I dived to the floor. A huge black crow fluttered above me with its beak open.

Aquila swooped in again, straight at the crow, and they collided in a chaos of feathers and chilling screeches.

The sight of them paralysed me. Was I hallucinating or–

"Get up real slow and put your hands where I can see 'em." The breath in my face was sweetened by alcohol, so I did as the man holding the gun to my head bid, taking my time, picturing where I'd put my revolver and wondering if I could reach it. The birds tearing at each other above our heads mightn't be real, but I had no qualms that he was.

"What's this about?" I said in a rusty whisper, as I got up off the floor. "You want money?"

He laughed. "You think I'd be robbing *you* if I wanted cash?"

"What then? I don't know anybody; nobody knows me."

"Seems you're wrong there. Now stop your gabbin' and listen." He began patting me down as he spoke. "We're going down in the lift and there'll be a car waitin' in the drive-through bay. You're goin' to get in it, nice and quiet, like a lamb, or I'll paste your brains all over the road."

My pistol was in the drawer beside my bed. I had no chance of reaching it, but there was no way in hell I was getting into a car with this guy. So I told him.

"No," I said.

"Whaddya mean, 'no'?"

I stayed silent.

He nudged me forward so I stumbled. "Move!"

I straightened up and shook my head. I was not about to be shot and killed at some lonely rubbish dump or in a derelict warehouse. "Fuck you."

Reckless? Hell, yeah. I should be being more careful with my life, but an overwhelming stubbornness took me. I wasn't going anywhere with this son of a bitch.

He cocked the pistol and his breathing accelerated. Above me, the crow had broken away from Aquila and circled the room. Aquila hovered protectively in front of me like an avenging angel, eyes yellow with hate.

"Do you see them?" I said.

"See what?"

"The eagle and the crow?"

"What are you talking about, you crazy bitch?" He grabbed my shoulder and shoved me so hard, I sprawled through the partially open doorway, banging my shoulder on the door frame as I went down.

As I rolled, my chin hit a pair of tan boots smelling of saddle soap, and a slow drawl penetrated my rattling brain.

"Put the gun down, dirtbag. Step away from the lady."

I didn't know whether to get to my feet or stay put. Some strangely detached part of my brain recognized Nate Sixkiller's voice and wanted to see what he would do, so I turned my head slightly so I could look up at him.

"Fuck off, cow*boy*," said my intruder.

"I'm not partial to cussin' in front of wimmen," said Sixkiller. I saw his hand move toward his holster and instinctively covered my head.

The shots were brief. One from Sixkiller and a stray from the intruder that pinged off my metal door frame as he went down. Then a hand touched my shoulder.

"You can get up, Virgin."

Of course I can get up, I wanted to say. I can take care of myself. I was just giving you a chance to prove yourself.

But that would have been hostile and not strictly true, so I bit my tongue and got upright as coolly as I could. I should have been grateful to him, but my stubborn streak just refused to allow it.

Then there was the shock. The intruder was on the floor, as dead-looking as the guy I'd seen in the park earlier in the evening. Two dead guys on a Friday; I was setting records.

I glanced up. The crow had vanished and Aquila had perched quietly on the top of my stereo speaker, beaking gently at her wounds.

"You're hurt," I said aloud.

"No," replied Sixkiller.

"Not you... I mean... er... him." I pointed limply at the dead guy. Death hadn't improved his appeal; white belly bulging from beneath his faded black T-shirt, a blue tattoo of a bird – a crow – inside a circle just below his belly button.

"*Hurt* is one way to put it. I'm assuming you don't know him." His drawl had vanished again and he spoke in a crisp but soft tone.

"You'd be right on that."

"What's your protocol for such situations?"

"Protocol?" I looked at Aquila again. She had tucked her head under her wing, exhausted, like she was going to take a nap. I wanted to go over to her and stroke her head, thank her for trying to help me, except of course, *she wasn't real.*

"She needs to rest. But she's not badly injured," said Sixkiller.

"Pardon me? Wha-at did you say?" I swung my stare around to him.

"Your disincarnate is not badly injured."

"Y... You can see her?"

"The eagle. Yes," he said. "She's beautiful and you are fortunate to have her."

"But she's not real."

"That depends, Virgin, on which reality you're standing in."

"Well, that's a kind of weird thing to say."

His mouth curved in an unexpected smile. "You're as blunt as they said you were."

"They?"

He walked past me into the room and looked around. "We should call your police."

I nodded slowly. "Yes. We should–"

"Virgin! Virgin, you OK?" called a voice from just beyond the doorway.

"Totes?"

The skinny tech was peering in, eyes on stalks, holding a Taser out in front of him. He lived three floors down and had never visited me before. "How did you know..."Then my eyes widened with comprehension. "You've got my apartment bugged?"

He blushed and the Taser-hand sagged. "Not bugged, exactly; just got some extra security up for you."

"What kind of extra security?" I moved closer to him.

"I... No... Well just a... sound decoder."

"What in blazing balls is a sound decoder?" I demanded.

"Picks up sound and sorts it into categories... you know... like you might be in trouble or somethin'... or like being shot at." His glance flicked to Sixkiller.

"Er... hi. I'm... er... They call me Total. Heard a lot about you. You've got some fearsome ancestors."

Sixkiller holstered his pistol and stepped closer to proffer a handshake.

I stared at the pair of them for a moment, not sure what to say next. When nothing came, I pulled out my phone and dialled 000.

THREE

The whole police thing took up way too much of the evening. I called Hunt, and he called his boss to stop them locking Sixkiller in jail while they did a background and credentials check.

I also told him about the murder in the park.

"Why didn't you call it in right away?" he demanded.

I gave him my lame reasons.

"Jeez, Virgin. Are you *looking* for trouble?"

"Like I said, I was late."

He gave an epic sigh. "I'll talk them out of keeping you in tonight, but tomorrow, you'll have some explaining to do."

Totes, Sixkiller, Caro and I ended up back at my apartment around midnight. I'd called Caro to pick us up from the Pol-Central. She didn't sleep much, and anyway, there was bound to be a story in it for her.

The moment she laid eyes on the Marshal, she began making suggestive faces at me behind his back. Considering the evening's events, I wasn't in the mood. But Caro lacked the sensitivity gene. That's what made her good at her job. In the battle between sensibility and story – story always won.

The body had been removed, leaving only the fluorescent forensic outline around where he'd fallen. The cops had taken a bunch of visual recordings and samples and given me permission to return but not remove the markings.

Caro had a good poke around the scene and aired some theories while Totes and I hunkered over a pizza in my kitchenette. Sixkiller declined any food and announced he was going back to his own room.

I saw him to the lift and stood there feeling awkward. "I… er… should… thank you."

He nodded. "You should have heeded your guide when it tried to warn you."

"What do you mean, 'warn me'?"

Even though it was the small hours of his first day in a new country, after a twenty-six-hour flight, killing someone and then a stint getting to know the local constabulary, he remained as phlegmatic and calm as if he'd been meditating for a week. Only the hint of a dark shadow under his eyes suggested otherwise.

"When the eagle appeared in the eatery to warn you."

"You saw it there?"

He stared at me as if *I* was acting crazy. "We talked about it. Remember?"

"Hey, you two, stop canoodling at the door and come and entertain me," Caro called down the corridor.

My skin warmed with embarrassment. "Probably not a good time for this conversation. I'll come by around lunchtime; Hunt told us to take the morning off."

"I'll be ready at 6am," he said.

"Fine, then." I sighed and trudged back into the apartment.

Caro and Totes were leaning in close, whispering.

"Time to go," I told them.

"Say what?" said Caro, helping herself to another piece of pizza.

I wagged my finger at Totes. "*You* I will deal with tomorrow. Go!"

He grabbed the last piece of pepperoni and cheese and scarpered with it before I could grab him by the scruff of the neck.

"So," said Caro, when the door shut behind him. "What the fuck?"

I stared at her tiredly and shrugged.

"Who's just tried to kill you, Ginny?"

"I don't know. Truly."

"When you get the ID on the guy, let me know. I'll do some digging around for you."

Caro had sources and then some. Years of building up a strong network of field specialists meant she knew people who could hack most databases and analyse any substance. I'd never asked her to use her contacts before. There'd never been a need.

"Thanks. But there's something else," I said.

She dropped her pizza crust onto the cardboard and wiped greasy fingers on my tea towel. "What's that?"

"I saw Aquila tonight."

Caro and I had first met in the reception area of a psychiatrist's rooms. She'd been getting treatment for PTSD after some time in a political hotspot, and I was seeking some explanations for the wedge-tailed eagle following me around.

It wasn't the kind of place you struck up conversations with strangers, but Caro was the most inquisitive person on the face of the earth, and she didn't make any exceptions for my leave-me-alone expression. Her scattergun approach to getting to know a person overwhelmed even my solid defences, and next thing I knew, we were having drinks on Friday nights at the Wild Turkey saloon in the Western quarter.

"Shit." Caro's mouth pursed and her smooth brow crinkled, making her look more her age. Most of the time her petite, blond-haired, blue-eyed innocent beauty passed for nineteen despite the fact she was two years older than me.

"Saw her when I took Sixkiller out to dinner at Yum Fat. I left and went home. When I got here, she was on the lamp shade outside here. I ignored her and opened my door. That's when the guy jumped me. While he was threatening me, Aquila was battling this huge bloody crow. I'm surprised there aren't feathers everywhere." I pulled a face at Caro. "Except, of course, *she isn't real.*"

"Concerning," she said.

A wave of tiredness took me. "Yeah. But listen, I need to get some sleep. Have to take Sixkiller into work first thing."

"You want me to stay?"

I glanced at the fluorescent markings on the floor. "I'm fine. But tomorrow, if you've got any theories on why Aquila's back, I'd like to hear them."

She leaned across the breakfast bar and hugged me. I wasn't the demonstrative kind, but Caro was. It came as naturally to her as being suspicious came to me. I'd had to school myself to not be bothered by it. Occasionally, these days, it was even a comfort. Like now.

"It'll be OK, Ginny. Just get some sleep."

I let her out, then I went into my bedroom, where I pushed my chest of drawer across the door. After checking the window was locked and doing a half-hearted scan for Totes' Peeping Tom microphones, I decided I didn't care. I slipped my pistol under my pillow and flaked right out.

FOUR

Nate Sixkiller had clearly been waiting for me. The door opened on my second knock and he stood there, immaculately groomed, hair long and straight, curling just the tiniest bit where it touched his shoulders.

In spite of my annoyance at him acting as if I was late, I noticed how shiny his boots were and that he'd added a set of chaps over the top of his denims. His shirt was plain black and buttoned through, showing a glimpse of the tan flesh at his neck. It pulled a little tight in spots, as though a half size too small. Blokes with muscles always liked that.

"You want to catch breakfast on the way?" I asked.

He shook his head. "I had mine earlier."

Earlier? It was only fricking 6am! "Well, I didn't."

We walked to the nearest Park bus pickup spot, and I bought a coffee and Danish from a street vendor while Sixkiller watched the traffic and those waiting in the queue.

They reciprocated, curious about his chaps and his Stetson but not surprised. We were too close to the Park perimeter and the Western Quarter for his garb to truly raise eyebrows. They probably figured him as just another waiter on his way to one of the saloons. Or maybe even an entertainer.

Their unworried glances told me that none of them realised that the six-guns in his holsters were the original Peacemaker series, loaded with live ammunition.

My revolver – a modern nine-shot– was inside my jacket. I never strapped it on my hip unless I was about to head into the park. Mine was a highly functional double-action Smith & Wesson. It didn't have a name. I didn't spin romance around it. It was protection, that's all.

The transit bus arrived and we climbed aboard. It was an express plunging resolutely out onto the ring road and stopping only at the park entries and exits. All the seats were taken, forcing Sixkiller and me to stand separately, something that didn't worry me too much. It gave me a chance to observe him for a bit. He wasn't short of admiring glances from both sexes, but he didn't seem to notice. His impassive expression and motionless stance, despite the rocking of the bus, were kind of eerie and mesmerizing.

I signalled at him that we'd be getting off at the next stop, and he followed me out and up into the hi-rise building opposite the entrance.

The Parks Southern office occupied all of a fifty-eight story high building – other than the thirteenth and twenty-third levels, which were given over to food courts and mini malls, and the thirty-third level, which was fitted with compact one-bedroom apartments and gym for execs on quick business trips. I'd tried to get Hunt to put Sixkiller up in them, but he'd insisted he'd be better off near me.

As we rode the lift to Bull Hunt's cubbyhole on the twenty-ninth, I wondered again if that had been a good idea.

Sixkiller wasn't saying much, but I got the feeling that was nothing unusual. At least he wasn't turning out to be a prattler. That, I couldn't stand.

Hunt's assistant, Jethro, led us through to his office. My boss was standing by the window, speaking into his cell phone. Tall, bald-headed and big-bellied with thick arms and shoulders that were still strong despite his middle years. I had no doubt Hunt could throw a horse if he had to. Bodies like his shouldn't be confined to offices.

"Yes, sir. Yes, sir. Yes. Yes. Goodbye," muttered Hunt.

He hung up and didn't speak for a moment, continuing to stare at the city vista so starkly divided by the park wall. Even from this height, it was impossible to see clearly into the park, which appeared as a massive splash of red and purple through the heart of the city's grey.

Sixkiller walked over to stand by Hunt. "Breathtaking, Director Hunt," he said. "I thought the Mojave was impressive until now…"

It was the closest thing to emotion I'd seen in him since we'd met. Even killing my attacker hadn't caused this much of a reaction.

Hunt held out his hand. "Pleasure to have you on our team, Nate. I'd like to thank you for protecting Virgin last night and apologise for the–"

"Protect me?" The words exploded out of my mouth as Sixkiller accepted his handshake.

Both men froze. Hunt uncomfortable, Sixkiller with curiosity.

"Now, Virgin–" Bull began.

But I wasn't going to let him get going on one of his monologues.

"For the record, I don't need nor will *ever* need protecting. I would have dealt with it myself. More importantly, though, why did it happen? This guy wasn't a random burglar, Bull. Have the cops identified him yet?"

"We expect a briefing from the police today. Until then, let's put this conversation on ice and discuss yesterday's body… in the park."

I frowned and glanced at Sixkiller, whose attentive, aloof expression had settled back into place.

"Nate is now one of our rangers, so he should hear what's going on," added Hunt.

Reluctantly, I recounted my version of last evening in the Park, leaving out the fact that the second guy appeared to turn into a crow that attacked me and then disappeared. I left it at two guys, one who killed the other then got away.

Hunt interrupted me here and there to clarify a few points. I knew he was recording our conversation; Hunt was the king of recording information. It's what helped him keep his butt so firmly on the eco-fence.

"And you've got no idea where the second person went and how they both got missed in the sweep?"

"None. Totes had done the sat scan, and I'd finished my visual rounds. The head count checked out – bodies in, bodies out. They shouldn't have been in there, Bull, unless–"

"Unless they'd been in there for a while," Hunt finished my sentence for me.

I nodded at the only explanation. "It's possible, I guess. We changed over sat systems a month ago. They could have slipped in then. But that doesn't make sense. How could they have survived and stayed off our radar? And why do that, anyway? Unless they got dropped in last night on closing."

"You know that can't happen."

I did. It was part of the reason you couldn't see the park properly even from Hunt's window. The company's technology division had devised a security filter that distorted the aerial view and restricted access to the park from above. No one could land a helicopter or plane in there on account of the electromagnetic field in operation. Top-level park security could switch the field off but not without a whole set of checks and balances. And Totes had clearance to do it to allow Emergency Services in. That was it.

Hunt ran his large meaty hand over his bald pate. I was fond of my boss, but he ticked me off when he started playing politics.

Right now, though, he was batting for me. I could tell.

"The carrion crew is in there with the police. Cops'll want to interview you about it, Virgin. Why don't you take Nate out on your rounds and be back here by mid-afternoon? I'll keep them at bay until then. We need some answers. An unexplained death in the Park will play havoc with tourist numbers... If there's even a whiff of murder..." Hunt drew his finger slowly across his throat in a dramatic gesture. "Visitors want to feel exposed to the elements in there but safe. *Murder*, Virgin, is not safe!"

FIVE

Sixkiller and I took the lift to the basement and walked the company subway beneath the ring road to the Park side, climbing the stairs to the stables entrance.

Totes was at his command post in the stall next to Benny and gave us a wave.

Calling Totes' cubicle a stall was a joke, really. Other than having the same basic configuration of the horse stalls, and the odd bit of straw that strayed in, there was no comparison.

Totes had some unidentifiably advanced geek gear going on in his nook: all dust-, vibration- and motion-proof. And mobile. If things got short-staffed, he could slide the whole desk console out into the doorway and watch the gate and the stables. If he needed quiet, he could shut the sliding bombproof door and forget the real world.

Usually, he and I shared a heart-starting coffee, but today I was too pissed with him, and anxious as hell to get out it in the park before the cops tied me up in interviews.

Totes had other things on his mind, too. "Virgin?"

"What?"

"Leecey's not here."

"Where is she?" I asked, looking around for our overly body-pierced stable hand.

"She's gone with the carrion crew and the cops to the morgue."

"Was it the eyelid studs?"

"Yeah. The cops took one look at her and decided she should go along for the ride and answer some questions, even though she was on a day off yesterday."

I sighed. Prejudice was stupid in so many ways. If anyone in the company could murder someone and leave no clues, it was Totes. But he looked so white-collar respectable and incapable of violence that no one would give him a second look. Leecey, on the other hand, was a punk throwback who favoured body art over clothes, perfect suspected-criminal fodder.

"I'm taking the Marshal on rounds. Back at the usual time."

"Hi, Mr... er... Marshal," said Totes a little nervously.

Sixkiller had done a circuit of the stables and had returned to stand at my side. "Is the horse in the last stable spoken for?"

"If you mean is he engaged to be married, not that anyone's told me," I said with a straight face.

"I'd like to take him."

Totes shook his head. "Uh-uh. Sorry, man. He's being shipped back to the trainer."

I squared up on Sixkiller. "He's dangerous. Threw me onto a pile of rocks and tried to stomp me. Chemical neutering failed big time." Sombre Vol didn't seem to understand he was supposed to have lost his man potency.

"May I?" He pointed to the tack room.

I looked at Totes and we both shrugged. Just what I needed, a guy that had to prove he could ride.

"You insured? I don't want Bull all over me with Workplace Safety," I said.

He ignored me and proceeded to gather a bridle and saddle in his arms. As he disappeared into #137 Geld's (Sombre Vol was the name *we'd* given the wild horse) stall, I grabbed Benny's lead and walked her out toward the gate.

The horses whinnied at each other and Benny flicked her tail. She rather fancied Vol.

I left the gates open and went through, not waiting for Sixkiller, seeking a few moments to myself in the Park.

Summer was no longer just hinting its arrival. The sun burned the sand already, causing me to blink away the reflected heat and light. From across to the palm line to where I stood was a mess of boot indentations and drag marks. The carrion crew wasn't allowed to bring a vehicle into the park, and they'd had to carry the body out by foot.

I mounted up and walked Benny across to the palms. In the daylight, my experience with the crow seemed so impossible that I wondered if I'd imagined it.

Maybe Aquila being back meant I was having a breakdown of some kind?

A whoop in my earbud caused me to wince. The shout was from Totes, but the action was all Sixkiller and Sombre Vol as they burst through the stable gate into the park.

Vol was a magnificent young horse, a burning red chestnut with an untamed temperament to match. I was commonly accepted as the best rider among the rangers, and even I was no match for this wild bastard.

Sixkiller, on the other hand, was a picture of calm as Vol tried to rid himself of the pesky rider. The cowboy didn't hold the reins but gripped the pommel like a rodeo rider, letting the horse have its head. With powerful, angry bucks, Vol sprang around the trough area on stiff legs, squealing with annoyance.

When the first of the horse's rage was spent, he barrelled over to Benny and ran circles around her, urging her out into the open country away from the palms and the murder site, past the windmill, giving Sixkiller and Vol room to move.

A short distance away, the tourist bus entry was a mere black outline in the graphene-reinforced Park walls.

To the north and west, though, aside from the buttes, there was only spinifex and dirt for as far as you could see. Vol sniffed freedom and went for it, galloping away. I followed at a canter, wondering at what point the cowboy would part company from the horse.

Benny kicked up dust and I settled in to enjoy the rhythm of her movement. Somehow, the graphene walls managed to extract the worst of the city smog, but it couldn't control the temperature, and by the time I caught up with the runaway and her rider, I was sweating hard.

Sixkiller was still upright on the heaving horse, leaning forward, patting his side, talking to him. Vol seemed to be listening, ears flicking back as he drooled into the sand. The horse would need a drink before we went much further.

Vol had run the Marshal out almost to the eastern butte, an unexpected granite outcrop shaped like upright fingers in amongst the iron stone. The other rangers called it *sandhenge* but I thought of it as *Big Hand*. Its official name on the park map name was *Los Tribos*.

The shadows from the rocks told me it was only about 8am.We had plenty of time to ride the local grid and be back by lunchtime. I pointed Sixkiller to the rock shadows.

"There's a trough over there. Best give him a drink." If he was expecting admiration for riding the wild horse, then he'd picked the wrong person. I didn't do performances.

I nudged Benny towards Los Tribos. When we reached the trough, I dismounted, leaving her to drink. She was trained not to wander, so I took the opportunity to walk among the rocky fingers. Other than some subtle erosion and the shifting levels of sand at its base, the Hand changed little. Not like other places in the park, which, like a beach, altered with the weather conditions.

Normally, I used the largest rock protrusion – the index finger–as my scouting post, but today, I climbed the middle finger because if offered a better view in the direction I'd left Sixkiller and Sombre Vol. It was hard going, with dry moss making the granite slippery. Halfway up, I stopped for a breather and to clear the flies from my face with a spray of repellent from my hip bag.

From what I could see in the distance, Sombre Vol had come to a standstill, head down, refusing to move, and Sixkiller had dismounted.

A smirk found my lips. He might have stayed on Vol's back, but what now, Mr Fancy Cowboy? Horses could be as stubborn as they could be wild.

I leaned back against the rock face, indulging in a flash of childish satisfaction while I swatted flies. But as I moved position, something sharp stuck into my hip, distracting me from the moment of satisfaction. Thinking it a loose rock, I reached around to brush it away, and my fingers connected something smooth.

I grasped hold of it and pulled it from its hiding place so I could see. It was a square black box with a dirty crystal lens.

"What the…?"

I twisted and slotted it gently back into the resting place that had been carved for it.

Getting my body totally turned around took a few minutes of careful maneuvering. When I was finally facing the rock, I studied the cavity the box had come from and the area around it. No doubt it was deliberately carved to fit. A camera of some kind, I thought, but nothing I recognized.

Someone had been illegally filming in my park. A little wave of anger surged through me. Whoever it was, this had been here a while. The case was caked and the lens smudged. But I wasn't going to mention this to anyone yet, especially Nate Sixkiller. Hunt might have welcomed him with open arms, might want me to trust him… but what my boss wanted from me, he didn't always get.

I took some photos with my phone and sent them straight to my home address. Then I removed the box from its slot and wrapped it in my handkerchief.

Climbing down, I tucked it in the bottom of my saddlebag. As I was rebuckling the strap, Sixkiller and Sombre Vol came trotting between columns of rock. The rider and horse, it seemed, had come to an agreement.

"It took longer than I anticipated," said Sixkiller. He didn't dismount, as if concerned Sombre Vol wouldn't let him back on.

"Yes, I saw you having a deep and meaningful conflab out there."

"Shall we continue?"

It didn't sound much like a request.

"There's a trough over by the thumb." I pointed to the stubbiest of the rock fingers. "Give him a drink and we'll move on."

He nodded then glanced at where my hand rested on Benny's saddlebag. "Did you find something? I saw you on examining the rocks."

"No. Nothing. But you've got keen eyesight, Mr Sixkiller."

He gave a sparing smile. "More than you could imagine, Ms Jackson."

SIX

I showed Sixkiller the extent of the home-zone territory, hectares of prime desert and iron rock, flecked with stunted bushes in some parts and just plain spinifex in others.

"The colours are real different from my home. We're more a yellow sand and flat-green kinder desert." He was back using his fake cowboy drawl, but his expression was rapt and sincere.

I'd seen video streams of the last deserts in North America. They were beautiful in their own way, but mine was so vividly red and purple that the spinifex took on a translucent green in contrast.

My heart swelled with sudden and inexplicable pride. *We did a good thing when we saved this for people to see,* I told my dad silently. *It was worth what you did. It was worth everything.*

Worth dying for?

Dad would have thought so. I hadn't given up finding who was responsible for his "accident". I would one day.

My mood soured. "Let's get on," I snapped. "Hunt'll be waiting."

We checked all the regular tourist stops including Little Canyon, Lost Gorge in the middle of the flatlands, Slate Hill on the southern end of my territory, and finally the Last Corral and the Paloma station house. I put the scanner over them all and got Totes to do a secondary.

"Looks clear, Virgin. Waiting on sat response, though; been feed problems today."

"What kind of problems?"

"You really want to know?"

I shook my head even though he couldn't see me. Totes' explanations could be like a foreign language spoken backward while coughing. "Just tell me when it's backup."

Sixkiller was standing over on the veranda at Paloma, the replica ranch/station house where the tours stopped. The inside was decked out with basic tin kitchenware and handmade tables and chairs. Even the legs of the cooling cupboard were sitting in little tins of kerosene like they used to back in the day – to keep the white ants from chewing through them.

Outside was a set of herding yards. Mostly, it was carefully aged to look genuine, but some of the wood was straight out of the museum. Lord knows how they got permission to use it; something to do with a Percentage of Authenticity legislation.

"We should head back," I called out.

He nodded and walked over to untie Sombre Vol from the railing. The horse began to edge away, but Sixkiller mounted at an unnatural speed that gave me a tingling feeling before he could take more than a couple of sideways steps. He'd seen Aquila, and then spied me examining the rock from a fair distance, and now this... freakish agility.

Something wasn't right here, but I was so overrun with thoughts, I didn't know where to file these ones. So, I put them aside. Sixkiller had saved my life last night; he could be as freakish as he liked for the moment, as long as he didn't get in my way on this murder investigation.

We rode abreast, cutting away from the main track and following a trail I'd cut myself, out of sight of the road. It meant a bit of winding around rockfalls and through some deep gullies (or gulches as the Marshal called them), but we got to see some of the wildlife that'd learned to avoid the tourist buses.

Sixkiller pointed out a brown tail disappearing into a low bush.

"They're vermin – fox and dingo hybrids. We've tried to trap most of them, but they're damned persistent and breed quickly. They eat other small native mammals," I said.

He nodded thoughtfully and I wanted to ask him what he was thinking, but we weren't on those kinds of terms yet, so I kept the conversation businesslike.

"If the sat images come back clean, I don't know what to make of it. We been through all the places someone could be hiding in this section."

"If your story is accurate, then there has to be something we're missing."

"What do you mean, 'if my story is accurate'?" My moment of goodwill toward him began to rapidly evaporate.

"You didn't tell Mr Hunt about the eagle."

I pulled Benny up short and waited for Sixkiller to stop as well. "Tell him what? That my imaginary eagle friend flew in to give me a heads-up that there was a killer in my kitchen?"

Sixkiller's expression became very still. "These are not matters to be flippant about."

"You're right," I said. "I take my mental health very seriously. It's not something I want the whole company debating over."

To my surprise, he sighed and nodded. "I understand," he said, nudging Sombre Vol forward.

"What do you understand?" I sent Benny after them.

The windmill and the semicircle of palms that signalled the Interchange station came into view as the horses climbed a last gully. There was a welcoming party of uniformed police standing in the shade. Hunt's physique stood out among them, and I could imagine him mopping his brow in irritation. It wasn't often Hunt got sand in his shoes these days.

"Hold that answer," I added. "And don't mention the eagle to anyone."

We rode the rest of the way in silence and I dismounted in front of Hunt. His gaze flickered briefly to Sixkiller when he saw which horse he was riding, and then settled back on me.

"You're late."

"We were thorough. And the horse wasn't obliging," I said, nodding at Sombre Vol.

Hunt grunted. The heat had purpled his face. He didn't get out of air conditioning much these days, either. "This is Detective Inspector Indira Chance. She's been waiting to talk to you. Both of you go downtown with her now."

I looked at the middle-aged woman in khaki. She had a biggish frame with a slight paunch and wrinkled brown arms. Her expression was sharp and lively, other than the panda patches under her eyes.

"Ms Jackson and Mr Sixkiller. Get in the van."

The order was accompanied by a decisive headjerk.

I headed through the Interchange first, handing Benny's reins to Leecey. Our heavily inked stable hand looked pissed off and tired. Her upper lip was swollen.

"You going with the cops?" she asked.

"Yeah. You OK?"

She licked her lip. "Yeah, nothing I'm not used to."

"You want me to go to Hunt about it?"

"Nah, just leave it. Hell, I wasn't even here when the murder happened. What's all the heat about? We've had dead bodies in the park before."

I loosened Benny's saddle while Leecey slipped the bridle off. The trough was full of oat-sprinkled hay, and the horse buried her head in it. "Heart attacks and stuff, yeah, but not a murder after close. You heard I got attacked in my apartment last night?"

"Shit!" she said, eyes widening. "No wonder Totes is acting like he's been skinned. Wouldn't speak to me when I got back from the station. Said he had to get the sat feed up."

I frowned. "Sat's still not right?"

She shrugged, then winced at the movement. I knew then that they'd body-punched her in places the bruises wouldn't show.

Anger toward Indira Chance boiled up in me. What had the DI let happen on her watch? Or what had she turned a blind eye to?

Caro told me that reporting channels at Aus-Police had changed and watchdogs had been set up to stamp out the more heavy-handed interrogation techniques. Obviously, no one had told Detective Chance. She looked old-school to me and proud of it.

"You should see a doctor."

She shrugged. "Like I said, I've been there before, Virgin. No big deal."

But it was a big deal– to me, anyways. I'd got Leecey this job on account of her being the ex-girlfriend of my irresponsible younger brother, Johnnie. Hunt hadn't wanted to hire her because of her police record. I'd talked him into it and I took it personally that Leecey was being victimised because of her criminal history and her appearance.

It was probably stupid getting wound up about that right now when I was the one about to be grilled over two murders. That's where my sense of disconnection came in. I didn't care so much about my predicament, but I did care about Leecey. She did a good job with the horses and she was clean of illegal substances – at work, at least. Why couldn't they just let her alone?

"They asked me a lot about you, though. Be careful, Virgin. That Detective Chance has got a giant bug up her arse. She's gunning."

"Thanks," I said. "And you lay low. They'll probably watch you while the investigation's on. Keep away from Johnnie." Warning her off my little brother was part of my daily salutation, but today I *really* meant it.

"You mean, no going to DreamWorks?"

DreamWorks was Junkie Central – a precinct farther west of the Quarter. "Yeah. That's just what I mean."

"I won't. And you should go easy on the cowboy. Anyone who can make peace with Sombre Vol has gotta be someways decent."

I scowled. "Why? What's Totes been saying?"

"Nothing much. Just that you're super fucking pissed-off that Marshal Sixkiller's here."

I punched her in the arm. She winced again, and this time I didn't feel bad for her.

"There's something wrapped in a cloth in my saddlebag. Can you drop it in my letter box at Cloisters on your way home? Carefully. I don't want it damaged."

She glanced around. "I gather you're not keen on sharing it with the detective."

"Not keen on sharing it with anyone actually, Leecey. You do this for me?"

"Course," she said. "You'd best get going before they come looking for you."

The silent ride across town in the arrest-wagon was punctuated by garble on the police band and a desultory conversation between the two officers in the front seat of the van. Detective Chance sat in the back with us, staring, not speaking, as if daring us to confess.

Sixkiller maintained his calm, meditative mask, while I occupied my thoughts examining the array of devices neatly compacted against the walls. The new broom that had swept through the force had obviously opened the coffers for some spending. I counted no less than a half dozen species of electronic restraints.

"You got some bitchin' tech going on in here, Chance."

"Detective Inspector Chance to you."

"Just passing the time," I said amiably.

"I thought rangers only talked about horses and sand fleas," she retorted.

Her comment was deliberately insulting and provocative, so I shelved my attempt to make conversation and looked at Sixkiller.

His eyes shifted to a spot above my shoulder, narrowed, then he looked away.

I broke out in a light sweat. I'd seen that look before. Aquila was here.

As casually as I could manage, I turned my head and took a quick look over my shoulder. Aquila was perched on the rack that held their thermo-jackets. She gave me a troubled stare and fluttered down onto the floor near Sixkiller's knee.

Leaning forward to rest his right arm on his thigh, he dropped his left down behind his lower leg and very subtly reached out a finger to Aquila. She inclined her head and he scratched her gently, above her ear where her feathers were grey instead of black.

I gasped and made a poor attempt to turn it into a cough.

"You swallow somethin' bad, Jackson?" asked Chance.

Sixkiller's lips caught in a tiny smile of amusement. He'd done it deliberately, to rattle me.

I hated him for it. Things were hinky enough today without me appearing skittish for no apparent good reason.

"Just thinking about all the time I'm wasting when I could be in the park tracking a killer," I said.

"Didn't do you much good this morning. And, of course, it could be that you *are* the killer."

I let my disdain show. "Yeah, right. I killed a man I've never even met before, for no good damn reason, and then pretended to find him on my work's doorstep. Guess I'm just a dumb psychopath in ranger's clothing."

Chance's look was hooded. "Psychopaths come in all sorts of fleeces. I've seen plenty of them. The worst ones are the hardest to pick."

The conversation dried up again after that and didn't restart until I was marched into an interview room somewhere on the edge of the Pol-Central building. Sixkiller had been taken elsewhere.

I was surprised that the interview room was as salubrious as it was. Two couches, face to face, and a small coffee table with a plastic water jug and cups alongside. What happened to metal chairs, handcuffs and the smell of stale fear?

There was no obvious recording device, so I figured the officer would be wearing it.

I lounged, or tried to lounge, on the couch, as if relaxed. Truth is, I was jumpy as a feral cat in a cage. Seeing Sixkiller touch Aquila in the van had messed hard with my sense of reality. If only he and I were seeing the eagle, what did that mean? Or had I imagined that he was scratching the bird?

Chance interrupted my crazy thoughts by entering and planting her backside on the seat opposite. She carried a small tablet, which she prodded at with the dexterity of a lame cow.

"I want you to tell me about last night, beginning from when you went back into the Park to get your phone. We have everything on the Park cams up until then."

I retold my story to make out that the person who stabbed the dead guy had already disappeared when I arrived. Y'know... rather than say he turned into a bird and flew away!

"Then why are there only two sets of footprints?" asked Chance. "Yours and the dead guy's."

I laughed. "Footprints? In the desert. You *are* shitting me."

"We can tell more than you think."

"People come and go through that Interchange all the time."

"But you just happened to go back into the park without any monitoring devices?"

"I was in a hurry to get to the airport."

"Aaaah, yes. Mr Sixkiller." Chance began tapping notes into her tablet. "So you claim to have never met the deceased before?"

"Which deceased?"

"Which one would you prefer to tell me about?"

"Tell you about? I've never seen either of them before."

"So you don't know Leo Teng, either?"

"Is that the dead guy in my apartment? Sounds like a bad alias. Nope. Never met or heard of him. Or the guy in the park. What was his name?"

She ignored my question. "What do you know about aliases?"

"Jeez, nothing. It was just a throwaway line."

Chance ahuh-ed and did some clumsy finger-play on her tablet.

"I've read your statement to the duty sergeant about the incident in your apartment. You claim the intruder was a complete stranger as well?"

I nodded. "Bad day, yesterday."

"Very bad day, *Ms* Jackson. Possibly the worst day of your life. I think that you're up to your neck in something. You arranged to meet someone in the park to receive or deliver an illicit item. It went wrong and you shot him. The ambush later that night in your apartment was his people trying to recover said item."

"You're a vivid storyteller, detective," I croaked. My mouth had suddenly dried up and my stomach had hollowed. Chance really wanted to pin this murder on me.

"The only reason you're not going to jail for a *double* murder is that the creepy little fuck you work with had footage of the events in your apartment showing Mr Sixkiller shot Teng in self-defence."

I tried unsuccessfully to swallow.

"The park killing is a different matter. We don't have proof that you did it, and you don't have proof that you didn't. So while you're going about your business, you'll remain a person of interest to us. I'm going to find a link between you and both these deaths, and then I'm going to send you down for so long, you'll need a memory stick just to remember your name."

She delivered her homily with such flat, hard-eyed dispassion that I wanted to throw up.

"But I didn't do it," I whispered again.

She leaned over and patted my hand, her eyes full of mockery.

I snatched my hand away and stared her in the eye. "Can I go?"

Chance got up and walked to the door, which she opened. "Step right this way."

Sixkiller had already been signed out when I reached the front desk. The detective with him shook his hand warmly before leaving and slapped him on the back.

"Was an honour sir," the man blurted." Can I drop you somewhere?"

What the…?

"We'll take a cab," I said shortly, and led the way out.

Once out of Chance's line of sight, I began to breathe a little easier. As we walked, I called Caro.

"Sweetie?" she answered.

"Leo Teng. Find out everything you can about him and a tattoo shaped like a crow with a circle around it."

"Is everything cool?"

"Nothing is cool."

"Then we'll make it so," she said, and hung up.

Sixkiller didn't proffer conversation, and when we got in the taxi, he just stared out the window.

"Which government posted your bail?" I asked him eventually.

"Bail?" He looked puzzled. "No one. They were very understanding. The visual footage collected by your… colleague clearly shows what happened was self-defence. No charges are being laid. Besides, the intruder was wanted for questioning in several murder cases and some illegal importation enquires." He turned his head a little so he could see me. "You had problems?"

The dryness in my throat, which had just started to ease, got all scratchy again. I told him, in short, quiet phrases so the cabby couldn't hear, what Chance had said.

"Do you flex?" he asked when I'd finished.

I flashed on the guys and girls in the gym windows who did their weights routine for the benefit of the passers-by on the street. "What the hell do you mean by that?"

"I mean that you should call work and tell them you're having the afternoon off."

A blank stare from me.

He sighed and gave me a patient father-to-confused-child look. "What I mean is… let me buy you a drink."

SEVEN

I rang Hunt and told him I was taking Sixkiller on an orientation of the Western Quarter. It was partly true, and he didn't argue with me.

"How did the interview go?" he asked before I hung up.

"About as bad as it could. They think I killed the guy in the park."

"But you didn't. Right?"

"Bull!" I was stunned that he was asking. We might not always get on but he knew me, and more importantly, he knew my dad.

"It's alright, Virgin. I've got your back on this. But make sure you're squeaky clean in every way."

He sounded just like me talking to Leecey. "Any cleaner and I could bleach your white undies."

He was quiet for a moment. "That's not funny. Be careful. OK?"

"Always." I hung up and paid the taxi, and we got out on the corner of Dry Ditch Boulevard and Tombstone Avenue.

The names in the Quarter were kitsch, as were most of the stage acts in the theatre bars, but there was an undercurrent to the place that was just the opposite. Beneath the mash-up of local Country Hicks and American Western-o-philes, something hard and unhealthy was going on here. Like the fusion had sprung some kinda screw loose in the patrons. I both liked and loathed it, depending on my mood.

We settled on some stools inside Beef and Horners. It was heading into closing time for most offices, and the place had already begun to fill up with sequined shirts, ten-gallon hats and shiny dance boots. An old Keith Urban track was on the E-box. Was that old guy even alive still?

"What'll it be?"Sixkiller was back in colloquial-speak, now he was out.

"You do that so easy," I said.

"Do what?"

"Switch from Cowboy to Yale in a breath."

"You've heard of Yale?"

"Last I checked, we were still part of the Global Village."

He smiled. "And you're having…?"

"A Dark and Stormy." Just how I was feeling.

The woman behind the bar planted the rum mixer and a schooner of beer in front of us, and went off to serve two middle-aged women in long boots and short skirts.

"I thought you didn't drink."

"Only on special occasions," he said.

"So what's the occasion this time? Me going to jail?"I took a long swallow that barely wet my lips but left the glass empty.

"You want another?" He hadn't had a sip of his beer.

"Sure," I said. "My buy, though."

Our unimpressed bartender lined two more drinks up and moved on, dabbing at bar stains with a dirty wet cloth.

My throat lubricated a little with the second rum and ginger ale, and by the third, I was able to speak without catching a lump. "That Detective Chance's got some kind of axe to grind or a quota to fill, and I think I'm in the crosshairs as the bounty."

Sixkiller shrugged. "Look at it from her side. The man in the park... you were the only one there."

"I thought you were supposed to be cheering me up."

"When did I say that?"

"You offered to buy me a drink. Out here, that means you're either hitting on someone or you're trying to cheer them up..."

His reply to that was a smile hovering at the edges of his mouth.

I felt myself blushing. Surely... Surely he didn't mean... Did he?

He drained his beer and placed it down. "There's a man sitting by the door, wearing a black felt hat. What do you call them?"

"Akubra?"

"Yes. He's been following us since the police station. You know him?"

I stretched and let my glance slide idly across the room. The lighting was dim but good enough for me to glean that I didn't know the person in question. Not a cop, though.

"That's why you suggested a drink?" I said.

Sixkiller gave a faint nod.

Heat warmed my cheeks. I'd thought for a moment that he'd...Why had I even contemplated such a thing? "Well, I've never seen him before. You sure he isn't following you?"

"No. But I've never seen him before, either."

I grimaced. "So where does that leave us?"

He got up slowly. "Reckon that leaves me and him having a private conflab."

"Oh?" This could be interesting.

He gave me an earnest look. "Virgin, wait here. Please."

With that, he threaded through the tables, past the small stage and the banjo and fiddle band that were setting up for the night, and approached the guy from behind.

He dropped his hand on the guy's shoulder, and the man's pained expression told me Sixkiller had pinched something tender. A moment later, he transferred hold to the man's elbow. They got up together and headed toward the restrooms.

"Leave our drinks here. I'll be back," I told the bartender, and hustled after them. My movements were a little clumsy after four drinks in as many minutes, and I collided with the roadie carrying a drum kit.

He swore at me but I wasn't in the mood to apologise. I shoved him out of the way so he fell onto the stage, hands outstretched to save the drum. Before he could recover, I was out into the corridor heading for the john.

The pair was nowhere to be seen. I searched the ladies' and then flung open the door of the gents', setting off a ripple of whistles and shouts. But no Sixkiller.

The only door left led to the kitchen.

I opened it and peered in, taking in the spilled gravy on the floor and smell of roasting meat and potatoes. The cook was blowing cigarette smoke out a window, lecturing the young guy dishwashing about something. His smoke curled around and back into the kitchen, rendering his attempt at hygiene null. I watched where the draught was blowing it and spied the wide-open back door.

As the chef stubbed out his butt and turned to stir his vat of soup, I skidded straight through and out.

The alley was a patchwork of shadow and light. One end opened into Tombstone Ave, the other was a dead end banked up with two overflowing skip bins. Obligatory graffiti and a bent *Do Not Park* sign decorated the walls.

Sixkiller had the man pinned up against the bricks, his Peacemaker pressed to the guy's temple.

"Nate!"I ran over to them.

"Hey, lady, this guy's a loony. Get the fucker off me."

Instant sobriety banished the warmer feelings alcohol had lent me. "Why were you following us?"

"I wasn't. Never seen you before."

I nodded at Sixkiller. "My mistake. Do what you have to."

He gave me a grim look and began searching the man's pockets. From inside the guy's leather coat he produced a wrapped object. I stepped closer to get a better look.

"Let me see," I said, pulling out my phone for light.

Sixkiller handed it over and proceeded to check the other pockets. I wasn't interested. The thing in my hand had me curious. I unwrapped the cloth and stared at a sharpened bone with a feather attached to one end.

I walked away from both men and called Caro. "I'm sending you a photo of something. See if you can find out what it is *now*." I hung up, took the snap and e-mailed it to her.

She called me back within a minute. "The closest I can find is a sharpened bone, no feather, which is a Vodun marker said to call the strongest of the Loas. Usually used before a battle. Where did you get it?"

"I can't talk now," I whispered.

"Are you safe?"

"Yes."

"Get back to me."

"Will do."

"And by the way, that tattoo you asked about... Local intelligence services have an alert out on it, but I can't get specifics. My source says the security clearance is beyond them."

"You think it signifies an active group of some kind?"

"My contact says yes but has no idea who."

A camera in the park, a random guy belonging to a new gang or cartel trying to kill me, and now this. I wondered if Indira Chance had guessed right on there being a connection between the two murders – but not the kind she was trying to make.

I wanted to talk it over with Caro more, but Sixkiller looked like he was strangling the guy.

"Laters."

I hung up, turned and ran back to them.

Too late, because the alley made like a dirty bomb.

EIGHT

OK, not nearly that bad, but enough to knock me hard against the skip. Momentarily winded and totally confused by a loud detonation and a lot of smoke, my first thought was how bad something stank.

A few blinks and head shakes later, I realized it was me, covered in some kind of red slime. Vegetable matter, I hoped, not human.

A hand thrust in front of my nose, motioning to help me up.

"I'm OK," I said, scrabbling to my feet. "Where is he? What happened?"

"A mild percussion device. Knocked me down, too, while someone snatched him."

Sixkiller sounded distant. Like we were talking though a door or window.

"Whaddya mean, *mild*?" I tugged at my ears a few times, and the near deafness improved to a ringing noise.

At the open end of the alley, a couple of passers-by peered in. Down at our end, the previously overflowing rubbish was now pasted on the walls, and the rear door of the bar hung off its hinges. The cook was pressed against the frame, a cleaver in his hand.

I gave him the reassuring thumbs up.

"He got away," said Sixkiller.

"No shit." I wiped some of the slime off my face. "Don't know about you, but I don't want a return trip to Pol-Central to explain the unexplainable."

He stared at me for a moment, then nodded. "Let's git."

He picked up the bone feather that I'd dropped and headed out past the curious young couple in ponchos and moccasins. I followed, stopping long enough to slip them all the remaining cash I had in my wallet.

"Drinks on me if you can forget this?"

We slapped hands in agreement and that was that.

NINE

"You find out anything from the guy before the boom?" I asked as we took the lift up to my apartment.

Sixkiller was insisting on walking me there, which irritated me more than I could say. I didn't need a caretaker, but I also wanted to keep him in my sights. Lord knows what he might do if he slipped the leash.

"No. Just the bone feather. I'll run it through our databanks see if I can identify it."

So, the Marshal wasn't going to share evidence. Figured.

"Right. Well, let me know what you turn up. And now tell me why I stink of kidney beans and you're hardly showing a scrape," I said as I thumbed my key lock.

He laughed, a dry, cut-off noise that could just as easily have been a cough. Glad something could amuse him.

I entered my apartment in a hurry to hit the shower but stopped dead on my cactus rug just in front of the fluorescent dead-guy outline, at the sight of a naked body lying curled on my two-seater, face buried in the cushions.

Sixkiller was past me before I could speak, slipping the muzzle of his Peacemaker into the person's ear, cocking the pistol.

"Stop!" I bellowed, recognizing the heart-shaped tattoo on the buttocks.

Sixkiller paused, flicked me a glance. "You know... him?"

I nodded carefully. Emphatically. So there could be no mistake. "Put the gun away, Nate."

He eased his thumb off the hammer and withdrew the piece.

My lover, Heart Williams, rolled over slowly.

"We all good?" Heart asked, taking in me and Sixkiller before he got up.

Another big nod from me.

Sixkiller holstered the pistol.

The moment it hit the leather, Heart sprang up from the couch and punched Sixkiller low in the guts.

The cowboy sagged a little, then straightened, murder returning as quickly to his eyes as it had left.

"Don't ever pull a gun on me again," barked Heart.

I stepped in between them before any more friendly fire could be exchanged.

"Marshal Nate Sixkiller, meet my... er... friend, Heart Williams."

Heart was as almost as tall as the Marshal and I but had a finely sculpted body. Every muscle defined. When you worked as a stripper for a living, you had to keep the bod in tip-top shape. It also meant you didn't get too worried about standing starkers in front of strangers. Right now Heart's manhood was on full display, and he looked as confident as if he wore a suit of armour.

If Caro had been here, she'd be gawking with delight.

"Do all your friends let themselves in and lie naked on your furniture?"Sixkiller sneered. His gaze swept my couch in a way that said he wasn't likely to ever sit on it again.

"Only her *close* friends," said Heart with equal weight.

I wasn't used to Heart bristling macho. Usually, he was just a cool, funny guy who was outstanding in bed. We slept together about once a week. It was great sex, but that was all. Some light pillow talk, maybe. But no dating, being seen in public together or acknowledgment that we had any type of real liaison going between us.

"Fellers," I drawled. "A mistake made from good intentions. Let's just get on with our day."

Sixkiller shot me a both a critical and questioning glance.

"I'll call you in a while, Marshal," I told him.

He let out a breath, spun on his heel and left.

"Did he just do that weirdly fast, or is just me?" said Heart.

I walked over and locked the door.

He still made no attempt to clothe himself.

I wanted to be mad at him for being in my place when I wasn't here (even though I'd given him security access), but in truth, I would have been pleased to see him under any circumstances. Our liaisons were the only time I felt connected to another human being, except when Caro and I got hammered and drunk-talked.

I guess that said a lot about me. I didn't relate well to the rest of the world. It's not that I didn't want to.

But since Dad had died... trust came hard. And before that... maybe I was just wired different.

"Looking good, Ranger," he said sarcastically, eyeing my slimy appearance.

I appraised his nakedness with equal attention. "Let me return the compliment."

He smiled. And that was unfair.

Heart without the smile was a good-looking guy with a great body. With the smile, he became a weapon of mass destruction. I never could understand why he worked as a stripper when anyone would have employed him. Then add polite and quick-witted to smoking hot. But it seemed like his current job was an index finger at anyone who ever had expectations of him.

I guess we all had our *thing*. The shoulder-chip that held us back in life made us act stupid.

"You hungry?" I asked.

He widened his smile and let his tongue rim his top lip. "Starving."

"Let me just catch a shower," I said.

"Let me help."

An hour later, we were dressed and sharing tea, leaning against my kitchenette.

"So who was the trigger-happy cowboy?"

"Visiting US Marshal."

"You get all the fun," he teased. "He here to keep you in line?"

"Something like that." Noncommittal was my default. We didn't usually talk about our work.

He took a sip of this tea and nodded toward the couch and the outline of the dead body. "So you gonna tell me about that, then?"

"Some crazy broke in here and tried to abduct me. Nate – the Marshal – shot him."

He frowned with concern. "You OK?"

"Fine."

"But the Marshal's a little touchy?"

"Actually, he was just doing what comes naturally to him. We've had a kinda bad day. I mean… I have."

Heart placed his hand to my waist and left it sitting there. "I've got no work this week. You want me to hang around a bit here? Keep you company."

I stared into his eyes. They were almost the same red-brown of the mesas in the park. "That's sweet of you, Heart. But I don't need a babysitter."

"Friend to friend," he said. "For company. I mean, you could whoop my arse in a fight, Virgin."

I thought of the punch he'd landed on Sixkiller. Heart had an athletic build, but he wasn't a fighter. At least, I hadn't thought so… "Not so sure about that. Where'd you pull that punch from?"

"Jeez, girl, I take my clothes off for a living. It's not the first time I've had to switch it up to macho."

"The other-man syndrome?"

His mouth twisted in amusement. "Well, sometimes from the ladies as well. But yeah… I've had more than one jealous boyfriend."

"Course you have," I sighed.

We stood for a bit, sipping some more. The tea brought a biting flavour to my palate; the sugar brought life to my limbs.

"Say, how long have we been doing this… thing?" he asked.

I tried to recall exactly. We'd met in a Western Quarter

bar where he'd been working on stage and Caro and I had been drinking. While Caro put a lynch move on some guy, I'd got maudlin about my dad. Heart had walked into my craziness and hadn't been fazed by it. That day was the best sex I'd had in a century."Bit less than a year, I guess."

"Yeah, well since that night we met, I've had six or seven more guys with ego haemorrhages come after me. Some of them bring their mates. So yeah, I'm learning how to stand up to them "

"You could always get another job." The words just fell out.

He took a sip of his tea and looked away, his mouth tightening.

"Jeez, I'm sorry Heart. I don't know where that came from. I'm the last person to tell you what you should do with your life."

He shot me a sideways glance, saw my apology was real, then laughed. "You sure are."

The moment of tension between us eased.

"So, should I be worried that the cowboy will come after me again?" he asked.

"Not at all," I said a little grimly. "I'll sort that out."

He nodded in satisfaction. "I have to go, but I'll come back tonight and stay for a bit if you like?"

Part of me thought the idea sounded nice. It was creepy living with a fluorescent outline on my floor and two dead bodies on my mind. But part of me resisted, not wanting to give up my privacy, even for my lover.

I liked Heart a lot and I *loved* being intimate with him, but I still didn't know him all that well. Not share-a-bathroom-every-day well, at least. And then there was Aquila to consider. What if my "disincarnate" aka imaginary friend decided to visit? I wasn't sure I could handle the strain of hiding my hallucination from him.

He could see me wavering.

"I'll cook," he said.

I felt my eyes widen. "Really?"

"Really."

I put down my tea mug and draped my arms over his shoulders. "Please. *Please*. Come back and stay."

TEN

Heart left me feeling better about some things and worse about others. It was almost dinner time and today had been a wipeout of police interviews, a few drinks and then the odd thing in the alley.

First, I went down to the foyer and unlocked my post box. The package was there, still wrapped in my scarf, and I tucked it inside my jacket for the ride back upstairs.

Once inside again, I set it on the coffee table and called Caro.

"Where the hell have you been?" she snapped. "I've been worried sick since you hung up on me."

"Ummm… Stuff… to deal with…"

"Where are you?"

"Home."

"Stay there, I'm coming around."

"No, Caro. Caro…?"

Crap.

I went into my bedroom and tucked the camera into one of my spare work boots in the bottom of my cupboard. As an afterthought, I pulled the bedcovers up and washed the extra tea mug. Caro had an eye for detail that made me nervous.

By the time she arrived, I was scanning tattoo sites on my tablet.

She followed me around the body outline back to the couch.

"I think we should make up a name for him," she said.

"He had a name. They told me down at the police station. Leo Teng."

"Not the actual dead guy; I mean the *drawing* of the dead guy. Two different things. Let's call him John Flat."

I frowned and shook my head at her. "You're certifiable, you know. Anyway, I hope they'll let me rub it out soon."

"That patch of floor will always be *where the dead guy lay*. You might as well give him a name and welcome him in."

She was probably right, but for now, I just tucked my feet underneath me so I didn't touch the marks.

She glanced at my tablet. "You find out anything more?"

"Not yet," I said. "You?"

"No. But I got a name for you. Kadee Matari."

"Who's that?"

"You'll find him in Divine Province."

"Yeah, but who is he?"

"I don't know exactly, but apparently, if you've got any Vodun happening, he's the one to talk to. Your bone feather might be in his wheelhouse."

"Your intelligence sources tell you this?"

She smiled in a slightly devious, very Caro way. When my friend had a purpose, she was straight and true. But the means by which she got there... well,

I'd made it my business not to ask. Rangers were too hamstrung by their connection to the law to approve of half the shit that Caro did.

"Divine, huh?" I said.

"You want me to come with you?"

"Absolutely not."

Divine spanned two or three suburbs south of the Western Quarter: Moonee, Calder and Mystere - a little slice of the city that had been market gardens back in the day. Genuine veggie growers first, then hydroponics druggies, naturists and hippies. After that, the alternative spiritualists moved in. Dad had told me a fair bit about its history because he had lots of theories about social demographics and city geography and crime.

Now, of course, there was no bare land to be had other than the park. Only varying densities of city living.

I hadn't been down that way in a while. Not since I'd been following a lead on Dad's death. Some parts of Divine were safe for strangers: the commercial section where people went for psychic and tarot readings. The rest was most definitely not somewhere you went without an invitation and a guide.

Ordinarily, I stayed clear of the place. The bundles of bones knocking together in the breeze, trippy music and smell of sacrificial animal blood were way too hostile for my taste.

The idea of going there with Caro set my stomach churning. She had survived war spots and even been kidnapped once in Afghanistan, but Divine... Her blond hair and bright attitude would be like offering a virgin to an angry deity.

"I'll take Nate."

"See what the man's really made of, eh?"

"Something like that."

"So, what did the police say?"

"You know a detective called Indira Chance?"

She frowned. "I think I have. Met on the Riggins case. Middle-aged, panda eyes, saggy tits. Bitch on a windmill."

"That would be her," I said. "Riggins? He was the one who murdered his whole family and boiled them in drums?"

"Yeah. She was running point on the mother's murder and getting nowhere when some young hotshot detective connected the dots. She didn't take being sidelined too well when the case broke. Decent detective but as vindictive as hell."

"Can you find out about her background for me? She likes me for the murder in the park. Actually, she'd like me for both deaths, but Nate is actually on video for one."

"Don't stay mad at Totes. He's a dick, but he did you a favour by having the place wired."

"It's still creepy," I sighed.

"You got to respect the level of his obsession with you."

"Totes isn't obsessed with me. He's just… a loser."

"That boy is way too smart to be a loser. You remember that, Ginny."

I made a contemptuous noise.

"But I'd be careful he doesn't get jealous of stripper-boy."

I gawked at her. "What are you talking about?"

"Heart Williams. You think you can keep that kinda thing from me, girl?" She lifted her chin, a gleam of triumph in her eyes. "Though I'm a little hurt you didn't say anything."

"You *know* Heart?"

"Darling, every woman with a pulse in the Inner City knows about Heart. He's the whipped cream and nuts on the ice cream and chocolate sauce."

I stared at her suspiciously. "You saw him leave my place."

"No. But the womanly grapevine is unfailing when it comes to something… *someone* so delicious."

My face burned. "Can we talk about something important?"

"Sure, Ginny. But let me say, I'm glad you're getting some."

I glowered at her. "This is why I don't tell you things."

"Prude," she said.

"Voyeur!"

She relented. "You should find someone in Divine who knows what the bone feather means. And maybe even the tattoo. When will you go?"

I checked my tablet for the time. It was still early. "Think I'll catch some dinner and head over there later tonight."

"And the cowboy?"

"Let me worry about him. You find me anything you can on Detective Chance. And Leo Teng."

"Yeah, boss girl." She got up and slung her bag over her shoulder. "Course, I could just go talk to her."

"What do you mean?"

"Well, last time I saw her, she was skulking around the sidewalk outside your lobby."

"Here? Now?"

Caro gave me a wave. "You're welcome."

The door shut after her with a bang. Caro loved an exit.

I tiptoed around John Flat and went into to the kitchenette. The fridge offered up a nub of salami, some blue-vein cheese and two soft carrots. I grabbed the cheese and sausage and carved slabs. Dropping them on a plate, I returned to my perch and did a bit more digging online while I munched.

The tattoo came up on a couple of forums but never associated with any explanation or comments, almost like it had been seeded there as a message or code.

Frustrated, I got up and retrieved the box from the park from my work boot. It needed a clean, so I took it into the kitchenette and wiped it over with a dishrag. Definitely a camera. But what had it been recording and how did I retrieve the footage?

A quick search online told me it was a pinhole security cam with a built-in motion detector that had been around for years but was still a big seller. Trouble was that the data card was missing.

Shit!

I put it back in my boot and thought about what to do next.

Food. Then Mystere, I decided.

I used the building intercom to call down to Sixkiller's room. No answer. It was possible he'd gone to sleep – jet lag and whatever. Even so, concern began to trickle into my stomach, imagining the damage he could do alone in the city.

I returned to my bedroom and grabbed a light black

overcoat. I didn't usually wear my piece after work, but the way things had been...

Within a few minutes, I was banging on his door. The guy in the next apartment came out in his dressing gown to see what all the fuss was about.

"You seen him recently?" I asked.

"You mean the cowboy with the TV twang?"

"Yeah. That's him."

He shrugged and turned to go back inside. "I mind my own business."

Right.

I pounded again, hard enough to wake him if he was sleeping. Still nothing.

Where...?

I called Totes. "Where are you?"

"Still at work. Police have been in and out all day, taking pictures and samples."

"Have you seen the Marshal?"

"Sixkiller? Only with you this morning. Why?"

"I can't find him."

"It's dinnertime, Virgin. He's probably gone out for a bite."

"He's not that sort," I said.

"You saying he doesn't eat?"

I thought of the soup he'd ordered at the food court. "Apparently not."

"You're not making any sense."

"Forget it. Just call me if you hear anything from him or about him."

"Always."

A thought occurred to me. "Totes, do you have his apartment wired, too?"

Silence.

"Answer me or I'll dismember Princess Puti."

Puti was his number one doll. The one he never took out of her dustproof, fireproof, shockproof casing.

"Virgin!" He sounded horrified.

"I mean it." And I did. I was still pissed at him for spying on me.

"Well, I had a surveillance bug in there, but he found it."

"Crap."

"That's what I thought, too."

"Is he smarter than you, Totes?"

"His detection technology is newer," he replied flatly.

I'd got under his skin about something. Good.

I hung up and thought for a moment. Not much I could do except get on with my own investigations.

I checked the time. It was just past the first sitting at most places for dinner. Maybe I'd go have a meal in the Western Quarter and then head on to Divine. See what information I could shake loose. I had a picture of the bone feather on my phone and I knew someone who might help.

My enjoyment of the T-bone and coleslaw at Dabrowski's Steakhouse was spoiled by the fact I had a cop sitting in the opposite booth pretending to eat curly fries. He'd been waiting outside the lobby of my apartment and had inexpertly tailed me this far. Indira Chance must have gone home for the night.

I forked mushroom sauce onto the meat and chewed slowly. Leaving through the kitchen door might be an option but was a pretty predictable way to try and shake a tail. If he was working with anyone else, they'd be watching the other exits. That left me only one option.

I signalled the waitress, Greta, over to me.

"You ready for your soft serve, Ranger Jackson?"

"No thanks, Greta. But I could do with a little distraction."

She poked at her ringlet-curled mountain of hair with her stylus and hitched her hose up by pinching at the waistband through her uniform. "You mean that copper drowning in chicken salt over there?"

"That's him. Is Chef Dabrowski in the kitchen?

She nodded.

"Time I told him personally how good his steak is."

She grinned at me. "So you should."

"If you could block my policeman friend's view of the front door for a few seconds, I'd be most grateful." I placed the cost of the meal and a generous tip into her hand.

She winked and made a beeline for the opposite booth. Just before her plus-size girth bent in front of the cop, I leapt up and headed for the door. Once there, I opened it wide and let it swing shut. Then I ducked back and around a pillar into the kitchen. The peep-through window let me see the cop push past Greta and race out the front door. She went straight after him, chasing payment.

After an embarrassed exchange of cash on the pavement, he disappeared into the throng outside.

I grinned and turned around to find the entire kitchen staring.

"I'm... er... just..."

Chef Dabrowski stomped out of his office to see what had caused the staff's paralysis and spotted me, saving them an explanation. His demeanour switched from stormy to sunlit in less than a second, and a moment later, he scooped me up and pressed me hard against his all-in-one chest and belly.

"My little girl," he crooned. "You never come to see me anymore."

I arched back a little to catch my breath against the raw garlic and onion on his breath. "Not true, Chef. I eat here once a week. I just don't like to bother you. You're a busy man."

"Just like your father," he cooed. "So humble."

I couldn't help but smile. Dad and Chef went back some ways. Not sure how it began, but Dad lent him some money to start the business. Chef paid it back years ago, but their bond had endured. You give a person a start in life and they're unlikely to forget it – the decent ones, at least. And Chef was more than decent, if a little overpowering. When Dad died, he'd sent me a home-delivered meal every Monday for a year until I insisted he stop.

The door behind us swung open and Greta waltzed in, balancing a stack of trays. "He's gone, Virgin. Lit out like a cricket up front of a tornado when I told him you'd headed Parkside."

I expelled a breath. "Thank you, Greta. Chef, I have to go, but the food was the best, as always."

His beam got wider and his grip loosened. "I launch ze new menu in two days. You must come and mingle. We drink Starka."

"*Na zdrowie!*" I lifted an imaginary glass.

"*Na zdrowie!*" he shouted in delight, flinging an arm back. "Bring a boy. Or a girl."

I blushed some. Chef Dab was almost as bad as Caro when it came to fussing about my love life.

"Ping me an invitation," I said, taking the opportunity to slip out of his armlock.

I pecked Greta on the cheek and headed right on out of there before he gave me a giant serdelki sausage and some sauerkraut to go.

ELEVEN

I couldn't help but feel a bit jumpy on the taxi ride out to Divine, constantly checking the rearview to make sure I wasn't being followed.

If the driver noticed my agitation, he didn't say anything except "I stop here!" when we got to the Laksha station.

The never-seen-better-days station house was the only stop along the rail line near Divine after it left the Western Quarter on its way south to Jesbo and Big Domain. It seemed like even the train didn't want to come in any more contact with Divine Province than it had to.

It had taken me almost an hour to find a taxi driver who'd drop me at Laksha after dark, and even then I'd had to pay in advance. I barely had time to close the door before he was spinning the wheels to leave.

That left me facing the chicken wire and splintered weatherboard of the stationhouse alone. Where a spluttering sodium light would've completed the uneasy atmosphere, a brilliant high-wattage spotlight perched and rotated on the roof instead – lending it a less seedy-slum and more concentration-camp ambience.

I wondered whose initiative that had been to put that up, Aus-Police or Neigbourhood Watch? The Watch had developed teeth as the police force's recruiting dropped off in the last ten years. Suddenly, no one wanted to be paid to enforce the law s of the country in general; everyone just wanted to join the Watch group and take care of their own small community.

Dad had seen it coming and been appalled. It was one of the rare issues we disagreed upon. I figured it was better when each community took responsibility for itself rather than relying on the government to make everything better for the whole. Dad said it led to bad decisions and persecution. I told him I thought there was plenty of that the way things were – how could this be worse?

I still think I was right, only Dad wasn't here to argue it with me.

My phone rang then. It was Caro.

"Leo Teng used to be a contractor working out of Indonesia and Japan, but he disappeared off the grid a while back. Seems like most people thought he was feeding fish in the Pacific, but now they're saying he was off finding a new religion. He's been out of town. Came in from North America a few days before your Marshal friend."

"He's not my friend," I said automatically.

"Colleague."

"So you mean Teng's a…*contractor* as in…"

"Yes, that's exactly what I mean."

"Then, someone hired him to abduct me?"

"Maybe? If he's supposed to have found religion, it could've been a belief-based act."

"How could my beliefs offend anyone? I don't share them around?"

"Maybe it's what you stand for… Honestly, Ginny, I don't know. I'll keep digging, but that's all I got at the moment."

"Thanks, Caro. That's more than the police would've shared."

"They may not even know some of it. I had to go pretty deep to get this."

"Hope you're not racking up too many favours on my account."

"Hope in vain," she said.

"In the name of friendship?"

"Whatever." She hung up.

I climbed through a hole in the chicken wire, ran up the stairs and checked the line. No train lights either way, so I jumped down and scrambled across the tracks to the other side.

It would have been easier to go the tourist route through the Coast bus route, but longer and fraught with drunks and excited tourists. My way was quick and quiet.

A ditch, an embankment, another falling-down fence and a long walk in the dark through an abandoned industrial site, and I was standing on one edge of Divine.

In all directions lights blinked, glared and haloed. Behind me, across the Western Quarter, those halos bled into a yellow-white aurora. In front, though, Divine shimmered like a bleeding rainbow.

I walked on, hand on my pistol, heading west according to my phone compass, toward Mystere, a dense plot of the Divine Province squeezed in to the lopsided triangle of Gilgul Street, Seer Parade and Mason Way. Not the real designated street names but those corrupted by the weight of local reference.

Common myth was an authoritative reality around here.

Dad had so much to say on the matter of common myths. He believed they were more powerful than any specific spiritualism or religion and that one day someone would realize that, stop waging wars on economic premises, and fight the real fight – the one about belief.

I could get arcane, too, when I had a half dozen beers in me, but I was still young enough to think that that kind of talk was also just a mask over bitterness and disillusionment.

Bitterness did bad things to people. Turned them into twisted-up versions of themselves. Or husks, sloughed off and left behind to blow away in the wind.

I never liked to think of Dad as bitter. But maybe he was, a little. Uncompromising, for sure.

Plenty of local and foreign tourists came to visit to Mystere on a daily basis. It wasn't exactly in the tour guide brochures, but you only had to ask a cabbie where to get a palm reading, or a rental car dealer where to find the more offbeat local colour, and you'd get the same instructions. *Go to Mystere but make sure you stay* inside *the triangle.*

The long side of the triangle was Gilgul Street, where every shop front had a layer of stalls in front of it like barnacles clinging to a jetty, hoping not to be swept away by the current (in this case, the waves of people rolling past).

One end of Gilgul intersected Seer Parade, the other, Mason Way. In the middle sat a wedge of hi-rise shopping, once glitzy, now gaudy and reeking of hashish and incense sticks. Clairvoyants and mediums competed like grocers, and the combined scents of street cooking and smouldering herbs slammed the back of my throat.

I'd been there dozens of times over the years, and each visit had me swallowing and sweating hard within minutes. The sweating was all about the way people looked at you in Mystere. Those who were selling wanted a piece of your mindspace. The rest were just wild-eyed, either pushing to get in somewhere or pushing to get out. Whichever way you turned, once inside Mystere's triangle, humanity became avaricious and urgent.

I stood by a hydrant, using it as a buffer against the tide of foot traffic while I decided where to go. Vehicles weaved along the road, slowed to a crawl. You didn't drive the streets of the triangle unless you were Delivery or Emergency, like Times Square without the homage to entertainment or the wholesomeness. Instead of thirty-foot screens blinking and yowling, the landscape was bright with glow sticks and fairy lights and plain old-fashioned wire-basket fires.

I knew a clairvoyant halfway along Gilgul who knew people, so I stepped out into the throng and let it propel me in her direction. The difficulty was cutting across to the right doorway at the right time. The normal rules of engagement people observed in crowded places didn't hold in Mystere. If you knocked into someone, they were likely to knife you or kick you down so that you got trampled in the undertow. If you didn't knock into them, you'd never make it across. Damned either way.

I edged sideways, minimizing contact, and then made a lunge when I saw the tiniest space appear the way I needed to go. I collided with someone trying to take the same gap, and a hand seized my elbow and pinched so hard, I stopped in my tracks. The owner of the hand rode up hard against me and for a moment, I thought we'd both be trampled. But suddenly, the tide of people parted, as if dividing around a pylon.

I swivelled, fist raised, and saw that the man who had hold of me was the same size.

"Sorry." Then the tattoo on the side of his thick neck drew my attention. A crow in a circle.

Without hesitation, I hoiked my knee hard into where it hurts a guy and threw myself sideways back into the people tide. Despite his size, my vision of him was swallowed in an instant as I scrambled to keep up with the traffic's pace.

Moments later, my clairvoyant's sign flashed over my head, and I made a second lunge shop-side behind a cluster of visitors all clothed in white robes and sequined animal masks.

That got me to the talisman stall outside the shop front, where I held fast to a pole covered in dreamcatchers and let my pounding heart recover.

"Crosses, Missy. Wands! Blessed teeth! Cat knuckles! Dung lockets! Best prices in Mystere," the vendor bleated in my direction.

"I want to see Corah," I called to him.

He kept his head averted, exchanging cash for trinkets with the precision of a factory machine. "Madame Corah has a price, Missy."

"Tell her it's Ranger Jackson."

He slanted a lopsided, unhinged grin my way and pulled an old-style microphone down from the folds of the stained silk drapery that served as a ceiling to the stall. I couldn't understand his dialect, but there was no mistaking my name in among the swallowed utterances.

With the other hand, he got busy wrapping a collection of animal bones in brown paper. A buyer handed him their One Card, and he passed the bag over.

"Corah be coming soon," he said, shoving the microphone back into its hidey-hole and jiggling the chimes above his head.

"You sell bone feathers?" I asked suddenly.

He stopped everything and looked at me hard. "What you say?"

The intensity of his stare made me uncomfortable. The stall vendors in Mystere belonged to an elaborate network of black market racketeers who gossiped like entertainment bloggers. Maybe I'd been indiscreet.

"Forget it," I said.

"Virgin?"

I heard Corah's husky accent behind me and turned to her with relief. She peered out from under the half-doorway entrance of her boudoir. A lot of the footings in Mystere had begun to subside due to dodgy earthworks on top and a mains water pipe malfunction up the line. Some buildings had flat out collapsed when the water seeped through; others just kind of sank.

Local government had tried to slap OH&S demolition edicts on them, but trying to stop or change anything in

Mystere was like trying to ban Akubras in the Western Quarter. Never. Gonna. Happen. Not. Worth. The. Hassle.

And so, premises like Corah's fell deeper into the ground, which made room for more buildings atop. On my rare visits, I always felt nervous in her place in case my visit coincided with another sink or collapse. Corah, on the other hand, seemed totally at peace with her surroundings, as if it was totally natural to work in a room where the floor sloped downward and the wall had a crack so large and full of dirt you could watch the earthworms getting busy.

I let go of the pole and ducked in after her.

She shut the heavy iron-hinged door behind me and we were alone in relative quiet.

"What would you be needing that brings you here at night?" she asked me with her charming Irish lilt.

She was a beautiful woman with a sheen of long hair and plump, upturned lips. I'm pretty sure that the beauty spot just below her nose was an affectation, but it added a kind of pouty glamour to her clothes and jewellery.

Her traditional beauty seemed out of place in a district famed for its weirdness and obsession with dangerous rituals, but Corah belonged here more than most.

She placed a tiny brass hash pipe in my hand. "Chillax, Ranger."

I handed it back. "Any more chilled and I'd be in a coma."

She sighed at that. "Still so lawful. Don't you ever get tired of yourself?"

"No more or less than you do, I expect," I said.

"Well, I guess it's good to know that some things in the universe are immutable."

Corah and I went way back to when we'd "hot-shared" lockers and a desk in staggered school classes. In our district, classrooms were on a roster system like beds on mining rigs.

Corah always left our desk smelling of patchouli and sandalwood, and spattered with sticky spills from whatever brew she'd been mixing. By the end of our graduation year, I'd regularly find joints and loaded pipes in there as well.

I never gave her up to the teacher but it made me mad, her inconsiderate carelessness. She wasn't the only one on scholarship. As payback, I'd sprinkle them into the palm pots that lined the corridors outside.

Our relationship had always been uneasy, but at the core there was something honest. We knew each other for exactly what we were.

"I need your help."

She faked horror, arching her pencilled eyebrows and rolling her eyes. I thought how much she and Caro would detest each other.

"What would I know about lawmaking, Virgin?" she mocked.

"Law*breaking* is what I'm asking you about."

She laughed at that. Almost spontaneously.

I glanced at the door. "Prefer not to be interrupted."

The mockery vanished and she moved past me to deadbolt the doors. "I have a client soon. Get to it."

I reached into my pocket, got my phone out and brought up the photo. "I'm guessing this is vodun, but what does it mean, exactly?"

Corah made no attempt to disguise her interest. She opened a drawer in her reading desk, pulled a sheet of film from a dispenser and slipped one hand into the sock shape. In a few seconds, the film melted onto her skin, leaving no visible signs of a glove.

"Didn't pick you for having OCD," I said.

"No offence, darling, but you're in law enforcement. I don't leave my fingerprints on anything official."

I snorted. "Thought only the police could get hold of dissolvable gloves."

"That's where you've got it arse-about, Virgin. The police can't afford *anything* after the last round of cutbacks. Hell, they don't even have a *policy* for managing Mystere anymore. They've *always* had that."

"You got sources inside, eh?"

"Of course," she nodded. With her protected hand, she took my phone and studied it.

I waited, giving her time to study it, watching her face for reactions.

"Strange. Which is rather delectable," she said.

I didn't comment.

"It doesn't look strictly African Vodun," she went on. "See the carvings on the knuckle ends... they're native Australian, and the beads where the bone and feather join, I'd guess they're Native American. And then there's this... the stone with the hole through it at the bottom of the beads..."

"What about it?"

"I'm not sure."

"And the feather?"

She shook her head. "I know someone who could identify it."

"OK," I said slowly. "So... no clue what it means."

"No. But how intriguing," she replied. "Where did you find it?"

"Around."

She sighed. "You really are infuriating, Virgin. Coming here, demanding my opinion, then you're not even prepared to share."

"I don't know anything, Corah. This here" – I pointed to where we stood – "is me starting from scratch."

"So, the guy that got wasted in your apartment has nothing to do with it?"

Now she had my attention. "How do you know about that?"

Her smile spread into heavy-duty smug. "I see things."

"Yeah. Right. You paying someone to watch me?"

She lifted her hand to my forehead and gently pushed my hair back out of my eyes. "Such paranoia is not healthy, my dear and oldest friend."

Her fingers were cool and dry against my skin. She used to do that at school to annoy me. Feign tenderness and lace it with a large whack of patronizing.

That was my read on it, anyway.

"Who can tell me about the feather?"

"Still wanting something for nothing?"

"What's your price, then?"

"I hear that Chef Dabrowski is having an opening night for his new menu. I wish to go."

"What? *Why?*" I stared suspiciously at her. Corah and I knew Chef both independently and together. For a while there, we worked the counter –a job-share arrangement – at his first burger bar. Chef sacked her for selling miscellaneous illegal substances from the kitchen door.

To my knowledge, they hadn't seen each other since.

"Let's just say that there'll be some interesting people there."

I vacillated for a moment. Chef wouldn't like it – he'd warned me off Corah many times when we were younger, but on the face of it, the request seemed harmless enough. It made me curious, though. Who could she possibly want to meet Uptown? "Fine. I'll message you the details, but make sure you come to it clean."

Corah walked over to the side table where her incense holder rested. Fishing in her pockets, she retrieved the brass pipe from her pocket and lit it from a smoking incense stick. The sweet hashish stench smoked through the room in a couple of puffs.

"Of course. Like a virgin."

I gave her a withering look. "Who can help me with the feather?"

"Papa Brisé runs Mystere these days, and a spiritualist called Kadee Matari has control of the rest of Divine over Moonee side. All the gangs answer to them, commercially and for permissions."

I raised an eyebrow. "Permissions?"

"Just like it sounds... who can go where in safety, what they can deal, what they have to pay for immunity. Brisé or Matari will know who's importing the feathers, if you can get past their gatekeepers."

"I could just ask around the stall holders."

"Asking questions in Mystere is more dangerous than drinking the water."

She was right. "So how do I get to them?"

"Do I have your word on the invitation?"

"Sure."

She turned and went over to a sideboard that rested under a 3D image of the rising sun. Taking a ring from her index finger, she keyed open a drawer and retrieved a flat box.

Then she came back to me. "Roll up your sleeve."

"What's in the box?"

"You want to talk to Papa Brisé or not?"

"Yes."

"Then give me your forearm."

Warily, I did what she asked.

She removed the lid of the box, took out a small black square and placed it on the sensitive flesh inside of my wrist, just above my pulse.

The instant it touched my skin, it began to burn in the way boiling water would.

I wrenched my arm away from her. "What the–"

"DON'T TOUCH IT!" she barked. "Pain won't last."

I bit my lips and glared at her through tear-blurred eyes.

Then, as quickly as the scalding sensation started, it went.

My muscles relaxed and I glanced down expecting to see burn marks. Instead, a tattoo undulated on my skin.

"Corah!"

"Relax, Virgin. It's a temp. Be gone in a few hours. That's how long you've got to find Papa Brisé and talk to him."

"You've given me a gang tattoo!"

"Technically incorrect on two counts. First, it will vanish like you never had it. Second, it is a parlay tattoo, not a gang marking. It means you've been screened to make contact."

"Screened?"

"Divine has its systems of checks and balances, just like you got laws uptown."

"You seem to know a lot."

"That's why you came to me, isn't it?" she said.

I guess it should be no surprise to me that Corah had questionable affiliations.

"Now use the parlay mark to get to Brisé. With Kadee Matari, you're on your own. I wouldn't go near her if my life depended on it. But if you put word out that you're looking for her, she may find you."

"*She?*"

She smiled. "Don't mess with the Stoned Witch."

TWELVE

"Shit is going down."

Outside, the streets were a fresh assault on my senses. The stall guy yammered on his microphone, noise projecting in short static bursts like a food blender.

I held onto the pole for a few seconds before letting the tide traffic sweep me up. The momentum took me down past Bambara's Emporium, where I had to skirt the edge of the human whirlpool created by people entering and leaving the popular arcade.

On the other side of it, traffic lights halted forward movement and the crowd bulged onto the street, waiting for the sequence to change.

I was six deep back from the curb and could only see glimpses of what lay ahead. Word seeped through, though, that something was happening.

"Jeez, do you see that? Three against one."

Arms began to rise above heads, hands holding camera phones, fingers tapping the *snap, reset, snap, reset* tattoo.

A surge of irritation made me consider trying to fight my way back against the flow. Then I heard the man in front of me say, "That guy in the hat has a gun."

I grabbed him by the shoulder and squeezed. "What kinda hat?"

He shrugged me off but I wasn't having it.

"Mate! What type of hat?"

"Who the–"

I flashed my badge at him before he let the profanity fly, only giving him a brief look at it so he didn't clock it as not being Aus-Pol.

The glimpse and my expression must have been enough, because he lowered his phone so I could see the screen. The photo taken a few seconds before might have been blurred, but there was no mistaking the scenario.

Or the man in the hat.

"Make room!" I roared, pulling my gun from the holster hidden by my coat.

The press of flesh melted away once shouts of "gun" and "she's packing heat" let loose around me. I suddenly had a free lane to the curb, and I ran through it hard before it disappeared, plunging out onto the street. The traffic had stopped and left an oasis of space right in the middle of the intersection.

The reason for the gridlock was four men. Three of them stood still, their backs to the other curb. They were dressed in baggy overalls adorned with patches. I didn't know all the gangs and mobs that ran in Mystere, but these guys clearly belonged to one of them.

My glance skittered along the upstairs windows and balconies with a vantage point. Someone had to be gunning for the fourth guy, who stood opposite the three statues, pointing two Peacemaker pistols. But the patchwork of window shadows and neon made it impossible to see clearly.

With my own piece raised, I stepped slowly onto the street, toward Nate Sixkiller.

"Marshal?" I said as evenly as I could. "What's going on?"

"Ranger," he replied without so much as a glance. "You made it."

I tried to swallow over the dry patch at the back of my throat, but it remained rough. "You were expecting me?"

"Gambling on it."

"You should get some help for that."

He didn't answer, but I fancied a faint smile touched his lips, even though his back was to me.

I raised my voice even louder. "Hoping we can sort this out now, gentlemen. These people want to get about their business, as do I."

"Then tell the fucking cowboy to holster his pieces," said the middle statue of the three.

"Nate?" I asked.

"Is it custom for thugs to set upon a visitor to the country and try and rob him?" he said loudly in reply.

That got the crowd caterwauling.

Someone shouted, "Shoot 'em and get on with it."

I drew alongside Sixkiller, knowing that his trigger fingers would be twitching, and noticed the blood trickling from his temple to his chin. Brown muck clung to the shoulder of his shirt as if he'd been rolling in something unsavoury.

"Sounds like you-all owe the Marshal an apology."

The middle guy spat on the ground and dipped his bald head so I could see his ink. *MY3*. I guessed that meant the three streets that made up Mystere. It wasn't smart to back bangers into a corner, but that's just what I'd done.

I straightened my aim. This could go way south and I didn't have a vest on. My stomach felt full of razor blades, and anger towards Sixkiller surged through me.

"Couldn't you just let it go?" I whispered out of the side of my mouth. "It's Mystere. Of course you're gonna get rolled, coming here in a hat like that."

He said nothing and I risked a quick sideways glance. His expression was hard enough to strike a match on.

"Shit," I muttered. "You cover the one on our right, and the one in the centre. I got the guy on the left."

A slight nod.

"But let me try something first," I added.

He didn't react.

Not sure if that was agreement or not, I stepped forward anyway, taking care to approach the three men from the side, so as not to get in Sixkiller's direct line of sight. I didn't know him well enough to judge whether he'd shoot me in an attempt to get at them.

The closer I got, the more little details stood out. The middle guy had a missing eye tooth and a thick silver earring though one brow, the small guy on his right had circular sweat stains under his arms and ribcage, and the guy on his right's fingers curled as if he was planning to grab something. I figured he had a concealed weapon of some kind, maybe a knife. The way his eyes darted to and fro suggested he might be estimating the accuracy of his aim over the distance.

All of them had killing in their eyes. And embarrassment. The kind of combination that led to impulsive decisions.

I took my shot at defusing the situation. "Y'all picked the wrong target today. I'm on my way to see your boss." I lifted my free hand so they could see my wrist plainly. "Hate to be telling him that you caused aggravation for a friend of mine. And a US Marshal at that. Could bring all kinds of heat."

Their eyes flickered to and stayed on the parlay tattoo Corah had given me.

"You'd be al letting the Marshal see your apology now, I'm guessing." I glanced back at Sixkiller, whose expression hadn't altered.

They glanced at each other, and the guy with the twitchy fingers began to reach.

I lifted my pistol. Behind me, I knew the Marshal's Peacemakers were a spit away from discharging.

The crowd had fallen silent, shuffling backwards, leaving space behind them, sensing the climax approaching. Further down Gilgul, the rhythm faltered, the vendors momentarily mute while the momentum within the triangle listed like a damaged ship.

"Don't waste your life over this," I said to the MY3 guys quietly. "He will kill you. I've seen how quick he is. His pedigree, you know. Comes from a line of true gunslingers."

The bald middle guy made a noise in the back of his throat, unintelligible to me but enough to communicate meaning to his compadres. Twitchy fingers relaxed and one by one, they all nodded their apology to Sixkiller. When the last one had finished, the Marshal slowly holstered his pistols.

And then, suddenly, it was over.

The bubble of invisible restraint on the curb burst, and people swarmed across. Like backed-up water pressure in a pipe, they spilled past, and I was once again caught in the swiftness of their flow. As I steered to the other side of the street, a hand seized my wrist.

I came around hard with my fist up and smacked it against a calloused, iron-hard palm, bruising my knuckles.

"Don't ever grab me from behind," I said with heat. Sweat trickled down between my buttocks. The stand-off had been intense.

He dropped his hand immediately. "I didn't want to lose you in the crowd."

I planted my feet to brace against the people brushing past us and looked at him. Not a trace of stress showed, only the underlying stern seriousness that was his default expression. He should have been handsome – the symmetry to his features and the compelling dark eyes – but Nate Sixkiller made me shiver. He'd killed the intruder in my apartment without a flicker. How much of a real human existed under his skin? There were plenty of psychopaths in law enforcement.

"You just can't do that here," I said. "Pulling your weapons when people do you wrong."

"Seems to me like the perfect time to do it." His deliberate contradiction made me want to smack him. "How did you get that apology from them?" He recaptured my hand and held my fingers in front of my face. "What's this marking mean?"

"Means I'm been working, getting some background that will help up with the Park murder while you've been–" I bit off the rest of my sentence, imagining Bull Hunt firing me three ways to Sunday for what I was about to say.

"Let's get something to eat and you can tell me about it," said Sixkiller suddenly.

"It's nearly midnight," I said, not wanting to tell him a damn thing.

"And your point is…?"

I let out a frustrated breath. "OK. There's a cantina just off Gilgul. Crowds aren't so bad there."

"Cantina? If that means beans and chilli" – he lifted his Stetson and patted his hair flat against his scalp – "then lead the way, ma'am."

I graced him with a withering look. "My *name* is Virgin."

THIRTEEN

Juno's Cantina was more tequila and corn beer and less fajitas and beans. But Sixkiller asked for a double order of vegetarian nachos to have at the bar and seemed happy with the result.

My double order was Mexican brandy and I'd earned it. Hellsakes, I wasn't on duty and I'd just prevented three civilian deaths. Even if they were bangers.

Neither of us said anything for a while, him busy scooping salsa onto corn chips, and me watching the methodical way he consumed the messy food.

"Sure you don't want some?" he asked as licked the last of the corn chips up from his fingers.

"It's getting late," I replied. "Can we get to it?"

"Sure thing, Ranger. Shoot."

"Fine. Why did you come here alone?"

"Just following up on a lead."

"Without me?"

He shrugged. "You were busy. So, what were you doing here?"

"Following up on a lead."

"Without me?"

"You were MIA."

We glared at each other for a bit. Then, surprisingly, Sixkiller offered me an olive branch. "Look, I thought it would be good for me to look around on my own. No harm intended."

"Of all the places you could have gone... why here?"

"The bone we found has vodun significance. My intel says this is where to find out about local vodun."

"Did your intel also inform you that wearing a Stetson on the streets of Divine might be the same as wearing a *you're welcome to shoot and rob me* sign?"

He pursed his lips and stayed silent.

I sighed. "Look, I have some contacts here who might help. Do you have the bone with you?"

He nodded.

Before he could comment, Sixkiller was jerked from his seat. I turned, hand to holster, and found a party of gun-toting gangers behind us.

Three of them I knew straight away – the MY3s from the street just before. And three others who might as well have been their clones with the same tattoos, piercings and palpable anger. The guy at the apex of the circle, though, was a different breed.

Taller than Sixkiller or me and sixty kilos heavier, he gave the term *man mountain* a baby face, an Hawaiian shirt and a thick plait.

"Who fuckeen hits on the MY3 in their place?" he rumbled.

I stood up. "Papa Brisé, my name is Virgin Jackson from uptown Parkside."

His frown appeared as two fold lines between his eyebrows. "The park ranger?"

I hesitated, blindsided by the fact that Mystere's main banger knew of me. How so?

"Yes. I'm… Ranger Jackson."

"Him?" The slight tilt of his head towards Sixkiller sent the folds of fat in his neck into a faint ripple.

"US Marshal on secondment. Working with me."

Papa Brisé blinked a few times in a way that suggested his mind was crunching through possibilities and outcomes. "Show me your fuckeen parlay, Ranger."

I lifted my wrist so he could see. "A mutual friend said it would allow us to talk."

"Your friend gotta fuckeen name?"

"Maybe we could discuss it somewhere more appropriate."

That got the giant man laughing in a hostile way. "*Appropriate*, eh? You come to my fuckeen house, Ranger. This is my fuckeen kitchen. Outside is my fuckeen street. We talk where I want to talk in *MY FUCKEEN HOUSE.*"

I folded my arms and lifted my chin against his intimidation.

The cantina patrons fell silent. I could sense Sixkiller's wariness to my reaction. I didn't care. Men like… No, *people* like Papa Brisé – jumped-up bullies – jammed my stubborn button all the way down. Dad always told me that was my Achilles heel.

Papa Brisé licked his lips and shifted the weight of his bulk from one leg to the other. His vest tightened across his girth, the palm trees on the print splitting apart where the buttons and buttonholes strained.

I snapped my gaze away from the puckered coffee-coloured flesh beneath it to see him lift a single finger.

His men seemed to understand what that meant, and three of them began ushering the drinkers out by waving their weapons. Soon, the only people left in the cantina were Sixkiller, me, Brisé and three of his guys. Even the barkeep had disappeared out the back.

"So speak, Ranger. Don't fuckeen aggravate me any more than you already have."

"Madame Corah gave me the parlay ink."

His eyes widened, lids disappearing under the fleshy folds of his eye socket. "You know Corah?"

"Most of my life," I said flatly.

That seemed to throw him. He licked his lips a few more times, and the perspiration grew thick on his upper lip.

If I hadn't been so caught up in the moment, I might have recognized his reaction to her name as lust. But as it was, my pistol hand throbbed with the blood that should have been in my brain but wasn't. I could feel a bad decision coming on.

It wasn't till he hauled an empty table over to the bar and sat his triple-plus-size butt on it that I calmed a little. Maybe Corah hadn't set me up to get shot on sight, after all.

"So, what you want to know?" he said.

I showed him my palms. "It's in his jacket."

"Put those pistols on the bar behind first. Both of you. Reach nice and slow for it," he said.

I did as he asked, nodding at Sixkiller to comply as well.

When our three pieces had been slid away by one of the gangers and we'd been patted down, Brisé nodded that I should proceed.

"Nate?"

The Marshal slowly withdrew a package from his pocket and handed it to me. I passed it to Papa Brisé still wrapped.

We both watched as he withdrew a long nail file from his vest pocket and used it to flip the folds of the cloth open.

"Corah said you would know about the origin of the feather," I said.

He poked at it with the file, rattling the beads and playing with the feather.

Then he blinked a few times and I saw the distortion of a magnifying filter slide across one pupil. He leaned in close and examined the object with the implanted lens.

As he straightened up, he'd blinked it away again and his eyes had returned to normal. "Where you get this?"

"Man followed us in the Western Quarter. When we tried to have a conversation with him, things got noisy," I said.

Papa Brisé raised an eyebrow.

"Percussion device," volunteered Sixkiller.

"You mean he threw a boom-boom and got away... from a Ranger *and* a US Marshal." He belly-laughed then, genuine mirth that made me squirm. "Glad this fuckeen country's in good hands."

I scowled a bit. "Yes, he got away, but not before the Marshal found this on him. Corah told me you would know about the feather."

"Mebbe I do. What you fuckeen give me to find out?"

"But Corah...?"

"Listen up! Your Corah gotta piece of this fuckeen big heart right here." He beat his chest. "But Papa Brisé don't do fuckeen nothing' for free. Feel me?"

I shrugged at that. What did I even *have* that he could want?

"Strikes me yer reward should be helping the law," drawled Sixkiller.

Papa Brisé blinked his piggy eyes at Sixkiller a few times then looked at me. "Fo' fuckeen real?"

"The Marshal's used to getting respect," I replied. "Australians don't get that so well."

"You speakin' out of school, Ranger?"

"Just an observation."

His teeth appeared, surprisingly straight and clean, as his lips stretched into a grin. "Bitch is fuckeen funny."

I let the "bitch" word slide on account of the odds and me still wanting something from him.

"I'm taking a fuckeen liking to you, Ranger, so I'm gonna take an IOU on this one. 'Cept you are gonna fuckeen owe me."

"I won't break the law for you," I said automatically. "As long as you understand that."

"Crystal fuckeen clear."

He poked at the stem of the feather with his file. After a bit of prodding, he stroked it. "See?"

I stepped closer. The feather had changed colour from a mottled grey-brown to a soft pink that gradually brightened to the saucy red that reminded me of sunset over the park.

Papa Brisé stroked it some more, and the hue changed to the purple of the mesa.

"Birrimun Park colours," I said without thinking.

"Your Park don't have the fuckeen monopoly on those colours, Ranger," said Papa Brisé.

"She's right, though," said Sixkiller.

I felt annoyed by the cowboy's support, and worse, a tiny bit pleased as well.

"Feather's from Manush," said the big man.

"What's that?"

"You saying it's Romani?" asked Sixkiller.

Papa Brisé nodded. "The original product, but is been tricked fuckeen out locally."

"How do you know that?"

"Fuckeen branding, Ranger. How else? Only one person know who do nano-lumes like that."

I arched an eyebrow.

"That fuckeen bitch Kadee Matari. And good luck with that."

FOURTEEN

I took Sixkiller home along the tourist route, picking the bus across the bridge from Gilgul and staying on the main line uptown. We got back to the Cloisters around 4am and parted in the lift with few words.

I drew my pistol before I thumbed my door open this time, but no one jumped me. Even Aquila was a no-show. The only sound I heard was Heart's breathing in the bedroom. I stripped, dropped my clothes on the floor, sank into bed beside him and mimicked his breathing pattern until I fell asleep with my forehead resting against his shoulder blade and my foot on his calf.

I woke in the same position a couple of hours later when my alarm went off.

Heart slid his hand back onto my thigh and stroked it. "Late night."

"Too late."

"That cowboy making work for you?"

I sighed. "In ways you could never imagine."

He rolled over to face me, so close that our lips almost touched. "You want to talk about it?"

I gave a slight headshake and a large yawn. A few

stretches later, I was able to speak again. "Not really. Just a case of a giant ego, a culture divide and some other shit."

"Can't help with the giant ego or the culture shock, but I cog 'other shit'."

I stretched and drew back a little so I could see his face. "Says the guy who dropped out of political science to become an exotic dancer."

His lips turned down. "You make it sound like I had a choice."

The sketchy picture I had of Heart's background went along the lines of huge education debt, private loan, no job prospects, no family. When the debtors started to chase him, he used his *attributes* to kick-start an income. Shame about it was he was good at dancing and good at women. Really good. Pretty soon, he was top billing at his club and the education took a back seat.

The night we met, Caro had dragged me out to a show, saying I was overwound. We got a bit crazy afterwards – whiskey highballs, beer chasers and salty peanuts – and I was still slumped at the bar when the night shift staff left and the strippers emerged from their dressing rooms looking for a liquid breakfast.

Heart sat on the empty stool next to me and I shoved him right back off. He got up and asked me why I'd done that. I told him I was drinking with my father and it wasn't polite to sit on his seat.

Anyone else would have written me off for drunk-crazy or just crazy, but Heart pulled up another stool and asked to be introduced to Dad. I told him he not to be a fucking loony and that my father was dead.

He laughed and a half hour later, we were in bed.

Course it wasn't the stupid conversation about my dad that attracted *him* to me. I worked out pretty quick that it was because I hadn't shown a single bit of interest in him when we met. When your job is to encourage women to paw at you every night, it's kind of refreshing when one kicks your chair over.

I didn't overthink what came next. Sure, he was attractive – inspiringly, if I stopped to think about it – but I didn't have any interest in a relationship with a pretty man. Just some way to let off steam and keep me connected to the human race.

The unexpected bonus was that we actually talked well together. In the brief moments before he left, or when he arrived, our conflabs covered the dissolution of individual states, the country's centralized government and the loss of our welfare system. Heart had an opinion and so did I. We often hit some kind of synchronicity.

"I know it's been hard," I said. "But things are better now. You've saved some dollar. Maybe you could consider alternatives."

"What? You don't like dating a stripper?"

"Is that what this is?" I said surprised by the quaint term. "*Dating?*"

He pulled me toward him so our naked waists touched. "You might have noticed I quite like you. Thought maybe we could spend some time together."

"Isn't that what we're doing?"

"I mean… while we're vertical."

"You want to go *out* on a date?"

"Yeah," he smiled. "For the novelty."

I knew I wasn't being very gracious about it, but I couldn't wrap my head around it. "Wouldn't that... y'know... ruin things?"

"It might make 'em even better." He'd started to move against me, his skin moist and hot.

"Can I take it under consideration?"

His smile grew wider and parts of him grew harder. "Always cautious, Virgin."

Cautious? Like my play against Papa Brisé's men, facing them down to stop a shoot-out. "Yeah," I said, softly. "That's me."

His hands began to move over me. "Let me help you with that particular affliction."

I reached down between us. "Let me help you with yours."

Less than an hour later, I was standing at Sixkiller's door, my post-coital calm waning already. The Marshal was not there or not answering again.

I stomped downstairs and hopped a taxi to the Park. Normally, I'd do the bus commute, but as usual, I was a step behind my charge.

To pass the travel time, I trawled irritably through my messages, accessing my work ones first. A priority from Bull blinked at me, saying my sector would remain closed while the murder investigation continued.

The message did nothing to improve my mood, but Leecey had Benny ready for me when I arrived. My horse snuffled and dribbled in my hand, her whiskers tickling my palm, reminding me I had some good things going on in my life.

"You look exhausted, Virgin" was Leecey's opinion as I mounted.

"Where is he?" I asked her.

"The Marshal? Went out about a half hour ago. Said you'd be coming in directly."

"Directly, huh? Where did he go?"

"Dunno. Totes has got the door locked."

"What?" I turned to her. Today her hair stood up in a golden-metallic crest, matching the colour of her jewellery piercings.

She shrugged. "Been knocking ever since the Marshal went out, but the little runt is ignoring me."

I let go of Benny's bridle and walked down the corridor. The scent of synthetic hay and antibacterial spray hung sweetly in the air, and the other horses shifted in their stalls to greet me. The stables at the Interchange felt more like home than my own apartment.

My office was set back between two stalls, masquerading as a storeroom. Or maybe it was masquerading as an office. Long and narrow and dark.

Down the far end, I kept a kickass office chair, worn to Virgin-fitting perfection, which sat in front of a large wall screen. My keyboard was a foldaway into the chair's arm, but it hadn't done that since the day after it arrived from the supplier. To one side, a table piled with paper maps inherited from Dad. To the other side stood a beverage caddy on wheels that harboured a coffee machine, cups, a Clean-Cubator and my supply of cream shortbreads and jerky.

The Clean-Cubator doubled as a mini microwave. I tipped coffee into a cup and changed the setting from CLEAN to HEAT.

How the cleaning nanites switched off and the microwaves switched on would remain ever a mystery to me.

I took the coffee out and sipped while I got the map up on my screen. All the horses were tagged, as were the Rangers' phones and the tourist buses. Visitors couldn't stray more than ten metres from the vehicle without an alarm going off, so we didn't individually tag our dailies.

My Park grid access gave me basic location maps of anyone in the park in the form of little green blips. Totes was the one with infrared and real-time satellite feed and all the bells and whistles data.

According to my Park map, the only blip in the Park – Nate Sixkiller – was halfway to the Paloma ranch house.

Why there? I wondered. And why without me? Did he have an agenda, or did he just not play well with others?

The only thing I really knew for sure was that the guy hardly needed to sleep. I'd caught about four hours last night, and a fog held my brain in suspension.

"Virgin!"

Bull Hunt's face suddenly appearing on my screen made me jump.

"Capt'n," I said.

He ignored the casual jibe. "I sent you details of an upcoming VIP visit. Need you to be there on the right day at the right time. *With* the Marshal."

"Why? Who's the VIP?"

"Just be there."His voice sounded strange. A bit choked off, like he was being strangled. Bull was feeling the pressure today. Even his skin had a choked hue.

I scowled by way of agreement.

"Where *is* the Marshal?" he asked.

"Halfway to the station house, according to Park-Track."

"And that would be because…"

"Honestly, Bull, I don't know. The guy doesn't talk or sleep much."

My boss's already purple face suffused to the colour of a bruised grape. "I expect you to stay with him."

"I'm trying to and he's trying his best to get shot of me."

"You telling me you can't handle him?"

I took that bait willingly. "I'm telling you he's making it difficult. Spent most of last night hosing down a situation in Divine."

"What in blue fucking blazes were you doing down there?"

"Trying to prove I didn't commit murder. He, on the other hand, was just out and about, wreaking joyful havoc."

"You telling me something happened that I should report?"

"No," I scowled. Much as he irritated me, I wasn't going on record about Sixkiller's trigger-happy ways.

Bull covered his face with his hands. "One simple instruction, Virgin, that's all. *Stay with the Marshal.*"

"Well, soon as I'm done here, I can do that!" I bit back.

Bull's face vanished as if it had been sucked away down a drain. I gave the screen the finger and slammed my cup down. The sticky Robusta bean liquid slopped over the sides, coating my fingers.

"Shit." I wiped them on my pants, grabbed my phone and made sure Park-Track was synced. Striding out of the office, I marched to the supplies store and checked out a phone for Sixkiller. When I caught up with the Marshal this time, there'd be no excuse for him being out of contact again.

I shoved it in my breast pocket and buttoned the top. Time to get moving.

Leecey had Benny down the corridor near the inner door, tickling the horse's nose with an oat stalk.

"Looks so real," I told her as I took the reins and mounted. It was against regulations to mount inside, but I was too bolshie to care.

"Tastes like crap, though," Leecey grinned, sucking on the straw for a second. She wasn't one to get wound up about rules, either.

"When doll-boy emerges from his hidey-hole, tell him I'll be back when I am," I said, nudging Benny's sides.

"You want me to crowbar his door open to pass the message on?" Her expression was hopeful.

"Nah. But can you tell him he'd better cough up a copy of his audio recording from my room, or I'll stick pins in Puti."

"But they're getting married next month," Leecey joked. "She'll be full of holes for the wedding."

I rolled my eyes, waved at the motion release and moved on through the inner door to the Interchange entry. As my sector of the park was closed to the public, I didn't have to worry about mapping a route to avoid the tourist bus.

Within seconds, Benny and I were through and I felt I could breathe again. The sense of suffocation had been worsening lately every time I left the park. My chest had been tight the whole time I was in Divine last night. And that wasn't just my irritation with Corah, or Sixkiller's impulsive draw-down on three bangers.

For the time it took to cross the Plains to Salt Springs and past Los Tribos, I let myself just enjoy being in the place I loved most. Sun-warmed and feeling the luxury of no tourists, I pulled my hat low and settled back to soak up the ride. Benny knew the route better than I did, and she picked her speed.

Paloma Station House was over an hour's ride, so I stopped at #3 trough to give her a drink and stretch my legs. Our arrival scared a large, open-mouthed bungarra from its perch on the ballcock, and a small party of galahs rose screaming to the sky.

Of all the bird life in the park, the galahs commanded my deepest affections. Not as noisy as the Corellas or as baleful as the crows, their curiosity and sense of fun made them an endless source of pleasure to watch.

The little flock I'd scared wheeled off in the direction of the station house. I wondered if Sixkiller could see them and had realized the reason for their sudden flight.

I imagined if the Marshal didn't want to be found, he could make it difficult for me, but this was a foreign country, and he didn't know the park terrain like I did.

Once back in the saddle, I urged Benny to a faster clip. All park horses had heart and muscular-skeletal enhancements, which meant they ran quicker and for longer than racehorses. The racing industry had embraced genetic enhancements for a decade or more and then decided they couldn't keep the playing field level that way, so they went old-school. Only horses to get upscaled these days worked for law enforcement.

My sense of being carefree diminished as the Paloma station house came into view. Sombre Vol was tethered and standing in the shade of the building, flicking his tail, one hoof lifted in rest.

What the hell was the Marshal up to out here?

The dry heat blistered around us, burning my skin. I pulled my Akubra down low and my neck scarf up, to shield my lips. We kicked up a fair dust cloud coming in and I didn't care. I decided that I wanted Sixkiller to know I was here and that I was pissed.

As I rode in past the stockyards, a large crow perched one of the posts extended its wings as if to take flight. Bigger than any bird I'd ever seen, its full wingspan surpassing the length of Benny's back, I caught the menacing flash of its eye.

Slowing Benny to turn back and take a look at it, I was stopped by something fanning my cheek. I looked up to see an eagle fluttering just by my shoulder.

Aquila? "What are you doing here?"

All the years I'd been imagining this bird, she'd never come this close.

A piercing cry drew me back to the crow again. It'd lifted from the railing, heading straight toward us.

Aquila gave her own protest call and rose higher, wings arched and claws forward, ready to engage. She was a bird of prey, but the huge crow moved with malevolent purpose.

I ducked down on instinct and turned Benny straight at the front porch of La Paloma, emphasizing the point with a kick in the ribs. She obliged me by surging from trot to gallop in an instant.

Over my shoulder, Aquila and the crow clashed. I glimpsed a tumble of feathers before they drew apart again and circled each other.

When we reached the steps of the station house, I reined Benny in and dismounted in one fluid motion, taking the steps two at a time. The front door opened before I could turn the handle, and Sixkiller hauled me in.

He slammed it shut after me and I flashed on a bunch of familiar objects – rocking chair, black iron pots on the wall, and the ancient paint-peeled food safe.

"What the...?"

Ignoring me, he took a large step across to the window.

I followed him.

Outside, Aquila ascended with the crow in pursuit. She soared in an almost vertical line, and I found myself holding my breath, willing her to get away.

"She's going to run into the Canopy," I said aloud. "What will happen?"

"Nothing," said Sixkiller. "Watch."

The crow gained on her and then fell back suddenly, veering and dropping, as Aquila kept on, disappearing straight through the almost-translucent vapour of the park's aerial barrier.

"What happened? Is she alright?" I couldn't see her anymore.

"Take a look for yourself."

"What do you mean?" I stared at him.

He pointed to the rocking chair where Aquila perched, feathers ruffled, beak open.

"How…" I brushed my eyes, and looked again. "But I just saw her go–"

"What you see depends on with which eyes you look," said Sixkiller in an infuriatingly obtuse fashion. "In the mind's eye, anything is possible."

The crow screeched again, drawing my attention back to the window. Robbed of its quarry, it plummeted back towards the house. Just when I thought it would plunge straight into the verandah and our window, it veered wide, pulling up to settle once more on the yard railings.

I felt my breathing slow a little, but it didn't help my dangerous mood. "Mind's eye? What kind of arcane bullshit is that?" I demanded.

He turned his head, revealing a bloodied deep cut along his jawline.

"And what happened to your face?"

"Arcane bullshit happened to it," he said calmly. "And your denial of what's in front of your nose is bordering on disturbed."

That sent my anger levels popping. I squared up on him, fists clenched. "Why are you even out here? You're supposed to be working *with* me, not riding solo!"

"Working with you does not mean we have to babysit each other," he said.

"Well, excuse me for saving your arrogant carcass last night."

"I came out to look around. The Mythos started hunting me at Los Tribos. I tried to outride it, find some cover."

"The Mythos? You mean the damned crow?"

Aquila lifted her wings at my tone. Her head swivelled, yellow eyes upon us.

"You're upsetting your disincarnate."

"My… *disincarnate*?" I grabbed him by the shirt front. "Stop using stupid bloody words–"

I was suddenly on the floor, with the wind knocked out of my lungs and Sixkiller's knee on my chest.

Gasping, I shoved his knee sideways, then rolled away and onto my feet.

The idea of shooting him plumed like a hot flash through me, but he already had his Peacemakers out and levelled at me.

"Calm down, Ranger," he said quietly. "Take a moment to collect yourself."

I tried to steady my breathing and my trembling. And failed.

Tried again.

"I'm writing you up for drawing down on me. You're a menace," I choked out, even though I'd been thinking about doing exactly the same thing to him.

"Listen up!" he said, without any hint that he comprehended me. "We need a plan to get out of here in one piece, and *you* need your wits about you."

"My wits are just fine, Marshal. Put your guns away," I said more steadily.

He pinned me with his stare, assessing my state.

"Don't mean no disrespect, ma'am," he drawled. "But people who lose their tempers make bad decisions. I just need you to cool down."

Cool down? Not in this lifetime. Not with him. Soon as I got him back to the stables, I was going to have him locked up. "Quit the fake cowboy drawl, Marshal, *and holster your weapons!*"

To my surprise, he did.

My shoulders sagged a little, and I quickly straightened them again. "So, you believe this... bird will actually attack *us*?"

We resumed our window viewing, side by side but apart. I slid my hand inside my jacket to rest on my piece.

"Talons that big'll take your face off. Not to mention spooking and possibly injuring the horses."

"Don't suppose we can outrun it, either," I said. "I just don't understand where it's come from. We have programmes that catalogue park flora and fauna. A bird of this size should have been flagged."

"Don't know any technology that'll track one of these," he said.

"What do you mean? Are you saying it isn't real?"

"Sure, it's real," he replied. "Same way as your disincarnate is real. Just need the right eyes to see it."

Anger reignited in my chest as though he'd struck a match to it.

"Stop fucking with me."I stormed over to the door and wrenched it open.

The huge dark crow cocked its head at an unnatural angle, lending to its sinister appearance.

I walked down the steps and pulled my gun. "Let's see how real you are," I breathed.

With a curdling squeal, it launched from the fence post and flew straight at me.

I stood my ground, determined to prove my own sanity. My fingers tightened on the grip of the pistol. Shooting native fauna was an illegal act, and not something I wanted, but my sanity was at stake. Sixkiller would be my witness that it was self-defence.

I got ready to squeeze the trigger. Four, three, two...

Aquila appeared high in my corner sight as I fired directly at the crow. But it kept coming as though untouched. I fired again. Nothing.

I dropped my gun and put my hands up to protect my face as talons sank into my shoulder, ripping my shirt and flesh as it pulled away.

I fell to the ground, the pain from the attack burning like hot coals pressed against my skin.

I screamed, I think.

Aquila appeared and flew at the crow, intercepting its next attack on me. This time, the creature's fierce talons interlocked with hers, instead of my body, in a vicious tug of war.

A hand clamped onto my uninjured shoulder and dragged me up the steps, my back scraping along the verandah.

Seeing its prey disappearing, the crow released Aquila and dived at me. I had a brief impression of Aquila dipping towards the ground, one claw hanging slack, before my arse got hauled inside and the door got slammed in front of my feet.

Nate Sixkiller stared down at me, his dark eyes unusually wide, chest heaving a little.

"Real enough now?" he asked.

I reached into my pocket with my good arm and retrieved my phone, dialling into the emergency frequency.

"Totes," I rasped.

"Virgin?" His response was immediate and reassuring.

"I'm at the station house. Can you do a sat'nal of the surrounds? I want to know what fauna – birds, specifically – are flagged."

"And this is an emergency?"

"Just do it!" I snapped.

As I waited, Sixkiller took off his shirt and rolled it up. Without a word, he knelt down, peeled back my torn clothes and examined my wound.

"You'll need glue," he said, proceeding to pack the bundled cloth against it.

I flinched and bit my lips, refusing to moan while Totes was still on the line.

"What was that about glue? Is that the Marshal?"

"Just tell me what you can see, Totes?"

"You OK, Virgin? You sound–"

"TOTES!"

"Jeez, settle down girl. Sat'nal shows a flock of *Cacatua roseicapilla* over at One Spring, and another at Los Tribos."

"You mean galahs?"

"I mean the pink and grey ones. *Licmetis* – the corellas – are all over in the Western sector today. Must be rain coming."

I forced myself to my feet and peered out of the window. The crow had settled on the fence post again, watching the house. Its beak was open and bloody.

"So, no other birds at all in the vicinity of the station house."

"No. Now, what's this about? I got audits coming out of my arse and you're calling on the EM line with ornithology requests!"

"Thanks!" I hung up and sagged against the window frame.

Sixkiller stood back now, arms folded, frowning.

"OK," I whispered. "I believe you. Now tell me what the hell this is all about."

FIFTEEN

Sixkiller produced a water bag from his kit and held it out to me. "You need medical help."

I took the bag and sank back down to the floor. The water was cooler than I expected and eased the constriction in my throat. The pain from the claw wound had settled into a persistent and excruciating throb. Would deep scratches from an imaginary, invisible crow infect, I wondered. "After you've told me what I want to know."

He read my stubborn expression and settled onto the table, shirtless. Perspiration coated his chest and arms in way that made his skin halo. Or maybe that was my blurring vision.

"You can't sit on that; it's a hundred and fifty years old. Even with the nanotube reinforcement, the original wood might break," I said through my pants.

Without a word, he came over and sank into a cross-legged pose in front of me. "What do you want to know?"

"Everything? All of it… starting with why we can see these… birds and no one else can."

"Take this first," he said handing me a small inhaler. "Pain makes it hard to think, and I need you to think so we can get out of here."

I wanted to say no but he was right; the throbbing was making it hard to concentrate.

I took two sucks on the inhaler and handed it back. The relief was blessed and almost immediate. The pain receded, leaving me feeling weak and a little nauseous.

"Tell me," I urged him.

He arranged his hands so they hung over his knees in the loose karmic pose of meditation. With his naked chest and hair loose, he looked like he'd just woken from a long, relaxing sleep. Only the blood on his cheek belied the calm.

"I imagine you know as much as most about the notions of the spirit worlds."

I shrugged and he went on.

"There are a few who believe. And then there are the rest who are entertained by the *idea* in the same way ghost stories amuse them. True believers are more in tune with other worlds, whether by genetic disposition or trauma or a life changing events. We are a minority, and even among us, only a few are truly connected."

"You're saying that you're psychic?"

"Just listen… please…"

I took another sip of water. The floor was hard and I wanted to lie down to get comfortable, but pride kept me upright.

"Something is changing," he said. "The divisions between worlds are eroding."

"You're saying other worlds exist. *With people*?" I knew as much astronomy as the next university graduate. We'd conquered the solar system to a degree, could space-travel to Mars and Saturn and Jupiter to sightsee. But that was it. No other substantial life forms had been discovered, and we were still hamstrung by the speed of light.

"In the manifold, there are many."

"You're insane," I said quietly.

"And your shoulder... how would you explain the blood and the pain?"

"I... I... can't... yet. But if you actually believe all this spirit stuff, then tell me what you are really doing here."

He tilted his head to one side as if releasing tension in his neck, and just for a moment, I thought he actually looked exhausted. But then his brow smoothed and the spark returned to his eyes. "Birrimun Park is at the hub of this weakening."

"The hub? So you're telling me that the US Marshal service believes in the spirit worlds and has sent you out here to investigate a breakdown in the... what did you call it... divisions?"

He stared at me, unapologetic for how crazy it sounded. Calm and confident as always.

"You're saying that the US Marshal Service polices the spirit worlds," I repeated.

"Whether you want to believe it or not, pretty soon it's going to be undeniable. It should be already." He gestured to my shoulder. "But some people are just pigheaded. And to save you getting your friend Caro to check up on me, I work for a division of the Marshal Service that monitors cultural anomalies and shifts."

I blinked a few times and let that idea roll around in my brain. My brain, however, had started to get foggy. "Cultural anomalies and shifts? What the fuck does that mean?"

"Virgin, you need to get that wound looked at soon."

I glanced down. Blood had seeped through the packing. "Why? Are imaginary birds more dangerous than real ones?" I said.

He frowned. "You're losing blood still."

My fingers were slippery from holding his shirt against the wound. Maybe he was right. I hit the emergency frequency code again.

"What now?" said Totes, clearly pissed with me.

"I need a medivac from the station house."

"Virgin?" His tone switched to concern. "Are you alright?"

"I've ripped open my shoulder pretty bad. Don't think I can ride."

"What about the Marshal?"

"He's with me, but he says I'm too heavy to carry back."

Sixkiller frowned at my silly lie and that made me childishly happy.

After a few silent moments, Totes came back to me. "Medivac's ETA is thirty minutes, Virgin. Just waiting for authorization for it to break Canopy into controlled space. You need anything in particular?" asked Totes.

"I..."The world receded and I fell into a grey, comfortable space. Sleeping right now seemed the thing, not talking. But I should check on Aquila first. "Nate... Aquila... is she..."

In the distance, I heard Sixkiller shouting something about blood. And then...

Bull was shouting at me.

No, maybe not at me... but right next to my ear ...Instructions about *priority care* and *PRIORITY CARE!*

I wanted to tell him to hush, that it was bad for his health to get so stressed out, but the words danced about on my tongue, then vanished every time I tried to use my lips. I settled for listening, pleased he was mad at someone else for a change...

And then I was back awake and screaming... SCREAMING with pain. Pain like no other. Pain to die from... to die.

Aquila came with me to that place. She screeched in unison. Her leg was broken, her beak damaged.

Birds don't survive injured beaks. Nate. Nate. Help her... HELP HER!

A cold, numb sensation snatched my consciousness away.

And then it was back again.

"She's awake, Bull, or at least the monitors indicate her brain activity is in a conscious pattern. I just don't think she's chosen to share that with us yet."

Who was that overinformed voice? Bothered that they knew I was awake before I did, I unglued my eyes.

Nate Sixkiller dominated most of my vision, but behind him, framed in the window, stood Heart.

"What are you doing?" I croaked.

Sixkiller put down a phone receiver and folded his arms. "Visiting you in the hospital, making sure you're alive. Hate it to be said I lost a partner on the job."

I wanted to disagree with his use of the term partner, but Heart brushed past him and sat on the bed.

"How are you doing?" Taking my hand in his, he pressed his lips to my skin.

In spite of the throb in my shoulder and the fact that my head felt heavier than a boulder, a wave of self-consciousness tingled through me. It was great to see Heart, but his solicitousness – in front of the Marshal – was awkward.

"I want to go home," I said. "Help me up."

Sixkiller walked around to the other side of the bed and over to the door. "Superintendent Hunt is on his way in to talk to you. I'll give you two some privacy until then."

The memory of La Paloma, the giant crow and the attack flooded back. "Umm... Marshal... er... Did you get me back here?" I asked.

"Came back in the medivac with you."

"The horses."

"Came home by dark. Your pistol's in your bedside table."

My relief was tempered by more concern. How in blazes was I going to explain what happened to me out there? "Maybe we should talk before Bull gets here?"

His eyelids hooded. "Sure thing, Ranger. I'll just go grab a drink."

Heart watched our exchange but didn't speak until the door shut. "Virgin? What happened?"

I wet my lips and tried to sit up a bit farther.

Heart helped me, plumping the pillows and brushing my hair out of my face.

"Don't fuss. I'm fine," I said lightly.

"You weren't fine..." he said. "The wound wouldn't clot. You've had a bunch of transfusions."

"I did?" No wonder I felt like the sweepings of the holocaust. "How long have I been here?"

"They brought you in thirty-eight hours ago."

I felt for my shoulder and winced. "Crap."

"You nearly died, Virgin. You were losing blood faster than they could pump it in."

Now I could focus a bit more clearly, I saw how exhausted Heart looked. "How did they get it under control?"

"Damnedest thing. They ran out of your blood type, were couriering some in from another blood bank. The Marshal insisted they take some of his blood. Turns out you're an identical match. Soon as they tubed some in, your blood started to clot."

"I've got… his blood? In me?"

Heart nodded. "Luckily. Yes. Doctors'll tell you more."

I nodded, feeling nauseous now and unreasonably ungrateful that Sixkiller had saved my life.

"How did you find out I was here…?" I asked.

He shrugged. "Your boss rang your friend Caro. She came and saw me at work."

"But they don't even…"

"You were dying, Virgin. You don't have a next of kin, apparently."

I wiggled my toes and fingers to make sure they worked. Toes were good, but the movement of my fingers sent knife stabs all the way up my arm. "Can you pass the water?"

Heart held a bottle and straw to my mouth. "Nurse said you need to drink a lot."

We sat in silence for a bit while I sipped and ached. I really needed to talk to Sixkiller before I had to answer a bunch of questions from Bull.

When Heart set the bottle down again, I led with "Thanks for coming in. I mean... you know... I appreciate it."

He took my free hand again and he flushed. "You kinda scared me. Didn't like the idea of not seeing you again."

My stomach flipped. Maybe there was something real going on between us. But right now, though, I had to sort out my story with Sixkiller.

"Heart, I need to talk to the Marshal privately... before my boss gets here. Do you mind?"

He hid a disappointed look by turning to look out the window. It was raining. Summer is coming rain. "Sure, lovely. You need anything else?"

"Nothing," I said.

"But, Heart…" I said as he got up and walked to the door. "I really mean it. Thanks."

His smile banished any hint of disappointment. "I heard them say you should be able to go home soon. I'll look forward to it."

"You want to come over and stay tomorrow night, then?"

"I have to work," he said. "But I'll call you. I'll let the Big Hat know you want him."

I smiled at him and waved. "Bye."

He blew me a kiss.

While I waited for Sixkiller to return, I went over the events at Paloma in my mind, including my attempt to prove that the crow hadn't been real. Though still impossible to believe, my body was the proof of it, and that left me with only one choice. Accept and deal… or ask for a psych evaluation. Eval would mean temporary suspension with no guarantee of being reinstated.

"Virgin?"

Sixkiller stood at the door, looking dead normal.

I made my decision right then. If he could be walking around acting sane but still believing all this, then so could I. "What are we going to tell Bull?"

He closed the door behind him and moved closer. "You got yourself figured out with this?"

"Short of offering myself up to the altar of a shrink, I can't see how not to be," I said.

One side of his lips curled. "Knew you were practical."

"You know nothing."

"I talked to the doctor," he continued. "They're saying you have some genetic clotting anomaly and that's why you nearly bled out."

"I do?"

"No," he said. "But it's fine that they think that."

"How do you know I don't? I mean... you got scratched on your face by the same creature, and it stopped bleeding."

"I've built immunity to the anticoagulant they inject. That's why my blood saved you."

"They?"

"The Mythos."

I blinked. This was too much. I wasn't feeling strong enough. "Back the bus up a bit."

He waited while I took a couple of breaths.

"What am I going to say to Bull?" I asked.

"Keep it straightforward. You fell on the steps and cut yourself. You've got a blood disorder that caused the clotting problems."

"Have you seen the mess my shoulder is in? No one'll buy that. The doctors–"

"They can't explain what's going on with your body, so they'll take what you give them," he said calmly.

I reached for the water bottle and had another sip. "Did your blood really save me?"

"Like I said. I've got some immunity."

"Well, I guess I should thank you, then."

"You know we are bound by blood now."

"That's a joke, right?"

His lips twitched. Emotion or amusement? It was hard to say.

"When it happened, I saw Aquila. She was hurt, too… her beak. She saved me from that… thing," I said.

"Your disincarnate will heal herself and return when you need her."

"Right," I said.

The man is crazy.

SIXTEEN

Caro visited after Sixkiller left, wanting precise medical detail.

I let her question me for a while, then sent her home, claiming fatigue and a fuzzy head from sedatives.

The nurse came in with dinner and more pain meds, and then I was alone, finally, with my in-room entertainment and a view of the rain-slick city. I got out of bed and sat in a chair by the window. May be Totes had been right about the Corellas in the Eastern sector.

I hadn't been in a hospital since Dad died, and the memory of it rebounded painfully. He'd fallen from the eastern butte, broken his back. They might have fixed the back but not the accompanying cerebral haemorrhage.

Those last hours I spent with him, he'd been drifting in and out of consciousness, his eyes flickering open, fingers curling in mine. At one stage, he'd whispered some words to me, but I couldn't understand them. His dying words and I'd never know what they were.

Even now, that made me angry.

The reports said he'd slipped but my dad had been murdered; of that, I was sure. And now someone was coming after me. Not coincidence. And not just bad luck. A connection.

My phone beeped from the bedside swivel. I got up and answered it.

"You haven't forgotten our deal, Virgin, I hope."

"Corah? How'd you get this number?"

"Really, Virgin?"

"If you know so much, then you might also know this isn't a good time."

"Good time or not, you owe me an invite to the opening. When can I expect it?"

I sighed. "I'll organize it now. Can I reach you on this number?"

"For a while, yes."

"And then?"

"We're a disposable society, Virgin. Move on."

The line went dead.

The meds had kicked in and I wanted to sleep but I fought it off a little while to search online for media about Dabrowski's reopening. Anything that might give me a clue as to Corah's interest in being there.

Chef Dab had a cult following in the Park precinct and the Western Quarter. It's not like the food was special; it was just good. Polish-Australian fusion with a smattering of Western flavours to catch the tourist.

Business had been good for Dab when others had struggled. He was a testament to consistency. People knew what they'd get and he didn't disappoint: sauerkraut and pork sausages on a hot roll, steak and smoked cheese, dumplings and seafood, ribs with mash and pickles – each dish as good as the last.

I found some articles featuring Dab in an apron, wielding a bread knife and a meat mallet. The articles talked about the redecoration of the premises and some new signature dishes. Apparently, the president of Birrimun Holdings would launch the new menu, accompanied by a smattering of judges and famous folk.

I frowned. Seemed an unlikely gig for the park's big boss, but then Dab's food struck a note with many stomachs, *and* the big chef really knew how to work a contact when he made one. Dab had a talent for making friends, while my dad had displayed a talent for pissing people off. I guess the latter was hereditary.

I leaned back and checked my messages.

True to his word, Dab had sent the invitation details through for me for a party of four guests. Even though it was for tomorrow night, and I knew I probably wouldn't make it, I hit accept on the invitation and then texted the details through to Corah.

Her reply was affirmative and almost immediate.

Out of curiosity, I waited five minutes, then sent another text to her number, asking her what she was going to wear.

The message failed. The phone number had disconnected.

Disposable, huh. Maybe it was time I changed my number, too.

I tucked the patient call buzzer in bed next to me and fell heavily asleep. Not sure for how long, but enough that my eyes felt stitched together when I woke.

I heard a faint rasping. There was concentration in it and more… fatigue. Labouring breaths.

I felt in the bed for the buzzer before I forced my lids open.

Detective Indira Chance sat in a chair close to the head of the bed. She was staring at me with her watery Panda eyes.

I wet my lips. "D-detective? Good of you to visit."

"Can you answer some questions?" She lifted her tablet to indicate she would record me.

"Depends…" I said, pushing myself more upright and scrubbing at my face.

I was suddenly wide awake. The sleep had sharpened my mind somewhat, even though my shoulder burned. "…on what you ask."

"Did you recently visit a psychic in Mystere?"

"You been following me, Detective?"

"I'm pursuing a line of enquiry, Ms Jackson. Can you answer the question?"

"I visited an acquaintance who lives down that way."

"And that friend has connections with a gang identity by the name of Papa Brisé? Is that who paid you to murder the man in the Park?"

My heart skittered. I'd been followed there, after all.

Then again, with the ruckus Sixkiller had caused in Gilgul Street, it wouldn't have been hard to find me. The familiar tug between annoyance and gratitude started up. How could a person be so competent and such a lunatic at one time?

"You wouldn't be questioning one of my people without the legal counsel present, Detective Chance?" a voice boomed.

Bull Hunt filled up most of the doorway, and his words filled the room.

Chance got to her feet, her hand instinctively reaching for her gun. When she recognized Bull, she let her hand rest on the hilt, sending a message that she didn't like or trust him.

"Just checking on the health of my primary witness, Director."

She nodded at me and deliberately stepped up close to Bull, who didn't back away. He remained still for so long, I thought she might draw on him.

"Boss," I said. "Can you pour me some water?"

He flicked me a glance, then stepped aside and let her pass. When she'd gone through, he shut the door after her.

I gave him a shaky grin. "Your timing is immaculate."

"Always." He walked over to me and dropped a light kiss on my head. "You're giving me ulcers, Virgin. You know that?"

His show of concern surprised me. Bull didn't do paternal kisses on the forehead or any other place.

He picked up the chair Chance had been sitting on and put it over by the window again. Sitting down, he gazed out at the rain-blurred city lights. A luminescent crown arced high above the nightscape, some trick of distortion thrown up from the Park's canopy. I guessed it was a little after 2am, because the crown had a silvery tinge. I'd long ago learned to read the time by its changing colour.

"Am I dying?" I asked lightly.

He turned his head little. "Poor taste, Virgin. Without Sixkiller's blood transfusion, you may well have."

"Aaah… yes… Nate."

Bull pinched the bridge of his nose between his fingers and closed his eyes. When he opened them again, he dropped his hand to knee and slapped it like he'd made a decision.

"Look, I'd hoped to avoid telling you this... figured the Marshal would sort things out. But things are getting out of hand, and you have a right to know... a right to protect yourself."

My heart did a skittering thing. "What is it, boss?"

"Your dad always told me there was a lot more going on in life than I'd ever let myself believe. And I always thought he'd spent too long in the heat without a canteen. I mean... I loved the man, Virgin, you know that. But your dad could be a zealot. I've tried to break you of that, but... looks like you will be whatever it is your genes dictate. Hang all that talk about nature and nurture. You're a clear winner for nature, Virgin."

I ignored the personal comments and tried to get to the core of what he was saying. "What has that got to do with me, us, or the Park?"

He took a deep breath. "This'll probably get me fired. But the dead guy in the park was an undercover guy that joint intelligence forces had planted inside an extremist group."

"I won't ask how you know this, but does the extremist group have a name, Bull?"

"I believe they call themselves Korax, something that originated with the word 'raven'. But don't expect to find anything about them online. To the rest of the world, they don't exist."

I took that in before I spoke. "So, maybe the Park was just a convenient place to–"

"The man Nate killed in your apartment was one of them… not a garden-variety thug. You saw the tattoo, Virgin. It might be that he went after you because they thought you saw or heard something in the Park. Or it might be for other reasons. All I know is that my park… my Ranger… are both caught up in something over my pay grade and out of my control."

"You saying you can't help me, Bull?"

"Not if you don't tell me the truth. I know you didn't injure yourself in a fall. Those are claw marks, Virgin."

"No, it wasn't a fall… but I don't know really know what it was."

"You want to *try* to explain."He scowled at me with a full-face-wrinkled, badass look that had scared a hundred Park employees.

I cast around for an answer that would satisfy him. Last thing I needed was to be sectioned for mental health issues.

"Someone knocked me out cold on the stairs at the ranch house. When I came to, I had these… scratches. Never saw who or what did it. Sixkiller was inside. He came out and found me."

"*Neither* of you saw anyone?"

I shook my head. "Not a damn person."

"Well, doctors say your clotting mechanism is normal now, and they can't explain why you wouldn't stop bleeding before. They're calling it an anomaly. Must be that your assailant injected you with something that was short-acting. Lucky Sixkiller was around with the right blood type. You'd already exhausted the local blood bank."

"Lucky," I agreed weakly.

"That bloke you're seeing. I'm going to have him screened."

"Which bloke?"

"The dancer."

He meant Heart.

"Bull!" I sat bolt upright. "That's my personal life. Stay out of it."

He got up out of the chair and lifted his chin so high I could see the age lines on his neck. "If you wish."

I nodded emphatically. "I do."

SEVENTEEN

Caro took me home from hospital the next morning early, insisting she had no urgent work and that we should spend some time together. Though grateful and all, time with Caro could be more tiring than a ten-mile run. By the time we reached my apartment, I was out of sensible conversation and onto monosyllables.

"So, you think there's a connection between the dead guy in the park, the guy Nate killed and this attack on you?"

"Dunno," I said. "Yes. Maybe."

She tucked a sheet around me rather too tight, to show she was peeved. "I get that you're shaken up, but don't play dumb on this, Ginny. How did it go in Mystere?"

I scowled. Why was everyone all up in my business? "Apart from the crazy US lawman, it was fine. Got a lead on the bone feather."

"You need to ask your boss for some protection while we figure this out."

"We?"

"Yeah. I'm good at what I do. Let me help you."

It was so tempting to tell her everything, but

friendship only stretched so far when one of the friends started blurting out crazy shit like "I was attacked by a giant imaginary bird that no one else can see."

"When I'm feeling a bit stronger, Caro. OK?"

I must have looked as pale as I felt, because instead of pressing me on it, she took herself out to the kitchenette to make some herbal tea.

It was such a relief to be home, away from the noise and surprise visitors of the hospital, that I dozed off as soon as she left the room.

A while later, a gentle sensation on my cheek woke me up.

"Heart?"

"How did you know?" His voice was low.

"You're the only person who touches me like that," I said sleepily.

"How sweet," said Caro.

I opened my eyes and saw her standing at the door with the tea. Embarrassed, I pulled the sheet up over my face like a little kid.

There was a clunk as she set the cups down. "The one on the left is ginger, one on the right is strawberry," said Caro.

I stayed right where I was, buried under my bed linen, and a few minutes later, I heard the front door shut.

Heart peeled the sheet off me.

I surfaced, feeling foolish.

"She's gone. How are you today?" he asked.

"Better," I said. "Tired."

He eased onto the bed alongside me and lifted the hem of my nightshirt up. With warm fingers, he traced shapes on my stomach. His touch made me feel a whole lot better, and I luxuriated in it until his breathing changed pace.

"Not yet," I said softly, pushing his hand away. "I have to get back to work soon as I can."

"Work? That's crazy. You've had multiple blood transfusions. You have to rest."

"If I have to rest, then don't tempt me," I said, smiling.

He shook his head, knowing he wouldn't win this conversation, and reached across me for the cup of ginger tea.

I took the strawberry, and we sat sipping companionably for a bit. Heart knew how to inhabit silence in style. It was one of the reasons I liked him.

"We're having a partner night at the club soon. You think you might come with me?" he asked.

"Which club?"

"The Outfit."

I knew the joint. It was a couple blocks from Beef and Horners. The clientele was a little younger and raunchier than at the drinking holes Caro and I favoured. "Partner night?"

"For the staff. Boss is closing up early, and we're having some ribs and beer on the house."

Me and a bunch of exotic dancers? I didn't think so. "Can I think about it? Got a lot on, y'know."

He didn't push it. "Sure."

I put my cup down and slithered under the sheets, closing my eyes. "Sleep and work."

He dropped a kiss on my head. "Don't go out on your own at the moment. Promise?"

"I'm fine."

I thought I heard him chuckle at that, but by the time I opened an eye to check, he was gone.

I woke again to my doorbell. My window view of the blinking lights on the tops of the Sanyo Triptych opposite the Cloisters told me it was almost dark. I didn't like shutting my blinds during the day, because the apartment was too dark. Right now, the sky was the colour of a thin spill of ink across dusty pink paper.

Slipping on a robe, I screened my caller on the sec-cam. It was Sixkiller; even with his back to the door, there was no mistaking him.

I opened up a crack and peered out. "What's up, Marshal?"

"You gonna let me in, Ranger?"

"Do I need to?"

He nodded.

I sighed and released the latch. "Please…"

He walked by me and straight over to the couch, where he plonked down without invitation.

I locked the door and leaned against it, arms folded. Being in a dressing robe around Sixkiller left me self-conscious and disadvantaged. Distance gave me some sense of control. It also meant I didn't have to navigate around John Flat.

He took his hat off, set it on his knee and shook his hair free from its elastic. It fell around his shoulders in a dead straight swathe. A movement designed to show he was letting his guard down.

I didn't believe it.

"You spoke with Superintendent Hunt?" he asked.

"He came by the hospital last night. He knows it wasn't a rock I tore myself up on, but that's it. I said I got knocked out and couldn't remember what happened. Then you found me."

I wasn't going to tell Sixkiller everything Bull had said. My boss and I went back a long way. Sixkiller and I went back several days only. Trust was something you built over time.

"That satisfied him?"

"Not really."

He snorted, and flipped one side of his hair back behind his shoulder. His sharp cheekbone brought a slash of definition to his face. And hardness.

"I have some information that may help us," he said.

Us? Well, I guess that was a start. "What's that?"

"The man in your apartment–"

"Leo Teng?"

He paused long enough to let slip his surprise that I knew. "Yeah... well, I've been told he's been living in a room above a club in your Western Quarter."

"Do the police know that?"

"If not now, then it won't be long till they do."

"We should go there and have a look around."

"Yes."

"What's the name of the club?"

"Jusco's. You know it?"

"I know it." It was next door to Dabrowski's Diner. My plans for *not* going to Chef's opening suddenly reversed. "You got a tuxedo?"

"Here?"

"Yeah."

"No, and are you going to tell me why I would need one, or am I supposed to guess?"

"The diner next door to Jusco's is having a big reopening tonight, and I have an invitation to go. It would be a perfect chance to look at the upstairs section of Jusco's where the apartments are, without being noticed."

"Are you fit to…?" He tapered off when my eyes narrowed.

"You'll need a tuxedo to get in to the event. It's a kinda mixed affair. Polish burgers, vodka, sequins and suits," I said.

"Are you wearing sequins?"

"Hell, no."

He looked relieved. "So, where can I get a suit?"

I grabbed my phone and scrolled through the city directory. "I'll book a mobile suit hire. They'll measure you when you arrive and outfit you inside an hour in your apartment. I'll meet you in the lobby aft–"

"I think it's best if I come back here and help you down," he said.

I wavered. I felt like crap and it would be a long evening. No point in being stubborn just for the sake of it. "Fine."

As soon as he left, I tried calling Heart, but his phone went to message bank. He had said he'd be working tonight, so I left a message saying not to come over later, because I needed the sleep. I didn't mention anything about going out to Dabrowski's. It was easier left unsaid.

Then I called Caro.

"Oh, so you're speaking to me now?" she said.

"Sorry, I've been… I've just been…"

"I know you, Virgin. When people start pressuring you, you get foetal. Nothing new in that."

"It's not fine. You're my… friend and I should be more grateful."

"Ugh. Grateful," she said. "What a disgusting word. So, you need company now?"

"Actually, I'm going to Dab's opening tonight with Nate. You want to come?"

"Are you sure you're up to that? You're pretty weak still."

"Yeah, Dad. I'm sure."

The "Dad" reference was our private joke, being that neither of us had had mums around when we were younger. Caro's was killed by insurgents in Thailand. And mine… well, who knew? She wasn't around, had never been, and Dad hadn't seen fit to dwell on it. I assumed she was a drunk or an addict. His sadness suggested it.

"Besides, I've got a reason to be going," I added.

A short pause. "Do tell!"

"Only if you come. Dress for hot sauce and sauerkraut."

EIGHTEEN

"And your plan is?" asked Sixkiller.

The strobe effect of the traffic and city lights on his face during the taxi ride to the Western Quarter didn't hide the odd expression on his face. I knew that look.

"What?" I demanded.

"Answering a question with a question is bad manners," he said.

"Staring at what someone is wearing is also bad manners. It's just a dress, OK?"

I swear he bit his lip right then, but it could have been the play of the fluorescents as they cast their fleeting patterns.

And then the taxi driver veered off the Park Ringway and onto the Western Quarter spur road, and we both stared out the windows, taking in the mad frizz of *Saloon* and *Beer* and *Girls* signs.

"My plan is to get upstairs in the diner to check out the apartments opposite above the club."

"Why not go straight in through the club itself?"

"Countless reasons, not the least of being that their security is tight and they hate any type of law enforcement. You've got it stamped on your forehead.

And me... well, I'm too well known in these parts. What number is it?"

"Apartment 5. What will you be able to see from upstairs?"

"They're old, narrow terrace houses, so the apartments all have windows. I should be able to just count along and find the right one."

"Terraced?"He looked confused.

"Built very close together," I said.

"How do we get in?"

I raised my eyebrows. "We go across, of course."

"Across?"

"It's only a twenty-foot drop."

"You won't go after him without me."That was not a question by any means.

"Unlikely, the way I'm feeling. But you'll need to run interference on the stairs while I look around first. Chef Dab– the owner – runs a closed house on the upstairs section on these occasions. A few drinks, and people who go searching out privacy end up stealing the silverware."

"Privacy for what?"

"It's a party in the Quarter with gallons of vodka. You work it out."

"You mean they're looking for places to... be carnal."

"If that's what you call it in Virginia."

Our conversation hit a major roadblock about then, and neither of us spoke again until the taxi turned right onto Virgil Earp Way and pulled into the loading zone outside Dabrowski's Diner.

As I gave the cabbie my One Card, my phone beeped an incoming text; Caro was already outside, waiting.

Sixkiller spotted her before I could get my thumbs free to reply, and unfolded himself from the car to stroll over.

I retrieved my card from the cabbie.

"Busy out tonight," he said. "You be wantin' a ride home? Might be best to book now."

"Thanks for the offer, but I'm not sure what time I'll be leaving."

He held up his I-code anyway.

I scanned it politely with my phone. "I'll beep you if I get stuck."

"Sure," he said.

Then I was out the door and he was pulling back into the traffic.

"A dress, Virgin; how sweet."

"Corah?" I turned to see the psychic standing behind me, dressed in a figure-hugging black dress and killer peep-toe heels. Her hair was floaty and almost at her waist, and huge circular silver earrings dangled from her lobes.

To add to the mystery, she had a bright circular red mark on her forehead. Last time I checked, there was nothing remotely South Asian in her ancestry, but it completed an intriguing image.

"I've clearly been spending too much time–"

"In the company of criminals?" I finished for her.

She screwed up her face. "So judgmental."

I bit my tongue on that. No point of getting into it with her on the sidewalk. The evening had a long way to go, and I was already feeling light-headed.

"Whatever. I got you your invite; now, you don't expect me to hold your hand all evening, do you?"

I moved towards the small queue of people having

their ID checked at the door. Caro and Sixkiller stood slightly to one side.

"I'm a big girl. But you will introduce me to *him*, won't you?"

With that, Corah cut right in front of me and slinked straight up to Sixkiller. Her loose hair flicked Caro in the face as she swung it back over her shoulder and tilted her head upward.

"I'm Corah, and *you* are delicious."

Caro's eyes bugged in disbelief, and she took an involuntary step backward.

"At ease, Corah," I said.

But the Marshal had already taken her hand and seemed in danger of drowning in whatever moist emotion Corah exuded from her stare.

"Caro Jenae and Marshal Nate Sixkiller," I said by way of introduction. "Meet... um... Corah."

"*Marshal* Sixkiller. What a shame... all the best men are always in law enforcement," she said, completely ignoring Caro.

"Well, I take that as a compliment, ma'am," said Sixkiller in his broadest drawl. "And hope you don't hold it agin' me."

"I'd like to hold many things agin' you, Marshal. Perhaps I could make you a list."

Sixkiller chuckled. A downright out-loud warm chuckle that sent my irritation levels skyrocketing. All this man had given me so far was grief and a superior lip curl. And Corah's sex scent had him *chuckling*.

I stepped right through the middle of their handholding huddle, knocking them apart.

"Let's go," I said over my shoulder. "I need vodka."

• • •

Caro was right at my shoulder as we passed security and inside.

"Virgin?" she whispered. "Who the f–"

"Later," I said.

A tray of shot glasses spun past and I retrieved one each for Caro and I. Sixkiller could get his own damn drink. I knocked it back in a gulp, hoping it would ease the knot in my gut. Corah had always had the power to twist me up.

As the waitress and tray reversed trajectory through the crowd, I secured another couple.

"Steady there, girl," said Caro. "You're barely upright as it is. You keep doing that and you'll be sailing more vodka in your veins than blood."

I ignored her and downed them both. The alcohol burned away the tension in my stomach but left me a little dizzy.

Caro took my hand and led me to a booth, where I steadied myself and looked around.

The diner had experienced some kind of makeover in the couple of days since I'd been there. The vinyl seats, plastic leader boards, rectangular fluorescent lights and cigarette-cauterised cafe stools had gone in favour of miniature chandeliers, freshly carpeted booths and self-regenerating gerberas in pots. Dabrowski's signature giant sausage still hung above the bar, though, and the smell of sauerkraut lingered.

I felt like I'd walked into a seriously messed-up food dream, the kind you had after eating Cool Whip on a pickle.

But the clientele was lapping it up. The Western Quarter loved a novelty look that didn't include upturned horseshoes and stirrup irons.

"You scared me to death, Virgin," said a voice at my shoulder.

Totes slipped into the booth alongside me.

"Hey," I said, and held out my fist so we could knuckle five.

He set his long glass nonalcoholic fruity extravaganza on the table in front of him and sucked with gusto through the straw. "I wanted to come to the hospital, but Bull wouldn't let me leave work."

"Nothing you could have done other than send the medivac for me. Thanks, by the way. Sorry I was so…"

He shrugged. "You're you, Virgin. That's all I ever want you to be."

Caro eye-rolled and mimicked a finger-gag while he was looking down into his drink.

"I'm still mad at you for bugging my apartment," I said.

"But now you're really grateful becuase it proved you didn't kill that dude."

I sighed. "Yes. But, Totes… why?"

"I… just… you know… want you to be safe."

"You invaded my privacy. It's… creepy."

His face fell. "I'm sorry."

"Just don't do anything like that again. OK?"

He perked up at signs of forgiveness. "On my dolls, I swear!"

"Right. Now get out of my face."

He gave me a salute, slopping his mocktail everywhere as he left.

"Cute," said Caro in a dry voice.

"Whatever."

Totes made a beeline for the food, passing by Sixkiller, who had made it to the bar according to his hat, which I picked out in the crowd. Corah's auburn crown of hair was just visible above his shoulder.

I looked away from them, searching out Chef Dab. He was holding court from the newly outfitted open-windowed kitchen, his belly resting on the vast stainless steel bench in front of him. Some kind of chopping demonstration was going on that involved a lump of meat, a wooden board and a giant cleaver. His audience was mainly business suits and cocktail dresses. I recognized some of the faces in them as corporate high-flyers – the CEO of the Australis moon shuttle company; an actor from the reality TV show *Wasters*; and Parks Southern's very own bossman. Then there was a judge or two, some lauded barristers.

Dabs food had always had a broad appeal, even if for some, it was a case of slumming it.

Corah had moved and was standing with the judges, watching Dab's antics from over their shoulders. Seems she'd dispensed with Sixkiller already. She wasn't one to dwell.

"You want some koreczki?" asked a nasal voice in my ear.

Greta stood dressed in a tight-fitting satin shift, lace-up boots and a floral wreath with trailing ribbons in her hair.

"Nice head thingy," I said.

"Chef's having an Andy Warhol moment," she replied sourly.

I gave her a quizzical stare.

"Pop culture meets stupid old traditions – instead of advertising. It's" – she used her free hand to gesture down her clothes – "supposed to signify I'm a waiter *and* a maiden."

"What's a maiden?" I asked.

"You serious, Virgin?" said Caro. "Maidens are unmarried women."

"That's sexist," I said, "and just plain gross."

"You gonna tell him that?" said Greta, dipping the tray so we could both seize some skewered cheese from it.

"Not while he's wielding a weapon of mass destruction."

"Wait till he does his knife-juggling demonstration," she said and tottered off.

Caro blew on the steaming hot cheese cubes. "Now tell me about that dreadful woman. Is that why you want me here? To keep her away from Sixkiller? I'd be happy to trip her up and accidentally step on her."

I savoured the image. "*That woman* is a psychic from Divine Province. We went to school together."

Caro's eyes widened. "She's the one you used to school-share with who–"

"Left smoke in our desk and got me busted. Yeah, that's her."

"Ahaaa. Good to know my instant dislike was justified."

I could grin now after three shots of vodka and a bite of fried cheese. "I owed her a favour and she wanted an invite to this."

"Why so?"

I shrugged, not really caring right now.

"You don't have the nose for a story, do you, Ginny? I mean, there's got to be something going on for her to want to come uptown for a diner relaunch. Could be newsworthy."

"I got my own stuff to deal with, and Corah stopped being interesting to me the year we graduated."

"Fair enough," said Caro, but her eyes narrowed with preoccupation.

"I'm here because we've found a lead on the guy who attacked me in my apartment," I said, trying to drag her attention back. It worked.

"And?"

"He was living in an apartment above Jusco's."

"Next door?"

I nodded. "I'm going to take a look from the first floor. Can you help Sixkiller and me by keeping anyone from coming up after me?"

"Might not be the only thing the Marshal needs a hand with – your friend has her suction pads set to warp."

I wanted to laugh at that, but a strong wave of nausea swept through me. Maybe I wasn't so good after all. "I'm going to say hello to Dab, then I want you to distract the bouncer on the stairs so I can get past."

"Fine. But why don't you just ask Chef if you can look around? You're on good terms."

"I could, but then he'd know what I was doing. I really don't want this coming back on him. You know the detective on the case is a bulldog."

"You mean her?" Caro tossed her head, indicating I should look over her shoulder out the window and onto the pavement.

Chance stood there, staring straight in at me.

"Jeez, did she follow us here as well?"

"Looks like it."

I got up. "Let's go say hello to Chef."

We left the booth and threaded through the partygoers, over to Chef Dab's stainless steel stage. He saw me almost immediately and blew kisses, which I smiled at, and nodded. He then glanced to my side and saw Caro, and his expression shifted to obvious disappointment that I hadn't brought a man.

That really made me want to laugh, but the nausea bubbled up in my throat in a way that made my eyes water.

I said in Caro's ear, "I need to get this done."

She lent me her shoulder to get back across the room.

"How about I go up?" she said.

"No, I know the layout upstairs. I'll be quicker."

"Not if you faint."

I grabbed another passing shot glass. "I'm fine."

"Virgin?"

Sixkiller was suddenly in my face, taking up space.

The room started to spin a bit, and I stumbled despite Caro's support. Sixkiller grabbed my other arm and righted me.

"Virgin?" Another voice.

I turned. "Heart?"

An influx of people though the door thrust us all together in a tight and awkward circle.

"Virgin, I didn't know you had it in you. Such outstanding male company," said Corah, piercingly clear above the chatter.

"What are you doing here?" said Heart in my ear. "You left a message saying you were staying at home to sleep."

His voice held all sorts of accusation.

"I'm going to be sick," I said.

I pushed away from them all over toward the bouncer at the stairs.

"Bathroom," I croaked at him.

"Over there." He pointed to the queue that had formed near the downstairs customer restroom.

"The lady needs somewhere private. She's unwell," said Sixkiller from behind me.

The bouncer folded his arms, not about to be told anything when Caro launched in on him.

"The girl's a friend of the Chef's and she's about to chuck her guts. You want the entire party to think it's something she ate here? The Chef be happy about that, do you think?"

He wavered and touched his ear to consult whoever was on the other end of his bud.

I let myself dry-retch out over his foot. It wasn't much of a stretch. The next time would be a hurl. I must have been convincing, because he stepped to one side.

"Make it quick."

Sixkiller took my arm to help me.

"Not you... her," said the bouncer, indicating Caro.

She took my arm from Sixkiller and helped me to the top step, where we paused to catch our breath. A glance behind me showed Sixkiller engaging the bouncer, and Corah already drifting off toward one of the judges again. Only Heart was watching me still, with curious intent.

"Where to?" Caro whispered.

"Bathroom's on the right."

Turns out I was going to need it. I made the pan just in time to lose most of the vodka and cheese. After a quick sluice of water across my face, I felt clearer in the head.

Caro stood by the basin and handed me a towel.

"Wait in here. Shut the cubicle door and pretend I'm inside."

She nodded. "Will you be alright?"

I squeezed her hand and slipped back out into the corridor.

NINETEEN

I'd been up here many times in the past and knew my way around. Chef's live-in suites took up the rest of the floor, opposite the restroom. The rooms on the other side were kept for visitors and the occasional live-in waiter. At the end of the corridor was a small stairway that led up to a room that always stayed locked. Dab liked to act out his kinky habits in a safe place. His version of a dungeon was more of an attic, a split-level room that you could only get to from the far end of the first floor.

The spare bedrooms would give me the view I needed into Jusco's. I tried the doors of the first two and found them locked. The third was open and being lived in. Once my eyes had adjusted to the dark, I saw a voluminous dress lying out on the bed and a collection of ribbons slung across it, suggesting the occupant was female and large. Greta, perhaps? She'd worked for Dab for a long time, but I knew nothing about her personal life.

The blind hung crookedly across the window like a broken arm. I studied it for a moment, the angle and height, and then pulled it up.

The side wall of Jusco's was only little more than a body's length away. It was like that with all the terrace houses in the area. Some even had tricky little bridges made from cast-off doors or planks joining the buildings.

I scanned the opposing windows and counted them off. Number five, the one at the very back, was in darkness. The good news was that its window was open. The bad news, the closest connecting room was Chef's private attic.

A whole bunch of things ran through my mind, the foremost being that the only way in, without a whole lot of hoo-hah, would be to plank it across. A bunch of doubts and reservations chased that thought, like I should get Sixkiller to help me but he'd never get past the bouncer; I was too weak to do something like this right now, but it had to be done; What if the bouncer came looking for me and Caro?; How would I get into Chef's locked room?

I had solutions to the last two, at least.

First, I texted Caro.

Tell Nate I need a distraction downstairs for 20 mins.

She replied quickly with an OK.

I headed along the corridor and up the steps to Chef's attic. The door was padlocked because Dab figured no one else used them anymore – we were all about bio-locking mechanisms these days. But then, he left a spare key outside – just in case.

Go figure.

I felt beside the door where the wallpaper met the wall panelling and found the piece that peeled back to reveal a little crevice .Chef had never shown me directly, but I'd seen him fumbling around here before.

It felt strange inserting metal into metal, and it gave a satisfying click when it opened. I put the key back into its hidey-hole and tried to leave the chain and padlock arranged in a way that didn't draw attention to it being open.

Negotiating the war zone of sex toys inside took a few moments. So did the struggle with the blind, which had clearly not been raised for years. By the time I had it up and the window open wide enough to climb through, I was slippery with sweat.

Planks were easy to come by, though. He had a set leaning neatly against the wall. Some with leather strands attached, others studded with hard plastic nails. I selected the biggest of the latter and levered it across into the empty apartment in Jusco's. It was only just long enough, catching on the lip of the opposite ledge.

I climbed out the window. No room for thinking too hard on this one. Either I did it or I got the hell out of there.

The nails gave the plank some grip at this end, but at the other, it slid around. I crawled along it on my hands and knees, concentrating on breathing evenly so that I didn't black out. It only took a few moments to cross the tiny distance, but it might as well have been as wide as a canyon.

Sweat dripped from every awkward place on my body. My hands and knees grew slick, making it a struggle to get enough grip to lift the window high enough to get in.

After several heaves that sent the plank into an unnerving sliding motion, the runners unstuck and I was able to crawl inside.

My heart smashed at my ribs so hard when I hit the floor, I had to wait for the dots before my eyes to fade. Normally, I was a fit, strong person, but climbing agility and long hours in the saddle didn't match up so well. Add some transfusion weakness to that, and I was running well below par.

My breathing finally slowed then foundered again on the rank smell of unwashed clothes, stale anchovies and an overly sweet high-end artificial weed scent.

Not planning on leaving trace evidence for Indira Chance, I retrieved a tissue from my underwear and used it to flick on the light.

Barely lived in. Weapons laid out on the bed. A battered pocket tablet on the bedside table.

Using the tissue again, I pressed it into life, and it opened straight to a set of photos. Me, and me, and me – leaving work, in a bar, on the street, in a taxi.

Looks like I had the right room.

I tried to search for other files, but the device seemed to be empty other than my pictures.

My phone beeped again; a message from Caro.

All hell loose. Chance on her way to Jusco's. Get out.

Shit.

I scanned quickly, looking for anything that could identify this guy. A quick rummage through his pile of dirty clothes revealed nothing but gum and a loose condom. His knapsack pockets coughed up half a hot dog and two strips of tablets. One was a prescription painkiller I recognized, but the other was had no brand. On impulse, I slipped them in my pocket.

Thumps on the landing outside the door told me I'd run out of time.

"There's someone in there!" A man's voice.

"Open the damn door!" Detective Chance.

I flicked the switch off and ran for the window, scrambling along the plank with no thought for balance or safety. If Chance caught me in there, I'd be in jail tonight, and maybe forever, no explanations required.

The back end of the wood began to slide off as my hand touched Chef's windowsill. I managed to get my knee onto the ledge as the plank fell into the skip bin below. Garbage bags muffled the sound, but I couldn't hear much above the blood rushing in my ears anyways.

I shoved the window closed and wrenched at the blinds. They fell with a clatter, and I grabbed them to stop them dancing around.

A slight lightening of the dark in which I stood frozen told me Chance had turned on the light in the room across from me.

"Out the window," I heard her shout. "Check... alley."

Dropping to my knees, I crawled across the room to the door, where I stopped to listen again.

"What about... next door?" said someone else.

"...search now."

I cracked the door and slid through on my butt, locking up the padlock as soon as I was through. My legs shook as I walked downstairs, but no one was watching.

The bouncer had deserted his post and most of the crowd had converged on the bar. From my vantage point of a couple steps higher than everyone else, I saw Heart attempting to restrain Sixkiller and the bouncer sprawled face-first onto the bar littered with broken glass and pretzel confetti.

The crowd seemed titillated by what was going on. Lots of catcalls and whoops. A brawl never failed to garner interest in the Quarter. Especially when the venue boasted free booze and mini chandeliers.

Chef, flailing his cleaver high in the air, climbed onto a bar stool and bellowed for order.

Spying Caro in the melee, I wove through the bumping bodies until I reached her.

"Thank the Time Fucking Lords!" she said.

"What's happened?"

She looked away from me. "You said you wanted a distraction…"

"Caro, what–?"

She turned back, putting her lips to my ear. "I might have accidentally knocked your girlfriend from Divine Prov into our bouncer friend."

Fatigue began to suck me down a drain, and I struggled to hold it off. "And?"

"He mouthed off at her and Mr Chivalrous Marshal took offence."

"What about Heart? What's he doing, getting involved?"

"Beats me, Ginny, but looks like it's not over. I'm thinking we should be heading home."

I glanced around and saw the crowd parting to let the police through, Detective Chance coming towards us, leading the march to the bar.

Seeing her, Sixkiller let Heart pull him back.

The crowd cheered some more and chanted something I couldn't quite understand. They were in a long, echoing tunnel.

Or I was.

I slipped the strip of pills I'd take from Jusco's into Caro's hand. "I might be held up for a while. Get out of here and keep these safe."

She arched an eyebrow and disappeared the pills into her own pockets.

Before I could check back on Sixkiller and Heart, a hand seized me by the back of the neck.

"Take her to the van and search her." Detective Chance was in a mood. Uniform creased and eyes puffy.

The police hustled me out onto the footpath to their mobile post.

The catcalls from the crowd got louder and more antagonistic. They didn't like the disruption to the party or the fight. I craned over my shoulder and saw that Caro, thankfully, had vanished.

I told myself to relax. The detective couldn't prove anything. The only person to see me go upstairs who would talk was out cold on the bar.

The constable halted at the door of the van and waited for Detective Chance to catch up.

When she did, she got straight up in my face, spraying me with spit. "I'm out pursuing a murder investigation, and who do I stumble on yet again?"

"You've been following me for days," I said. "I'm not sure that qualifies as 'stumbling'."

She gave me the benefit of her nastiest smile and gestured into the open doorway of their mobile station.

I stepped in, ducking my head.

Part tall surveillance van, part Photos While U Wait booth, it reeked of stale pies and solvent.

The detective followed me and as she shut the door, I glimpsed Heart's anxious face among the spectators.

Chance pushed me into a chair and activated the console on the wall behind her. A lap belt snapped tight on my legs and another across my breasts.

I flexed against them, furious. "What are you doing? Am I under arrest?"

"Just want to talk, Ranger."

"Then take these restraints off me."

"We find they help to focus agitated felons."

I stopped myself from swearing at her. She didn't need an excuse to take me downtown. "I am not a felon and I have nothing to say to you."

"Your cooperation would make this a whole lot better."

"You don't want cooperation, detective. You want a conviction. Even if it's the wrong one," I said calmly.

She ignored that, turning her head away to speak to whoever was at the other end of her communication channel.

I glanced around while she was preoccupied. The van had several segments, from what I could see. Three guys sat hunched in front of screens down the far end, running some type of facial recognition scans on the patrons out on the sidewalk.

The middle section was a semicircle of fixed stools, all set up to receive pull-down sensory helmets. Both those sections were divided by a transparent partition. The third section held Chance, one of her officers, and a row of restraint chairs like the one I was in, a place for short, sharp street interrogations away from the public eye. Was it old blood spatter on the walls or spilled coffee?

She swung back to me, hands on hips, small enough to stand upright in the van, even though her officer had to stoop a little. "Tell me what you're doing here."

"I'm friends with the owner. Chef Dabrowski and my dad were friends. He invited me to his opening."

She tapped an intercom link. One of the techs down the end nodded and got busy verifying my statement.

"You look sick. You wired?" she asked.

"I don't take drugs. You know why I look sick. I've just gotten out of hospital after having multiple blood transfusions."

"An innocent person would be home in bed," she commented. "A guilty person would be out trying to mop up their trail. I know you were in that apartment in Jusco's."

"Pardon me for saying, Detective, but you seem a little fixated on me. Perhaps you should cast your net a little wider."

She folded her arms and blinked in anger. "Search her!"

Her constable ran a body scanner over me first, then patted me down and checked my pockets, removing my One Card and the tissues.

"That's it, detective," he said when he'd finished.

"What were you looking for in that apartment? What did you take?" she demanded.

"No idea what you're talking about. I've been at Chef's party."

Her expression suggested she wanted to strangle another kind of answer out of me, but instead, she told her officer to step outside the van. Then she followed him.

Through the open door, I heard her organizing a search of the alley and a warrant for Chef's place.

A throbbing, mind-melting headache descended over my eyes. I needed to lie down badly and sleep. My mouth began to water and without any other warning, I threw up on myself. The vomit pooled on my lap and then ran down my legs, dripping from the hem of my skirt.

I groaned with embarrassment more than anything else.

"Is she under arrest? Then I insist that you bring her out here where I can see her!" boomed a voice from outside.

A short silence followed. Chance leaned into the unit and pressed a function key on the panel by the door. The restraint snapped open and back into its holder.

She curled her lip at the sight of me and beckoned.

I got up and kinda fell out of the door into the waiting arms of Chef Dab. Despite the vomit, he held me fast.

"Chef, I got sick, let go."

"Are you alright?"

"I'm fine."

The flush spreading up his neck told me he was not. "You come into my place without a warrant, abduct a guest and traumatize her. That is kidnapping, Detective."

"We were responding to a complaint about a violent incident and therefore needed no warrant. Your guest agreed to speak with us. Besides, how can it be kidnapping when the person in question is standing right next to you? No need to be melodramatic, sir."

"*Melodramatic*?" Chef's voice rose to a pitch that threatened the sound barrier.

The crowd on the pavement fell still and silent around us. People watched. Cameras out and recording.

"Chef, let it go," I said softly. "It's OK."

The hot puff of his breath glanced off my cheek and he set me on my feet.

"However, Chef Dabrowski, in a matter of moments, I'll have a warrant to search your premises. In the meantime, I request that you step back inside and provide full cooperation," said Chance.

"I will do nothing of the sort," said Chef. "You will present your warrant to my solicitor and they will accompany you on your search. In the meantime, *you* shall wait outside my premises."

He clamped his arm around me and ushered me back inside.

Most of the party was out on the pavement, and Chef unceremoniously waved them off by locking the diner's doors.

"Greta! Help Virgin clean up and then bring her to the office."

Greta emerged from behind the bar and offered me an arm. I glanced back outside as I took it. No Sixkiller or Corah or Heart in evidence among the bystanders. Caro, I hoped, was already home and examining the strip of pills I'd given her.

"You had a tough night, honey. Here, let me sponge you down," said Greta.

My grateful smile was about as watery as my mouth. Together, we washed the worst of the mess off my dress, and she gave me a fresh kitchen coat to cover it.

"Now let's go see Papa Bear," she said.

Chef was drinking neat vodka in his desk swivel when I shuffled into the office. He'd changed his shirt.

"Sit, Virgin. Talk."

I shut the door and eased down opposite him. The quiet in the room was divine.

"It might take a while," I said.

He poured another measure into his glass. "I'm a good listener. Vodka?"

I shuddered. "No."

We were done an hour later. I told him about the murder, the Marshal, my trip to Divine Province and how I'd just crawled across into Jusco's from his attic looking for a clue to who'd sent Leo Teng after me.

"Why didn't you just ask me to help?"

I shrugged. "Didn't want to involve you. But I guess that didn't work out so well, huh."

He sighed. "Did you find anything?"

"Yes, and I gave it to my friend Caro. She left the party as they dragged me out. The only thing they'll find is one of your paddles, down in the alley. It fell as I climbed back."

"You went across from my playroom?"

"Yeah, sorry. It was the most direct route."

He grunted. "I'll say I threw it out there yesterday."

"It will have my DNA on it."

"Then you'll just have to admit to having a penchant for older men."

I nodded. "You'll cover for me?"

"Of course."

I nodded at that. "Thank you, Chef. I have no right to–"

"You have *every* right to. I told your father I would watch out for you. And that is what I will do. Is there anything else I should know?"

"Your bouncer, the one who the Marshal knocked out... he knows I went upstairs."

"He is on his way to Saint Gilliard's Clinic with a broken jaw. He will not be speaking to anyone for a while, and when he is, I will make sure it's not mentioned."

My gratitude evinced itself as stinging tears behind my eyes.

"This detective, she wants you bad?" he asked.

"I think she just needs an arrest. I don't know. Maybe there's more to it. Either way, I need to find out the truth myself."

"I will send my lawyer to visit you. He is good."

"Superintendent Hunt wants me to use Park lawyers."

Chef made a rude noise. "Bureaucrats. My man knows how to win a fight."

I hesitated. It would annoy Bull, and I needed my boss on side, but Chef had a point. Park lawyers were all about conveyancing, property and environmental law. Their kind of crime came in shades of white. They could be a bit underdone if left to handle a murder.

"Just meet with him, Virgin. Humour me."

I smiled and nodded.

"Good girl. Now we get you home before Detective Heavy Boots comes kicking through my door."

I hugged him. "If you hadn't come and caused a scene, I'd still be in that van."

"For that, you must thank your young man. He came to me, said what I should do in front of the cameras."

"Young man?"

"Virgin," he said with a sigh. "I see you with your girlfriend, I think that maybe she is your partner. Then the boy, the dancer, he comes and tells me who he is and what I should do."

"You mean *Heart?*"

"Yes, Heart Williams. His name I'm not so sure about… but the rest I liked."

Chef's revelation took me by surprise. "Do you know where he went?"

He shrugged. "Perhaps he is outside still?"

I pulled out my phone and called him, but it went to message. "Call me, please."

Greta poked her head in the office. "They're at the door."

"Take her out the back and put her in a taxi," said Chef.

Greta and I headed down the stairs and out through the kitchens.

"You'll have to walk a block or so to catch a taxi," said Greta.

"No need," I said pulling out my phone again.

I called the taxi who'd brought me to the club. "You free now?"

"Just a block over from the diner," he said.

"Come to the street behind. I'm out back."

"Be there soon," said the driver.

Greta waited with me, not saying much. There was something soothing about her.

"None of my business, Greta, but are you and Chef…"

She lifted her shoulders a little. "We have an understanding. You know how it is."

I thought about Heart. There'd been an understanding between us too, but that seemed to be changing and the ground had become shaky.

"Here's your ride," said Greta as the taxi pulled into the alley. It surged over the speed bumps and stopped right in front of us.

I gave her a quick hug and jumped into the back seat.

"Destination," asked the driver.

"From the pickup address earlier. The Cloisters, Park South." I settled back, overwhelmed by relief to be going home.

"Rough night?" he asked.

"Rough week," I said. "Going to shut my eyes for a bit. Can you wake me when we get there?"

"Sure thing."

And with that, I slept.

TWENTY

A noise woke me. An eagle's cry. Distressed and urgent.

I lifted my head from the sticky vinyl seat and wiped saliva from the corner of my mouth. The headache had returned but as more of a dull ache at the base of my skull. I rotated my head to either side, stretching the tendons in my neck, and looked to see where we were.

"Hey," I said, sitting bolt upright. "What's going on?"

"Traffic jam on the ring road; I'm taking the southern bypass."

"Oh, sure, of course." I settled back for a moment, waiting for my senses to sharpen. My phone clock said I'd been in the taxi almost twenty minutes. If we'd gone the way he said, we should be almost back at the Bypass and Ringway convergence by now. Instead, it looked like we were driving south toward either Divine Province or Coast City.

I stared at the back of the taxi driver's head, a prickle of fear across my skin. As carefully and surreptitiously as I could, I tapped his driver number, illuminated on his visor, into my Safe Travel app. It came up with an alert that the number was fake.

As he slowed for the next intersection, I grabbed

the door handle and tried to shove it open. Nothing happened. It was locked.

"Settle down, Ranger," said the man in the front seat. He leaned an arm back over the seat and aimed a SIG 9mm at me.

I probably should have done exactly what he said, but my adrenalin-whizzed survival instinct had other ideas. I chopped down as hard as I could on his forearm with both hands, forcing his elbow to bend at an unnatural angle. The pistol discharged into the floor. Could have been me, but it wasn't. Dumb luck.

I chopped again and brought my boot up to heel-jam his hand against the seat. Then I wrenched the pistol from his fingers and shoved the muzzle against his throat.

"Pull over!" I twisted the barrel into the soft part under his jaw where it met his ear to make my point.

He swerved to the curb, and the cars behind blared their horns in fury at us.

"Unlock my door. One hand, slow so I can see," I said.

He reached for the release button and pressed it. With my free hand, I pressed the handle and kicked the door open. "Who are you working for?"

He kept silent and stiff.

"Tell me," I shouted at him.

He tilted his head away, bracing against me pulling the trigger, but refused to answer.

That left me with a decision.

I wasn't going to shoot him, and the longer I prolonged this moment, the more chance I had of something going wrong.

"You follow me and I'll shoot your face off," I said.

With that, I was ripping my heels off and out on the street running.

It didn't take long to lose my kidnapper… and myself. After a few alley zigzags, I found my way onto a wide road lined with endless used-car lots, low brick utilities buildings and gas stations. The Million Mile, they called it.

The East Coast had nominated lots of areas where only public transport, delivery and emergency vehicles could go. But the freeways still linked commuters to their work, and they got there by a combo of drive, park and ride. Which meant you could still buy cars.

The Million Mile sold mainly electrics, but some still specialized in the old-style guzzler V8s and diesel devils, more as collectors' items than anything else. Like wearing animal products around Liberationists, driving gassed cars in certain parts of the city could get you dead real quick by the hand of anti-vehicular fanatics. Car lots along here all boasted electrified fencing and black box image recognition sec-ware. You came in through the security checkpoint and left the same way. Everything was monitored.

I checked the safety on the pistol and tucked it in the inside pocket of the Chef's whites with trembling hands. Whoever the hell the taxi driver was, he would still be out looking for me. I had to get off the main road.

Flashing signs ahead wooed me with names like Burger Beast, Chicken Chow and a Round the Dick's. I slipped my heels back on and headed for them.

A quick reconnoitre told me that Chicken Chow offered teriyaki and rice and a darkish corner to hide, so I headed in, keen to be off the brightly lit sidewalk. I ordered a regular meal with an upsized drink and took it to the corner table. The food tasted better than I expected after two vodka vomits and an evening full of stress, but I made myself eat slowly, giving my stomach time to relax and accept the peace offering.

My phone vibrated in my pocket and I pulled it out."Caro. I was just about to call you."

"Where the hell are you? I've had Delicious Williams and the Marshal demanding I tell them where you are. Like I can pull you out of my pocket! Why haven't you answered your phone?"

I glanced about. The few late-night diners didn't seem interested in me or my conversation. "I'm in Chicken Chow on the Million Mile. I think I need a ride home. Public transport might not be safe."

"The Million Mile! What the–"

"Chef sent me home in a taxi while Chance was off getting a search warrant. The taxi driver took me south. I got out, but he's still looking for me. Caro…"

I didn't need to finish my thought; she caught my tone. "OK. Right. I know a guy who has a car. Sit tight; I'll get back to you. Meanwhile… *ring those men.*"

Caro always knew a guy. Always.

I leaned back on the booth seat and sipped on my Sprite, thinking. This thing that I'd got caught up in was not going away.

I considered what I knew. Leo Teng and the guy who tried to grab me in Mystere both wore the Korax gang tattoo. The alley guy was carrying a warning talisman. The dead guy in the park was some kind of government spy. If they all tied in, I still didn't see what the connection with me was, nor did it explain Aquila or the Mythos.

The Mythos attack in the Park, my injury and blood loss, and Sixkiller's obvious ability to see everything I saw… well, that still defied my logic.

Keep moving forward, I told myself. Something will click.

Papa Brisé and Corah and Caro had mentioned the name Kadee Matari. I guess that meant I had to go back to Divine Province and make this woman's acquaintance. She could know something more that could help me.

And the more I thought about it, the more I realized so must the Marshal.

I prodded at my shoulder. It ached worse than hell now after slamming the taxi driver's arm. My phone buzzed against the plastic tabletop.

I picked it up. "Yes?"

"My guy'll be there in an hour, wearing scrubs under an overcoat. He has your picture. I'd come but it will be quicker if he doesn't have to wait for me."

"Thanks, Caro."

"You be safe until then? You got protection?"

I felt the pistol pressing into my ribs. "Yeah."

"Use it," she said.

"Why? Do you know something?"

"You're stranded in the Million Mile, Ginny. People take guard dogs to go shopping there. Just get back here in one piece, alright?"

"That's the plan," I said.

I went back up to the counter, bought an apple turnover and a coffee and retreated to my corner again.

Two sips later, a posse of guys, talking loud and waving their hands about, came in and ordered up big. They'd been test-driving a car from one of the lots, or so I learned from their conversation – an old V12 Chevrolet – and it didn't seem to bother them that the whole place knew about it.

I kept my head down but they weren't having any of it. Female alone equals good hunting.

They took the two tables across from me.

I hunkered down, wishing to be invisible, but some fries landed in my lap. I flicked them away and didn't look up.

The next few bounced off my chin and landed in my drink.

The gun against my ribs began to burn into my skin.

Leave me alone, assholes.

I could get up and go to the counter, call the manager, but that meant walking past them to get there. Grabbing hands would be waiting.

Were they harmless? Too hard to tell. In here, they wouldn't try assaulting me, but it could be a long, aggravating hour.

The only refuge was the restroom, which also meant walking past them.

A condom packet skittered along the floor and landed at my feet.

I got up, deliberately crushing it under my heel, and walked the few feet to the entry of the restroom. As I pushed open the door, one of the guys ran over and bumped into me.

Smaller than me but thickset with pill-pumped muscles, his jawline showed the puffiness of 'roids use. Behind it all, though, he was just a kid. The tight jeans and tee he wore looked like his mum might have pressed them.

"Seeing as we're going to the same place, darlin', you wanna share?"

"I'll wait." I stood back.

He giggled. "Nah, you go. Just fooling."

I hesitated, then went on through. Soon as the door shut, he burst in after me and threw his jacket up over the sec-cam. With one hand, he grabbed at my breast, the other at my crotch.

Predictable.

I pulled the gun from my inside pocket and pressed it against his balls.

"Out," I said. "And leave me the fuck alone."

"Whoa!" He put his hands up and backed away. "Nothin' meant. Nothin' meant."

"Course," I said. "But learn some manners. And remember how I didn't blow your nuts off."

He nodded vigorously. Whether out of panic or agreement, I'd never know. Fumbling backward for the door handle, he vanished through it.

I sagged against the hand basin. Tonight had been too long in so many ways. Now I just had to survive until my ride came.

I sat in a cubicle, laid the pistol on my knees and set my alarm for fifty minutes. Caro's ride would be here soon after that. Then I leaned back and closed my eyes. It wasn't sleep, but it was rest of a kind, and the alarm beeped at me what felt like almost immediately.

I scrubbed my face and checked the display. Time was up.

The boys had gone, leaving their tables piled with wrappers and burger entrails. A black trickle of spilled cola dribbled onto the chair and puddled onto the floor.

The lone counter person glanced up at me from behind his sec-screen.

"You alright, ma'am?" he asked over the intercom.

I gave him the thumbs up and took the same seat. My apple turnover had gone, but the drink sat there, flat and ominous. I pushed it away, not willing to risk what the boys might have dropped in it.

Finally, the door opened and in came a guy matching the description Caro had given, wearing a hospital uniform covered by a hooded greatcoat. He scanned the few remaining patrons and nodded recognition at me. He was younger than I expected – thirty-plus, but with a lean body and already-grey hair.

I got up and walked to the door to meet him. Closer up, I saw his grey eyes, tanned skin and an unreadable expression. He held his head back at an unnatural angle and I realized he was keeping it out of the sec-cam's view.

"This way, Ranger," he said. That was all.

We exited Chicken Chow into the parking lot and I followed him toward a dark sedan.

He beeped the remote lock and climbed into the driver's side.

"Pistol girl!" shouted a voice. "Safe travels."

I glanced over my shoulder. The boys were on the far side of the lot, drinking on the bonnet of their new Chevy.

What startled me was that Aquila was with them, perched as if waiting for me. I hadn't seen her since the park, and in the artificial light, it was hard to tell if she still looked injured.

Suddenly, she took off toward me at full tilt.

I flinched. *What…?*

The question remained only half formed in my mind as someone shoulder-charged me from behind. I went down with a howl of pain but came up swinging.

It was the fake taxi driver from before. He took me down again, hands at my throat. "Where's my gun, bitch?"

I writhed in his grip and looked for my ride.

"No!" I shouted as the sedan driven by my rescuer reversed out of the parking lot. Where the hell was he going?

Aquila screeched louder. She was above me somewhere, wings beating hard.

The boys on the Chevy started shouting too, hollering encouragement as the taxi guy and I rolled each other. But he was bigger than me and I was exhausted. I couldn't free my hands to grab the gun in my coat.

Instead, I brought my knee up and jacked him between the legs. Breath evacuated his lungs into my face as I connected with his soft bits. I followed up by headbutting him hard. The two moves loosed his grip enough for me to break free.

I stumbled to my feet and ran toward the boys.

"Shoot him," shouted my friend from the rest room. Enjoying the sport of it all.

I fumbled for the pistol, but my fingers caught in the pocket seam.

A knife clinked next to my foot, and the boys scattered to hide behind the wide girth of their V12.

"Stop!" shouted the taxi driver. "The next one won't miss."

I did as he bid and turned slowly. He had held a second knife ready to throw. His shirt sleeve was ripped from our scuffle, and I saw his crow-and-circle ink. *Korax.*

"What do you want?" I cried.

But the taxi driver wasn't interested in conversation. He advanced on me–knife high, mouth wide in a smile. He'd been waiting out here for me the whole time, I reckoned.

Should I run? Would he kill me right here? Or later? *Aquila! Help me!*

Then wheels screeched high and hot on the bitumen. The sedan swung back into the lot from the street, taking the speed bumps at a fast clip, careening straight at the taxi driver.

He turned, saw it, tried to run, but the sedan kept coming, knocking him down. The wheels pummelled his body, and the knife spun free of his grasp.

"Fuck" and "Holy fuck" and "Fuck me" from the boys behind the Chevy.

The sedan braked and reversed over the taxi driver, silencing his groans. The guy in the scrubs leaned across and flung the door open.

"Get in," he said.

I didn't argue.

TWENTY-ONE

I got back to Caro's apartment sometime after 3am. The guy in the scrubs pulled the sedan into the loading bay around the back of her building.

"Leave his gun with me; I'll deal with it." It was the first time he'd spoken.

I dropped it in the drink holder and got out. But I couldn't leave without asking him one thing, so I knocked on the window.

He rolled it down and waited.

"Why did you leave me in the parking lot and then come back?" I asked.

He pointed to the back seat and his long, dark kit bag. "Magnetised license plates. Best change them if you're going to run over someone."

"Oh," I said.

He nodded and pulled away into the traffic stream.

I watched him go with numb exhaustion.

Caro must have been watching, because she rang while I stood there.

"Come up," she said. "Gate's open."

I walked the foyer, lift and corridor on automatic pilot.

She opened the door before I could knock, and I staggered past her to her couch.

"Who was that guy?" I whispered.

She looked me over and went and poured me three fingers of whiskey. "He specializes in retrievals."

"*Retrievals*? He ran my abductor over. Twice! I heard his fucking bones snap. Then he didn't say a damn word to me on the way back."

She frowned then helped herself to an equal measure of spirits. "You'd better start from the beginning."

The story drained out of me in a matter of minutes and left me staring at the rim of my glass, savouring the slow burn the whiskey had left in my belly.

"Aquila was there, just before the attack. Then she vanished," I added. "She was in the park, too."

"Strange you should be seeing her again. Must be the stress."

"I guess." I wanted to tell her more, but the words just wouldn't come. "I have to sleep now."

"You want the bed?"

"Here's fine," I said, stretching out.

"Did you call the Marshal and dancer boy?"

I put the glass on the floor and rolled over. I may have answered her question. But I don't really know...

And then I was awake again and the sun was fighting with the edges of the blind. I felt too exhausted to do anything other than open my eyes.

"Ginny?" Caro was curled in a chair opposite, her tablet on her lap. On the table to her side sat a box full of disposable phones. Another on the floor by her feet.

"How... How long?"

"It's 3pm," she said.

"I've been asleep twelve hours."

"Pretty much. What do you need?"

I sat up suddenly. "Work, it's…"

"I called Superintendent Hunt. Told him the basics of what happened, leaving out the incident with my guy. He said to tell you you're on leave for the moment. He's sending a protection detail here."

"But I don't want–"

"You should eat before you start arguing."

I stopped and fell back, overwhelmed by a sense of weakness. "Fine."

She got up and went to her kitchenette, which was even smaller than mine – no more than a sink, a microwave and a fridge. From it, she somehow produced toast and guava juice.

When she handed them to me, I noticed how pale she looked.

"How are you travelling?" I asked.

"Finish your food."

I nodded, sipping the sweet juice and crunching the toast in greedy bites. The blackness receded from around the edges of my eyes, and the world gained a little more colour. When I was done, I put my feet on the floor and brushed my hair back. "Talk now."

"I'm having the pills you gave me checked out. They're clean-skins – produced and packaged directly for the black market. No batch numbers, no brand, which means we won't be able to get a location trace on them until the ingredients are fully analysed. But straight up, I can tell you that they were made in one of the eastern US states."

"OK, so Leo Teng's been in the States."

"Good chance, yes. Interesting thing is, his passport, which I got a look at courtesy of Aus-Police's less-than-spectacular firewall on the Evidence Collection Repository, doesn't tell the same story."

"Have you been hacking enforcement sites?"

"Me? Heavens, no. That's what BC is for."

"BC?"

"Short for BitCoin. It's a personal joke."

"Did you call BC on one of those?" I asked, pointing to the box of burners.

"My guys, you know, Ginny. They guard their privacy."

"Not so good if the police searched here, Caro. Looks like you're running a drug empire or an illegal import business."

"I've got a good hidey-hole," she said, unperturbed.

I sighed and returned to the puzzle at hand. "What about if he's been given the meds by someone else, and he hasn't been there at all?"

"Possible," she said. "But it still suggests a connection."

I nodded. "Bull says the dead guy in the park was an undercover intelligence officer infiltrating a dangerous group called Korax – the crow and circle. He never said which country the undercover guy was working for, though. Maybe he was from the US."

"That would explain the Marshal's presence."

"Yeah."

"Ginny, that detective worries me."

"Did you find out any more about her?"

"Nothing on the record. But there is a whisper around that her family was illegal immigrants. Not something she'd want coming out. Under retro-immigration laws, they could be extradited."

"Good reason to be testy, but why come after me?"

"Maybe someone is squeezing her about that."

I took in a long, deep breath and concentrated on letting it all go, pushing my diaphragm out hard. *Steady. Steady. Steady.* "Your guy, Caro. He killed the taxi driver. I should report that."

"Are you crazy? He saved your life. And if you report any more dead guys, Detective Chance will throw away the key on you."

"But there were witnesses. Some guys... and lots of sec-cam. The guy in the takeaway joint may have even seen."

"Hamish has dealt with that already. Trust me."

If there was anyone in this world that I *did* trust, it was Caro, but it didn't make me feel any better. "What's it costing you, though?"

"This one's for free. Hamish and I go a long way back. But Ginny, that's the second attempt to kidnap you."

"Third, actually. Happened in Mystere as well."

"You have to start carrying... permanently. And don't go places alone anymore."

"I have to meet this Kadee Matari. The talisman we got off the guy who followed us to Hoofs and Horners, she can help us identify it. There's something else, too. I found an illegal recording device out at Los Tribos."

"What? When?"

"The day after Nate arrived. It had been fitted into the rock. No battery and no card, though."

"You should let me look at it. And you should let me come to meet this Kadee Matari with you."

"No. Not in Divine Province; you'd attract too much attention out there."

Caro made an irritated noise. "Then take Hamish."

"No. He runs over people."

A knock at the door saved me from her reply.

She screened the visitor from her sec-cam. "Looks like your bodyguard is here."

"Comforting," I said with sarcasm, wondering which security company Bull had used.

Caro opened the door and Sixkiller strolled in. He tipped his Stetson. "Ma'am. Ranger. How are you both today?"

"*You're* my bodyguard!"

"Come to escort you home and stay with you around the clock, courtesy of Parks Southern and the US Marshals Service."

Bull, I thought with feeling, I'm going to strangle you.

A half hour later, we were standing outside my apartment door. "I'm going to find this Kadee Matari in Divine Province. You want to go get the bone feather and pick me up when I'm showered and changed?"

He shook his head. "No deal, Ranger. My instructions are very specific: *around the clock.*"

I clenched everything that would clench. "Whatever."

It took me an entire shower to loosen my jaw. So far, Sixkiller had caused me only aggravation and anxiety. I doubted that was going to improve anytime soon.

Dressing in jeans, a jacket and boots made me feel a whole lot better. I strapped on my shoulder holster and slipped my badge in my jacket. My job gave me the right to carry a weapon. Outside the park, though, my power to arrest was limited, but my badge would identify me as law enforcement and *maybe* buy me some benefit of the doubt.

I found Sixkiller sprawled out on the couch, his feet apart, and avoiding touching John Flat's outlines.

"When they gonna rub this out?" he asked.

"Like Detective Chance's going to confide in me?"

"Yeah, right, thet woman's got a bug up her ass." He straightened up, elbows on knees, feet tucked in. "I'd like to hear the details of last night, Ranger."

I folded my arms. "And I'd like to hear the truth about what you're doing here and everything you were briefed on about the trip."

We stared at each other in the kind of passive impasse where the silence hung and hung.

Into it intruded a quick, loud knock. And the door opened.

Heart.

This uncomfortable little threesome was getting together way too regularly for my taste, so I dispensed with any niceties. "Wait outside, Marshal; I'll be there directly."

Sixkiller shrugged, got up and stalked past Heart, closing the door behind him.

"Virgin?" The dark rings under his eyes sucked the anger from me. I stepped forward and wrapped my arms around his shoulders.

He stood silently in my embrace for a bit, then kissed me on the cheek. "I came here and waited for you last night. You didn't come home."

"Unplanned detour," I said into this hair. "My taxi driver decided to abduct me as I left the diner. Managed to lose him out on the Million Mile. Things got messy after that, and I crashed at Caro's."

He pulled back from my embrace and took my face in his hands. "That's the quick and sanitised version, I'm guessing. Are you alright?"

"Tired, sore, pissed off but alright. And I owe you... Chef said you told him how to best back the detective off me."

A little colour seeped into his face. "I've found that cops respond best to the threat of news coverage. They can't afford not to manage their profile these days, with the whole regional vigilante thing going on. But you don't owe me anything; I owe you an apology. I had to leave right when you were being questioned. When I came back, you'd gone and the police were searching the diner."

"Something wrong?"

The emotion in his eyes cooled. "Just some aggravation with a client."

I kissed him on the mouth. "Well, be careful with that. I have to go now, but I'll call you later."

"With the Marshal?"

I pulled an unhappy face. "My boss has assigned him to watch me round the clock until things settle."

He surprised me by saying, "That's a relief."

"You don't mind? I got the feeling you didn't like him."

"I want you safe. If he can do the job, then I'm happy."

"*I* can keep me safe, Heart. I don't need anyone else to do that, but it seems my employer has other ideas."

He smiled and put his lips to mine, kissing me in a lingering, loving kind of way that was different from the usual passion between us.

"What was that?" I asked.

"Just let him help, Virgin. Please!"

"Oh, is *that* what you call it? My mistake."

"Fond farewells?" said Sixkiller while waited for a taxi at the Cloisters rank. Hump day in this part of the city was one of the busiest for tourists, and the queue was longer than usual. I wasn't in the mood for self-cleaning business suits and early-bird travellers.

In Divine Province, on the other hand, people observed siesta at midday on midweek, which made it the ideal time for me to go hunting Kadee Matari.

"And it would be your business… why?" I asked.

"You seem particularly hostile this morning, Ranger. Would you care to enlighten me why that is so?"

I glanced around. The queue had spread back into the Cloisters' foyer, but most people were on their phones, distracted. No one seemed to be listening, so I dropped my voice.

"You've been forced on me with little or no explanation. Then I have to get you out of one scrape after another. Last night, when I really could have done with your help, you spend the evening staring down the cleavage of the woman who I wouldn't trust to make my toast, and then you KO the bouncer who's offended *her honour*. Meanwhile, I've been detained illegally by the police and then kidnapped by a taxi driver. And just to add some flavour to the whole scenario, you've spun me some wild yarn about other worlds and other-worldly creatures that are here to effect some monstrous change to our society. I think you're completely off your nut and they've sent *you* to protect me!"

His eyes grew wider and wider as my rant went on. When I'd run out of steam, he said nothing. Then he burst out laughing.

I hadn't heard him laugh before. It was a wildly abandoned sound from deep in his chest.

"Do. Not. Laugh. At. Me," I ground out.

He mopped his eyes and reined in his mirth. "My sincerest apologies, Virgin, but I've never met anyone who speaks their mind like you do. It's disconcerting… and downright funny."

"I'm feeling anything but downright funny, Nate."

The laughter fell from his face. "And so protecting you from the attacker in your apartment and giving my blood to help you recover from the Mythos scratches were unacceptable actions? From where I stand, you're blessed that I was there."

"Well, that's a matter of opinion. But in the spirit of the greater good and coming out of this alive, I will continue to work with you, but only if you tell me everything."

"Everything?"

Right about there, my remaining shred of civility vanished and I raised my voice. "Don't be so fucking obtuse. Either tell me what's going on… or *get fucking lost*."

"There's no need to be vulgar, Ranger."

I folded my arms and tried to burn him alive with my stare.

A taxi pulled in and retracted its doors, rescuing us from increasingly curious bystander glances.

"Only get in if you're going to talk to me, Marshal," I asked softly.

He hesitated, then nodded. "After you, ma'am."

I let the *ma'am* slide. He folded his body into the back

seat after me, and we didn't speak until we reached the connecting bus that would take us the normal tourist route to Divine Province. I wasn't giving my shortcut up to the Marshal. I didn't trust him enough.

The bus offered more privacy than the taxi, so I reopened our conversation when we got clear of the Western Quarter. There were only a few people on board, and none of them sitting close. The driver sat behind his everything-proof shutters, watching a football game on his screen, while the bus steered itself along the coastal freeway.

"You said you work for a division of the Marshal Service, so tell me about it."

He stared past me and out the window. "My division watches and analyses unexplained trends in human behaviours. Pattern changes. We're not the only ones. Most intelligence agencies have a similar section. The Marshals liaise directly with a fraternal group at Langley."

"How does that work?"

"Mostly, in practice, they issue edicts to us and we enact them. But we have expertise in Native American culture, so they defer to us on things pertaining to it."

"So you're saying that every country in the world has a division of their spy service devoted to spiritual shit."

"An unsophisticated and simplistic summary… but yes."

"Since when?"

"I haven't seen any official record on it, but my guess is that the secret services *began* with the Spiritual Divisions."

I digested that for a bit, letting the swaying rhythm of the bus rock me. The air conditioning blew cold air onto my face, causing the back of my throat to itch.

"And how do you define spiritual?"

He let out an impatient breath, and it was hard to miss the look of irritation on his face. "The Marshals Service's definition is a hundred-and-fifty-page document. But if I can condense for you, it means anything *not* classified as Traditional Human Reality."

I mirrored his irritated look. "That's pretty fuzzy and weird."

"I don't claim to know about everything that exists beyond the mundane, but I do know some things. In my time with USMS, I've investigated or tracked over fifty different kinds of Mythos or talismans."

"Talismans?"

"Sometimes the talisman is more powerful than the creature."

"Like the bone feather from the guy in the alley."

"Maybe. If we find out exactly what it means."

"Which is why I'm sitting on a bus with you."

He nodded and fell silent, but I wasn't prepared to let it lie yet.

"So you came here because our secret services think we've got trouble from the spirit plane."

"Patterns have been emerging that point to this city and its fringe groups, with Birrimun Park as the focal point."

"So your intel thinks I'm just collateral damage on that? Wrong place, wrong time?"

"Actually, no, Virgin. We think it has something to do with your father."

That kinda froze over all my organs. "Dad?"

"Yes. He had connections deep in the community here among many of the spiritual groups. If I tell you something, can you keep it together?"

"I don't make deals like that. But if you want my compliance… my assistance… you'd better not stop now."

He hesitated just long enough for me to glimpse the indecision behind his self-assurance. He was taking a risk here. On me.

"We believe your father's death was not an accident. We think it was the beginning of a push by the Mythos."

My heart blazed, melting my insides alive again. My breathing accelerated and the pounding in my ears drowned out all other sounds.

Dad. He knows something about Dad!

I wanted to grab him by the shirt and shake more from him. I wanted to know everything. *EVERYTHING.*

But somewhere underneath my erratic emotional reaction, my brain still ticked over. I tucked my shaking hands under my thighs and turned a cool expression to him. Did it fool him? I couldn't tell. "And now the 'push', as you call it, involves me?"

"Honestly, we don't know. I'm here to both protect you and learn about you."

"You're spying on me?"

"Not the way I see it, Virgin. And if I was, would I have told you this?"

He had a point, but then I didn't really know how tricky Sixkiller could be.

"We're getting off at the next stop," I said, shutting the conversation down for now. "Please don't pull your guns on anyone unless you absolutely have to."

TWENTY-TWO

Oil-streaked, privately-owned Velora Line buses sat parked like spokes in a wheel around the Mystere bus stop. They waited there for the visitors to transfer across and plant their butts on the soiled vinyl seats. Once full, they'd rumble them over the bridge into Divine Province.

Everyone who stepped foot on these Velora Lines had to DNA-accept a personal indemnity waiver. The city was quite sure it wasn't taking responsibility for citizens and tourists who decided to get their kicks on Gilgul Street.

I led Sixkiller off the city commuter bus we were on and bypassed the Veloras, heading straight for the bridge on foot. "We'll walk across this time. I don't really like Velora Lines. You could catch anything travelling on them."

He strode easily beside me, his head swivelling left and right as he scanned and evaluated the location.

I tried to see it through his eyes. Bus depot, light industrial buildings and chicken wire compounds right up to a rivet-heavy bridge. Dull water squeezed past underneath. Sun biting our backs. And flies…

Ahead, the piecemeal urban sprawl of Divine was given context by the scent of a thousand incense burners. Not beautiful. Not ugly. But somehow a very badly conceived juxtaposition of landscapes.

The sound of fluttering wings and a stir in the air alerted me to Aquila's presence. She glided down in front of us, landing on the Mystere side of the bridge's handrail.

I glanced at Sixkiller. He saw her, I could tell from his smile.

"Your disincarnate is solicitous."

"And yours isn't."

"I've been in many threatening situations over the years. Mine is… selective."

"So it doesn't turn up to warn you anymore?"

"Only when things are… precarious. How do you plan to find this Kadee Matari?" he asked.

"It's siesta time in Mystere. Quiet on the streets and in the bars. We cross through there quickly and into Moonee. I'm pretty sure she'll find us."

"Pretty sure?"

"You got better intel than that?"

"Kadee Matari is in on our watch list, only…"

"Don't tell me: you can't find her to watch her?"

"You truly have a way with words, Ranger."

"Yeah," I said. "It's called being direct. You should try it sometime."

He chose to ignore my barb, lengthening his stride so I had to keep a quick pace to stay abreast of him.

We brushed past some dazed revellers trudging home by the bridge walkway.

"Hard night," observed the Marshal.

"Or week," I said. "Gilgul Street… can be hard to break free from once you're there."

He made a noise in the back of his throat. Disbelief or disapproval? Hard to know where the Marshal's moral code truly lay.

I just kept on walking fast anyway.

Gilgul Street was just as I'd told him it would be – down to a trickle of pavement gawkers. Many of the street stalls were hooded or shuttered, and the neons, though switched on, were a dull, barely perceptible gleam in the glare of midday sunlight.

The bridge led directly into the intersection of Seer Parade and Gilgul, and I veered to the Seer side of the triangle. Though the music on the sidewalk changed at each premises we passed, the whining melody of spirit music seemed to underpin each tune. It made me sweat a little harder and walk a little quicker.

Welcome to Mystere, where you can meditate your way into madness.

While Gilgul was normally three deep in trinket and food hawkers, Seer Street was five deep in mystics and mediums. Corah had been smart, locating her business on Gilgul Street. It set her apart from the rest – gave her visibility.

I wondered what had happened to her after the diner opening. Last I'd seen her, she'd been appreciating the Marshal's testosterone display with the bouncer.

Why had she wanted to come to Chef's opening, anyway? That question still bugged the hell out of me.

Not quite as much, though, as the bombshell Nate Sixkiller had just shared with me – my dad and the

Mythos and the secret service and… murder. That little sequence of notions set my guts on fire. I tried putting it out by asking about Corah.

"What happened to Corah the other night?" I asked casually.

"Your friend?"

"Corah is *not* my friend. She's just someone I've known for a long time."

"Like Ms Jenae?"

"No," I corrected. "Caro is my friend."

"I escorted your *acquaintance*, Corah, out for some supper."

"W-what!" I spluttered.

"She seemed a mite upset, so I found a place that served refreshments. The host had hustled you off and shut the restaurant. Nothing more to be done thet I could see."

"You weren't curious to find out whether I managed to locate Teng's apartment? That's why we went there, as I recall."

"Figured you'd had a rough night and might need some time."

We walked on in silence until we reached the end of Seer Parade, where it connected with Mason Way. Just before the intersection, I deviated into an alleyway heading west and encountered a rusted metal gate. I gave the gate a shove and it opened, sliding along well-greased tracks.

"Gets some use," said Sixkiller.

"By certain sorts."

"So, you located the apartment Teng was in?" he asked, following me.

I bit my lip to hold back showing my satisfaction. "Yeah. Got inside there, too. Nothing really to show for it, though, other than a near miss with the police. You were busy defending Corah's honour, I hear."

"Damn fool cussed her out."

"You should learn to let people fight their own battles, Marshal."

"That's where we'd be in some disagreement, Ranger. Not everyone can do that."

I stopped just before the end of the alley. "Well, let me tell you something, Corah isn't one."

From the other end it looked like a blind alley, but from down here, there were thin gaps at the side of the wall that led into another narrow lane.

We squeezed through single-file. The hidden lane was piled at one end with crates.

We walked toward them slowly. Halfway along, I paused and turned to him. "From here on in, the rules change, Marshal. Trigger-happy could equal dead. You got me?"

He raised his hands, fingers wide in a gesture of placation. "Your place, your rules."

I stared at him. Was he taking me seriously? His deadpan expression made it so hard to tell.

"Look," I said in earnest. "I'm sure you've been in more than your share of rough places and no doubt handled some mean hombres. But to get by in this part of Divine Province, you need guile and a lot of luck. Not firepower."

"You've been here a lot?"

"No. Once or twice only, when I was following up leads on my dad's death. But I'm native to this area of the city. I *get* the undertones."

"I'll follow your lead all the way, Virgin."

I nodded. "Thank you."

Deep breath, and I climbed over the loose barricade of pine crates into the area the locals called Moonee.

TWENTY-THREE

Moonee was a tiny pocket of the city's coastal mass that hadn't been affected by the shift away from terraced hi-rise, hi-density living.

Other than some office clusters in what had been the old central business districts of individual cities, Moonee was one of the few high-rise residential builds left on the East Coast.

Of course, the old CBDs didn't exist anymore. Or at least, the buildings were still there but not as markers for individual downtown hearts. But Moonee had been built as a detention facility for illegal immigrants. When the city had subsumed the entire eastern landscape, the refugees had stayed on here, but the money for services had evaporated. Utilities were still extended to the area, but maintenance and policing were hit and miss.

It became a cauldron of cultural and spiritual splinter groups. Once you entered one of the terraced high-rise buildings, there was no clear exit. Entire floors were taken over by factions, which meant that homemade stairs had been attached to the sides – none of them built to safety standards. Sometimes, they were little more than a rope and some chinks in the wall.

More people died falling to their death in Moonee than from any kind of crime.

You had to know where you were going here; it was too easy to stumble onto the wrong level of a building and wind up assaulted and pushed out a window.

I didn't know where Kadee Matari resided, but I knew someone who could probably get word to her. Though I imagined that the moment we stepped over the crates in the alley, she'd known there were strangers in Moonee.

Sixkiller's hyper-awareness had me on edge as we walked the almost-empty street that ran between the dozen tenements. Up on the balls of his feet, fingers flicking at his sides; I sensed he was itching to pull his guns. Maybe he could feel the thousand eyes on us as well.

"Easy," I said quietly.

"Where are we going?"

"Across the road. Tenement number four."

The guy I wanted to see resided in the bottom floor in what had once been a foyer with a reception desk and lift wells. Now it provided living and storage for a man who ran Moonee's communication hub, selling access to the local CC network and wireless Internet.

Which meant he already knew we were coming.

I crossed the empty street and stopped in front of a rectangular advertising sign covered by scratched plastic. The girl in her underwear had long brown hair and a coy look. I stared straight in her eyes. "It's Ranger Jackson from Park South. I want a meeting with Kadee Matari."

For a long, long moment, there was no answer. Maybe he was out, maybe he'd died. Maybe someone else had taken over as gatekeeper and feed provider in Moonee.

I slipped my hand inside my jacket and rested it on the grip of my pistol. Some movement in the undercroft of the opposite tenement caught my eye. A door opening, perhaps.

"Welcome back, Virgin. I missed you," said a deep, mellifluous voice emanating from around about the poster girl's mouth.

"Can you help me, Rombo?"

"I already have," he said.

I heard Sixkiller's quick intake of breath, then felt the prickle of something sharp at my neck.

"Keep still," said a clipped, foreign voice in my ear. I complied, hoping Sixkiller would do the same.

A hand fished inside my jacket and removed my gun. Then it propelled me sideways past Rombo's foyer to the narrow conduit between buildings four and five.

I found myself looking up at a gate and stairs made from steel rods of varying lengths. A rough spiral of wire circled around them like a cage.

"Climb," said the voice again.

I angled my head just enough to see that the man who had possession of my gun and held a long blade knife to my throat, had long hair knotted at the base of his neck and a face pierced with gold chains.

Behind him, two men with similarly styled hair held guns at Sixkiller's head. His holsters were empty and so was his expression. Something told me it was a look that might be dangerous.

"What about my colleague?" I asked.

"He stays. Insurance," said my chaperon.

"Let me speak to him."

The man nodded once and let me turn to look at Sixkiller. "Please just wait. I will be fine, but I need the bone feather."

The Marshal moved his hand very slowly to his jacket. He withdrew the talisman and handed it to me.

I slipped it into my pocket and turned back, placing my foot on the first rung. "How far?"

"Until I say."

I hated heights, really. That is, I loved to stand on a mesa and watch the sunset, and to climb the rock fingers of Los Tribos. But this kind of situation flat-out turned my insides to shitty water– slippery foot pegs, barbed wire to catch me and a weapon at my back.

Coward! I chided myself. This might lead you to Dad's killer.

That thought alone got my legs working.

I concentrated on each step without looking down. My arms and legs burned with the effort, and sweat blurred my vision. Slow, slow progress took me up past the fourth floor until the pegs literally ran out. The building ran ten or fifteen stories high at least, but this particular staircase had run its course.

I looked straight ahead along the length of the wall and saw other stairs dotted across the width of the building. Not all of them reached the bottom or the top.

What kind of crazy system was this?

"What now?" I called back.

"Wait," said my escort from below me. "Hold."

I clung to the top peg and hunkered against the wall, not sure what to expect.

A rope and hook flew past my face, lodging in the corner of an open window above us. The face-chain guy climbed over me, using my body for purchase, and swung lightly through. A few seconds later, a rope flew down and lassoed my shoulders.

He poked his head out. "Tighten at the waist."

I did as I was bid.

"Now get your hands on the ledge and pull yourself in."

I was neither agile nor imbued with killer arm strength, but the threat of falling to my death proved a powerful motivator. I latched onto the ledge and heaved arse.

Between my desire to get off the ladder and the face-chain guy hauling the rope around my waist, I catapulted through the window in ugly but effective style.

It was hard to hide how badly I was trembling when I righted myself. I badly wanted a toilet.

The face-chain guy had other ideas, though, pulling me up by the lasso and tugging the rope in a way that meant I had to follow him. I stumbled after him, looking around. Most of the internal walls had been gutted, leaving a large open space, partitioned by clusters of wooden and brass statues and curtains of dreamcatchers.

I smelled hashish and sandalwood and meat cooking, each scent fighting for dominance and yet mingling to create something organic and holistic as well. On one side of me, over near the front of the building where the windows were, three large ovens squatted next to each other. Pots bubbled on the cooktops, and the oven lights flickered. Without getting any closer, I could tell that it was curry in the pots and hash cookies on the cooling oven trays.

A busy kitchen's a happy kitchen.

The face-chain guy brushed through drapes of chimes and feather charms, and stepped around large Buddha and Shiva statues and rearing brass serpents. The serpents creeped me out the most with their bright green eyes and tarnished skin.

When we were almost, I guessed, at the other side of the building, we reached one of the few internal walls, which was painted with Indigenous artwork. In front of it sat a young woman on a worn but one-time-quality armchair. The right side of her face was quite beautiful; the left, a mess of scars. On one knee she balanced a tablet; on the other, a jewelled pipe. She tapped slowly at the tablet between sucks on the stem.

The face-chain guy slung me down on the floor in front of her.

She didn't lift her eyes for several more puffs, but when she did, I was mesmerized by them. Glassy green like a sea creature, and the force of her personality radiated through, striking me hard.

"You've had little rest of late, Virgin Jackson."

"You know me?"

"In the way that a person knows about history," she said.

I had no idea what that meant. "I've been told that you are the one who could help me with the answer to a question."

"And were you also told about the dangers of coming to me?"

"I've been here before. I know the dangers."

She sucked thoughtfully on the pipe again. "Aaah, yes… about your father."

I did a bad job of hiding my surprise, but she went on anyway.

"You expected I would just give you what you want? Why is that?" she asked.

"Because I think that my question affects you. And that I am connected to the answer. It may be that you have things you can learn from me as well."

Her laugh went off like a crack of thunder in the room. "A sense of conviction is a gift like no other, Ranger. You have my attention, so ask me."

Strange as it was to be treated as child by a woman younger than me, I reached slowly into my jacket pocket and brought out the bone feather. "Can you tell me the significance of this?"

"Where did you find it?"

"Taken from a man following me in the Western Quarter."

She frowned, shifted both the tablet and the pipe to a side table and took the object from me, rolling it in her hands, sending the feather into twirling flurry. The bleached white bone stood out starkly against her olive skin.

"Tell me how you see yourself to be part of this."

"First, a man tried to kill me in my home. He wore the tattoo of a group who call themselves Korax, after the raven. Then a creature attacked me in the park. I came close to bleeding to death from my wounds."

"What creature?"

"It looked like a crow but much larger; I've been told it is called a Mythos."

She closed her eyes, appearing to drift off to sleep, then she blinked them open. "Do you believe, Virgin?"

"How is what I believe relevant to any of this? I just want to deal with what's happening. People are trying to kill me."

"That's where you are wrong," she said. "Belief is everything. Belief is the foundation of our reality."

I narrowed my eyes at her. "I *believe* that my father was murdered, though it was made to look like an accident. I *believe* his death is somehow connected with the recent attempts on my life and a man I found murdered in my park. And I *believe* that you know something that can help me with these problems."

She rested the bone feather on her lap and retrieved the pipe.

I waited while she sucked at it and her eyes grew even glassier. It took all my self-control not to tear the stem from her lips and toss it across the room. The face-chain guy stood close by, though, ready to tug the rope around me tighter, and I sensed others in the shadows.

"What you've brought me is a *varna*, an object of warning. But this one is different... special, I suppose you could say."

"How so?"

She lifted it high in the air. "The bone is a native animal. The kind that our local vodun might use. The feather is from the coastal Romani, but the nano-lumes are Druze. These nicks that appear as straight lines are inscriptions by the Indigenous tribes." She brought the feather to her nose and sniffed. "The feather has been soaked into cannabis favoured by the Rastafarians and the beads are Yoruba and Akan – African."

"You're sure?" I was impressed.

Her green glass eyes sparked. "I'm always sure."

"What would one of the Korax be doing with this kind of a collective warning?"

"Are you sure he was part of this Korax group you speak about?" she asked.

My eyes widened when it dawned on me that I'd *assumed* he was, but I'd seen no actual tattoo. "If he wasn't Korax, then who was he?"

She blinked. "You seem clever, Virgin, but maybe I am wrong."

"And you seem to practise being obtuse, but maybe I'm wrong," I snapped back.

The face-chain guy lifted his knife, but she waved him down and passed me the talisman. "Take this; go home, Ranger, and don't return here. Find out what it is that you believe in. That will serve you better than anything I can tell you."

"I'm facing a murder sentence for a crime I didn't commit. How can what I believe in affect that?"

"Talk to your companion. Perhaps he can help you understand."

"Which companion?"

"The tall one guided by the bison."

"Nate? But how do you know...?"

She shrugged, put the pipe back to her lips and closed her eyes. Clearly, I was dismissed.

Face-chain guy pulled me to my feet by the rope and along in a different direction from the way we'd come. I brushed past rows of bead curtains, glimpsing weapon racks behind some of them and ultraviolet enclosures behind others. When we finally stopped in front of a double door, my inner compass told me I was on the other side of the building from where I'd climbed the stairs.

The doors slid open and revealed a lift.

I turned to face-chain guy. "You're shittin' me. You mean I…?"

He grinned and the chains tinkled. I so wanted to rip them out.

Instead, we rode down in silence. When the doors opened at the bottom, he removed my lasso and pushed me out without a word.

I found myself at the back of tenement number four, looking at a landscape that stole my breath. A wide tract of bare, churned earth punctuated by mounds of burned bricks and charred remains amid glowing coals. From the choking smell, I knew at least some of them were animal or human. It was a burning ground, a body incinerator made all the more ghastly by how public it was.

I walked away quickly, heading for the nearest corner to take me down the side of the tenement and back to Sixkiller. Halfway along, I heard voices behind me. A quick glance told me that a posse of guys had rounded the corner after me, carrying spears and clubs.

My walk became a sprint past the stairs I'd climbed previously.

No Sixkiller.

I'd almost reached the front corner when the first spear thudded into the ground at my heel. I bowled around the edge of the building and collided with Sixkiller, who was sitting with his legs out and his back against the wall.

"Spears…" I gasped. "Clubs!"

He sprang to his feet. "We take them."

"Be my guest," I said stepping around him.

"Virgin!" he shouted after me, but I wasn't stopping. I didn't plan on ending up on a pyre in the burning grounds.

As I reached the other side of the street, I heard his boots on the pavement, catching up with me. Thank heavens for that! It would be have been tough explain losing him in Moonee to Bull.

"Hurry," I called over my shoulder.

We were almost at building number three, and I could see another gang emerging from the foyer. These guys had aluminium baseball bats and shivs as long as small swords.

A voice bellowed through a loudspeaker from above. "Ranger!"

I glanced up and saw a mini-drone with the wingspan of an albatross heading straight at my head. I ducked, still running, and it landed lightly on the pavement a few meters ahead of Sixkiller and me.

Three pistols were strapped into the carrier on its back. I broke stride just long enough to free my 9mm and toss the Marshal his Peacemakers.

"Don't... fire... unless... you... abso... lute... ly... have... to..." I puffed at him, and veered back across the street to avoid the guys with bats.

Spears rained about my feet. One nicked my shoulder, and I heard Sixkiller grunt with the impact of another.

"Don't shoot," I said. "We're nearly there."

The previously quiet enclave was now rampant with screeches and cries that sounded like they might come with a free scalping.

Nearly. There. The alleyway that led back to Gilgul was a tantalizing few lengths ahead, but the guys with shivs had crossed as well to head us off.

Ten strides. Nine…

Whump!

Someone took me out from the side and I went down heavily, cracking my head on the pavement. The world went grainy for a second, then brightened. I heard two pistol cracks followed by soft thumps. A hand touched my shoulder and rolled me over.

I lashed out, connecting a punch with Sixkiller's jaw.

I realized what I'd done when he swore.

"Nate!"

But he'd had already sunk into a crouch, one pistol drawn.

The guy who'd tackled me lay dead on the ground, a shiv near his open palm.

The rest of his gang had fanned out around us. Lined up behind them were the spear throwers.

The two gangs exchanged some excited street dialect that I didn't understand. The gist of it was pretty plain, though. They were fighting over who had the right to claim us.

Sixkiller fired a warning shot in the air.

"Git back!" His voice was hoarse and steeped in bad intent. Enough to make my skin prickle.

"Be calm, Marshal," I said.

"Never been calmer, Ranger. Now git into the alley."

Only a few steps backward and we would climb the crates – the line between death and the relative safety of Seer Parade.

I got to my feet, lifted my 9mm and stepped alongside him. "After you."

He made an irritated noise in the back of his throat. "This ain't the time for—"

"One step back at a time *together*," I said. "On my count…"

My sideways glance caught his brief nod.

"One…"

We stepped backward.

Three pistols against spears, shivs and bats. It seemed like we were on the winning side.

"Two…"

My sense told me three more steps would do it. I could smell the rotted fruit from the crates.

So close. "Three…"

Our pursuers surged forward, suddenly forgetting their differences as their prey appeared about to escape. Spears lifted. Shivs, too.

"Four…"

Then suddenly, we had a much bigger problem. Around one end of the semicircle stepped a guy with a bare chest. The tattoo on his breast was large and unmistakable— a circle encompassing a crow. Korax.

He lifted a semiauto to his hip.

From nowhere, I heard a thundering noise. In the corner of my eyes, I saw a bison galloping towards us.

A bison. Had to be.

Nothing else in my mind matched with the shaggy shoulders and fierce spray of saliva from its mouth.

"*Ohitika!*" gasped Sixkiller.

If that was his disincarnate, then we were seriously—

"Five!" I yelled, firing at the guy with the semiauto simultaneously.

Then Sixkiller and I turned in unison and dived over the barricade of fruit crates.

A fierce rain of spears and bullets pelted down after us.

I kept rolling as I hit the ground, using momentum to get me as far into the alley as possible.

The semiauto chopped the crates to bits. Wood chips sprayed me, and I glimpsed Sixkiller lying on his stomach, returning fire. The sight of the bison standing over him, fierce and protective, added to my acute adrenalin rush.

I loosed a couple more shots, more a fear reaction than anything particularly effective against a semiautomatic weapon, and scrambled on my knees toward the blind alley and Seer Parade.

I reached the false wall still on my knees. Sixkiller was close behind me, and the guy with the semi was kicking decimated crates out of his way.

A volley of fire started, this time above my head, coming from the direction I was crawling, two guys leaning against corner walls looking back at us.

One of them nodded and beckoned. I got to my feet and sprinted around the corner, where I collapsed, my back up against the wall, sucking in air. Sixkiller rolled out behind me, and suddenly we were side by side again, staring out at curious passers-by.

My whole body shook from exertion. The Marshal seemed calm other than the fact he was panting.

On the other side of the alley opening, our armed allies had slung their rifles over their shoulders and were busy sliding the metal grate across the gap. It locked into place with a *thunk*, and they snapped a heavy bar into place.

Everything went quiet. We'd made it back across the invisible line.

"I think I shot the guy with the semiauto," I said.

"Not damn quick enough. He near took my head off."He nodded at the guys securing the gate. "Hadn't been for them, though, we'd be stone-cold dead."

"Hadn't been for your disincarnate scaring me half to death, I might never have pulled the trigger at all."

He frowned at me. "What do you mean?"

"The bison. I saw it."

"*You saw Ohitika?*"

"Saw it come hell for leather at those guys. Then it was standing over you in the alley. What did you call it? Ohi…?"

"Ohitika. Means *brave*," he said.

I nodded. "Fierce, alright. Don't think you'd want him around all the time."

"Ohitika only reveals himself to people he chooses."

"Oh. Right," I said. "That's… um… nice."

Sixkiller shook his head and swallowed, seeming at a loss for words. He pinched the bridge of his nose with his finger and thumb.

One of the guys approached us. He wore shorts, a dirty singlet, boots and a satisfied smile. "Best you get up. Papa Brisé wants to talk."

TWENTY-FOUR

Sixkiller held out a blood-wet hand. I took it and we helped each other up.

"Sure," I said to the guy. "And thanks… y'know… for that."

He patted his rifle as if it were a pet. "Can't have the fucking Moonees up in our place. We got business to conduct. Shit is bad for tourists."

I felt relieved at that. Order among the disorder.

"How did you know we were there?" I asked.

"We watch their side. They watch our side. Way it's gotta be."

"The gate was unlocked, though."

"Yeah, we leave it like that for the most. We lock it, they get the message." He sauntered off down Seer.

"You're bleeding," I said to Sixkiller as we limped after him.

"So are you. Shoulder."

I looked down at myself. The peak of my adrenalin had begun to fade and things hurt, the shoulder that the Mythos had attacked, and now the other one, right at the top of the arm, where the spear had grazed me.

The increasingly familiar sense of having been tossed around and mangled returned.

"Nate," I croaked. "You need a hand?"

If my request surprised him, he didn't show it. He shook his head.

Together we limped along Seer towards Mason Way. Before we reached the end, Brisé's guy threaded between a real-animal-hide stall and a tarot reader, and went up a set of removable stairs hooked to the awning in front of a bar called Sage.

The stairs were a tough task in my present condition. I gritted my way up them, drawing on the handrail and innate stubbornness to get me through. From Sixkiller's periodic grunts, he was feeling it, too.

We passed through three pairs of guys with guns before our guy left us in a small room with two big couches and a large wall screen. The ashtrays on the armrests overflowed, and the stale smell of cigar added to my woes. I stayed standing, conscious of the blood on my shoulder and hands.

Sixkiller propped against the wall next to the door we'd been brought through, not about to be ambushed again.

I estimated he had about three rounds left at most. I had two.

They hadn't taken our guns, so I guess that was something.

"Ranger and Marshal!" boomed Brisé's voice.

He sprang to life on the screen, not in person. "Someone will fix your wounds soon. But first, explain your fuckeen selves."

Medical help? I wondered if Papa Brisé was looking to build allies. Might be a smart move. And somehow, for no good reason, I trusted Papa Brisé a whole lot more than Kadee Matari. Not that *that* was much a measure.

"We went to speak to Kadee Matari. Find out more about the bone feather talisman," I said.

"You got fuckeen front, Ranger, I give you that. What did the Stoned fuckeen Witch have to say?"

"That it was a collective warning from Romani, Africans, Druze and others. Then she said I should find out what it is that I believe in."

"As clear as my fuckeen whiz in the morning," said Papa Brisé with a sneer.

"That's all I got from her. Some gangs chased us out of Moonee with spears and shivs and clubs. But someone showing crow-and-circle ink joined them last with some real hardware."

Brisé's face folded into unhappy lines. Not concern for our welfare, I guessed, but concern for his territory. The huge man stroked an imaginary moustache on his face. "That she spoke with you at all is fuckeen mystifying. You must be fuckeen charmed, Ranger."

"Who are the crow and circle, Papa Brisé? I've heard they're called Korax."

Sixkiller stiffened and lifted his head when I said that, suggesting he had heard the name too.

"I know as much and as little as you, Ranger. They are here and fuckeen there. Selling fuckeen hardware, fuckeen shit, fuckeen everything," Papa Brisé moaned.

"They're locals, you mean?"

"Some. We hear accents like the Marshal's as well," he said.

"Is it affecting you?"

"I fuckeen run Mystere. It has been that way since I took it from Lobo Smith ten fuckeen years ago. There are drugs and deals and bullshit... all fuckeen normal. But I control the flow. You fuckeen feel me?"

I stared and Sixkiller gave a slow nod.

"These Korax they're coming and changing the fuckeen flow. They talk to Kadee Matari. Maybe planning something. These last few days already... fifteen fuckeen murders in three streets, and not one is mine. The Stoned Witch is trying to take me down. I'm losing control of my own fuckeen place."

His admission might have been either darkly humorous or personally damning at another time. Right now, it was just plain frightening.

"But what's it about?"

"That's why I save your fuckeen life, Ranger. You find out for me so I can stop the Stoned fuckeen Witch. She burns the shit of fuckeen babies in her pipe and smokes it."

The screen went dead, and Sixkiller and I were left staring at each other.

"Korax?" he said.

"I hear stuff," I said, shrugging. "What do you call them?"

"That name might fit."He glanced away from me, and I suddenly realized how truly bloody he was. And pale.

Before I could retort, the door opened and a young woman with white hair, wearing a halter top that showed off her violet tattoos, entered. She opened the case she carried, took a plastic sheet from it and spread it on the ground. Then she set the case on the coffee table and selected a short, bulky object that she unfolded into a small stool with three legs.

She motioned to Sixkiller to sit on it.

"Why would I do thet?" he asked.

She opened her mouth and pointed to her tongue. Or what might have once been a tongue. Now there was a lump of tissue split into two short peaks, like the ears on a dog. They wiggled freely, independently of each other.

When he remained where he was, she made an angry noise and rummaged in the case. After a moment, she held up an aerosol can and a tube of antiseptic.

"For chrissakes, let her fix you up before you bleed to death, Nate." I sat down on one of the couches as I said it, suddenly tired beyond my ability to fathom.

Sixkiller's shoulders sagged a fraction, and he moved stiffly to sit on the stool.

With quick and efficient hands, the woman swabbed and applied the plastic bandages to the scratches and scrapes on his skin. She took her time on the deeper spear wound, squeezing it full of antibiotic and anti-inflammatory goo into it. When she'd finished that, she pulled a plastic bag out of her overalls and handed both him and me a square cookie each.

I declined but Sixkiller took one, smelled it and handed it back.

She shrugged and popped it in her own mouth. While she chewed, she motioned the Marshal off the stool and me onto it.

The same quick, sure hands dealt with my injuries. When she looked at where the spear had sliced my shoulder, she rummaged in the bag again and produced a tube of skin glue.

She set the stubs of her mangled tongue between her teeth, concentrating on pulling the skin together in a straight line. I tried to imagine what her story was as she worked. When she finished patting the wound dry, I found myself asking, "Why are you working for Papa Brisé?"

She paused for a moment, then snapped the lid on the glue and began packing up her gear.

"Virgin," said the Marshal softly from his post by the door. "We should go."

I stood up. The glue must have had its own anaesthetic, for the wound no longer throbbed as much. "Thank you for helping us. I'm the Ranger in the south-east sector of Birrimun Park. If you ever need somewhere to go, come to the Park offices on the Ring Road. I'll do what I can for you."

She blinked as though having difficulty absorbing what I'd said.

"No strings," I added, forcing a smile. "One good deed, you know…"

She gestured that I should step off the spills sheet. By the time I'd joined Sixkiller by the door she had packed it and the stool away and was re-shouldering the pack.

We stood together in a brief, awkward silence. Then Sixkiller and I left.

"Why did you say that to her?" he asked as we headed back over the bridge toward the bus depot. "She works for a criminal."

"Because I did," I said, way too tired to be explaining myself.

He shook his head and let it drop. Thankfully, he didn't speak again, even after we boarded the commuter bus heading north.

The other travellers aboard kept a wide berth of us and our bloodstained clothes, but I was too tired to care about that, either. Sixkiller's arm against mine was warm, and the seat was comfortable, and the drowsiness beset me almost immediately.

I woke to find the bus had gone quiet and my nose was pressed into the leg seam of Sixkiller's jeans. The smell of dried blood and stale sweat pervaded my senses.

I sat up and looked around. The bus was empty apart from the auto-cleaner and the driver backing up his credit machine. The cleaner skittered over the seats with a low-pitched hum as it gobbled up rubbish and sprayed disinfectant and odoriser.

"Why didn't you wake me up?" I asked.

"Thought you needed it. And to tell you the truth, thought you might use that on me if I startled you."

I followed his glance to my right hand. My fingers were clenched around my pistol's grip.

Carefully, I unkinked my forefinger and slipped it off the trigger. "Jeez, I could have shot myself."

"Or someone else," he pointed out.

"Definition of a bad day," I said as I tucked it back into the holster under my jacket.

Sixkiller took a long deep breath, as though he hadn't had one for a while.

"Sorry about that," I added.

He got up and stretched. "Been a day, alright. I need a wash."

The thought of a hot shower was motivation to get moving, so I followed him off the bus, and we flagged a taxi to get us home.

Watching the late-afternoon world along the Ringway flash by, I felt a strong sense of dislocation. Business as usual. Orderly tourist retail in progress, and a kaleidoscope of flashing motel *Vacancy* signs. Moonee, Mystere and even the Park might as well have been from different dimensions.

I wondered how Sixkiller felt right now, so far from home and constantly under threat. Maybe that's what a Marshal's life was? Maybe he thrived on it? Maybe his calm exterior hid a need for risk? Maybe he was deeply screwed up?

I decided right then and there to ask Caro to spare some of her investigative energies for Sixkiller. I needed to know the man who was stuck at my side in this battle.

And his bison disincarnate. What a powerful and terrifying sight. Even now, my gut cramped up at the memory.

"Virgin?" Sixkiller was standing, holding the door of the taxi open.

I paid the driver, got out and headed straight for the lift, desperate for my own space. But the Marshal stayed until it pinged open on my floor, then he walked with me to my door. I think he would have planted himself on the couch if Heart hadn't been there waiting.

"You staying the night?" he asked Heart. "She needs someone with her."

Heart nodded. "I'll be here until you come for her in the morning."

I wanted to snarl at them both that what I needed was privacy. This sudden unspoken agreement to share bodyguard duties on me was a cheese grater on my skin.

When Heart shut the door on Sixkiller and deadlocked it, I didn't wait to chat but disappeared straight into the shower, unbuckling my pistol and dropping my stained clothes in the rubbish chute, not the laundry.

Heart sensed my mood and left me alone.

When I emerged in a tank top and my most comfortable shorts, he had a tumbler of rum and some pretzels waiting on the coffee table, which he'd shifted so it sat right in the middle of John Flat.

"Inspector Chance won't like that," I said.

"Stupid that it's still there. They've done their forensics. She's just playing the intimidation game with you."

"Caro says I'll see the outline there forever, so she's given it a name."

He raised an eyebrow and held out the tumbler.

"John Flat," I said, sipping and edging around the table to sit next to him. The alcohol burned for a bit and then softened my knotted gut. I sank back into the cushions and tried to relax.

"You want to tell me about the blood on your clothes and the wound glue on your shoulder?" He let his fingers trace lightly the new wound.

"In this case, knowledge is not a good thing," I said, sipping again.

"I'm no stranger to trouble, Virgin. And truly, I want to help you."

I took his hand and squeezed it. He looked almost as tired as me, his face a little thinner than a few weeks ago and his eyes a little swollen. "Have you been sleeping?"

"Don't switch the attention on me," he said. "I mean this."

"I'm sorry, Heart. It's just been a really crappy few days."

He drained his rum and took a deep breath. "Look… this is not something that I really want to say out loud… but shit, Virgin, I *care* about you."

I let go of his hand. "I… don't…"

He raised his hand up to stop me. "I don't need anything from you right now. Just trust me a little. Let me in."

To my dismay, my eyes moistened. I didn't cry a lot, and I wasn't about to change that. But my face had other ideas. My eyes brimmed with tears and my lip quivered. I poked my eyes with my fingers and bit my lip to help get control of my emotions.

Heart didn't say a word, just watched me until the wave had passed.

"I'll tell you about it," I said. "But in the morning. After some sleep."

"But it's only just gone dark."

"Put me to bed," I said. "And that's an order."

TWENTY-FIVE

My phone woke me early. Heart lay on his stomach, head turned away, sheet down around his haunches.

I dragged my blurry eyes away from the magnificent sight of his nakedness and rolled over to answer the call. A squint at the display told me it was Caro, so I climbed out of bed and staggered out to the couch.

"You sound half asleep," she said.

"I am half asleep."

"I've had a pingback on the meds. They were mixed in Baltimore, Maryland."

"You got any kind of more specific location? I'm guessing Baltimore is a big place."

"Heading up to a million bodies."

"That narrows it down."

"Patience," she said. "I don't have an address, if that's what you're asking, but the ingredient batch numbers were shipped from a warehouse in Washington to the North Baltimore area. Probably a dummy address, but I guarantee wherever they're mixing their pharma will be close to that."

"I guess that's another piece of the jigsaw. Not sure if it's the sky or the water, though." I tried not to sound despondent. It must have cost her some resources to find that out. "When I see Nate, I'll tell him. It might mean something to the Marshals Service."

"You working *with* the Marshal now?"

"We had a rough visit to Moonee yesterday. I'm going to have to trust him a bit... for my own health."

"You want me to dig around a little on him?"

"You read my mind. And Caro... thanks."

"You're my friend, Ginny. And 'sides, I smell story."

I laughed quietly and both my shoulders hurt.

"You're still on sick leave, remember. Get some rest," she said.

"Yeah. But I may go parkside today. Need some air."

"Last time you went out there, you came back *needing* a blood transfusion."

"I'll be careful," I said.

"You don't even know what that means."

"Sure, I do."

"Liar." She hung up and left me staring at the coffee table, which still sat in the middle of John Flat. She was right. I was never going to forget someone died there.

With a sigh, I got up and put a mug of water in the microwave to boil for tea.

A faint noise outside the door had me reaching for my pistol. I checked my sec-cam and got an eyeful of Totes' butt as he bent down to put something on the floor.

I flung the door open. "What the...?"

"VJ," he said, popping up. His eyes widened when he saw my 9mm. "Thought you might like some brioche and coffee." He'd been placing a small takeaway tray on the floor. Next to it sat a little doll wearing a checked shirt, jeans and riding boots. Her hair was pulled up in a ponytail and her features were solemn.

"Who's that?" I asked poking at the doll with my toe.

He picked her up and handed her over in the most reverent manner.

"Is that me?" I asked staring into a plastic-doll replica of my own face.

"You like her?" His face lit up. "I made the mould myself. Got the clothes made on Verve Street."

Verve Street was Fifth Avenue on a small scale. "She's wearing my favourite shirt."

His eyes shone. "Please take her. I'll feel better if you do."

Creepy didn't even begin to describe it, but even my blunt nature wavered at the sight of his ecstasy. "Sure, Totes. And thanks for the coffee and food."

He lingered, but I wasn't weakening that much.

"Got company," I said. "I'd better go."

He nodded his head a few times, turned on his heel and wandered off.

"See you at work. I'll be in today."

He flashed me a grin over his shoulder.

"Who was that?" asked Heart from the bedroom door as I brought the doll and the food in.

"Totes. He's left me a good-luck charm."

Heart came and took the Virgin doll from me, turning it over in his hands. "Pretty. Hope she's not bugged as well."

I snatched the doll back and shook, squeezed and prodded it until I was sure it was harmless.

"Every girl has one, you know," said Heart, watching me.

"Has one what?"

"A creepy guy."

"He's OK, really. He's just smart and screwed up. Can't hold that against him."

Heart gave me a funny look. "I guess not."

I handed him a brioche. "Tea or coffee?"

"Coffee," he said. "And conversation."

I handed him the pastry and coffee and went to finish making my tea. Pouring hot water and mixing milk and sugar gave me time to work out what to share with Heart. When I was done, I carried my mug over to the couch, careful to walk around the blurred edge of John Flat.

"I went to Moonee with the Marshal yesterday."

"Moonee?"

"In the Divine, near Mystere. But away from the tourist strip."

"You mean *burning-grounds Moonee*?"

"You know about that place?" He surprised me sometimes. But then, I guess I didn't know much detail about his life outside our bedroom encounters.

"I hear stuff, you know. Strippers do."

"Even a stripper from the Western Quarter?"

"People travel a distance to see this boy dance," he said, pointing his thumbs at his chest.

"I believe it."

He took the coffee from me and set it on the table. "That's how you got the wound on your other shoulder."

"Spear. Some primitive shit goes on in Moonee."

"And are you going to tell me why you went there?"

"Nate and I found a talisman that we think's connected with the murder in the park and him." I tapped the floor to indicate the body outline. "Finding out about it meant a trip to Moonee."

"And?"

"The Marshal thinks it might have some link back to my dad, which means me."

Heart lifted his head with interest. He seemed to choose carefully before he spoke again. "Why would your dad be involved?"

"He was an outspoken man. A hardliner on many things. When he was lobbying to get the land designated as a park, he made a few enemies. Property developers and some politicians. Other than that, I have no idea. But I'm going to go through his journals today. See if I can find anything."

"Your dad left journals?"

"I haven't been able to bring myself to open them. But now… well, I think it's time."

"You keep them here? In your apartment?"

He asked the question quite conversationally, but I couldn't help my defensive response.

"Yes. Why?"

A shrug. "Nothing. I mean… you've talked about him a bit, but you never mentioned them. Hey, listen, I have to head out to work. You coming to the partner dinner tonight at the club?"

I groaned. "Still on, is it?"

"Still on." He threw a cushion at me. "And you promised."

"Fine. I'll meet you there, though. What time?"

"Seven."

"Date night, eh?"

He grinned. "Yeah, something like that."

We finished our hot drinks, fooled around on the couch a bit, and then Heart showered.

"Call Nate; let him know I'm leaving," he said when he emerged with wet hair and a smoking aura.

"I just did," I lied.

"I'll wait," he said.

"He's on his way. You'll probably pass him in the corridor."

"Promise?"

"Promise."

He shrugged into his shirt and kissed me. "See you tonight."

I waited just long enough for Heart to clear the building, then I hightailed down the fire escape.

By the ground floor, I could barely breathe and my boots were like lumps of concrete on my feet. I didn't ever take the stairs, and the transfusion had really knocked me around. To add to it, yesterday's spear injury still stung like a nest of green-ant bites.

Not in good shape, Virgin.

But this was something I had to do alone with no one looking over my shoulder. I'd avoided answering Heart about Dad's journals for no good reason other than I'd never tell anyone where they were. Not even Caro.

And there were a couple of reasons for that. One being that burying anything in the park was highly illegal and against Heritage rules. The other, that they'd been too painful for me to go near, so I'd put them somewhere safe for when I was ready.

I'm not sure that I was ready now, but the time had definitely come.

My police tail today was a short, heavyset detective in jeans and a baseball cap. He was eating an apple and watching the traffic as I left the building. I headed straight into Cloisters next door and led him around the food halls, finally losing him in the restroom near Dim Sum Delight.

Exactly ten minutes later, I was at the stables, standing in front of the security scanner.

"Virgin!" squeaked Totes over the intercom. "Thought you were kidding about coming in."

"Open up. I gotta get out in some fresh air. This off-duty shit is killing me."

He bleeped me in, and I was saddling Benny when he ambled along the corridor to find me.

"Think you're up to riding?" he asked. "How're your shoulders?"

"Shoulder," I corrected. Wasn't about to tell him about the spear wound.

"You know you're not meant to be going out there, anyway. Sector's closed, orders of the Po-Po," he added.

I bestowed him with an exaggerated eye-roll. "Listen. I'll take full responsibility with the boss and the police. Just tell Bull that I disengaged Benny's GPS and snuck through while you were in maintenance mode or something."

He gave a big, exaggerated eye-roll of his own. "Like he'll believe me."

"He can't prove otherwise. And anyway, it won't come to that. I just want to destress. I'll be back soon."

"Leave your phone's GPS on, just for me."

"I don't want to be logged."

"How about I track you in my duplicate system? No one sees that."

I raised both my eyebrows. "You have a dummy back end?"

"It's my personal backup. Gotta have somewhere to practise tweaks."

"Fine," I said, not feeling fine about it at all. "See you in a while."

I led Benny down to the Interchange, mounted and walked her through. As soon as the gate closed on me, I took in a deep lungful of air. Without Sixkiller to worry about or any tourist buses, it felt like the first time I'd had any peace in days. Even the memory of the Mythos attack dimmed against my relief to be out here alone.

I rode out past the trough, the palms and the windmill and headed straight for the butte. My skin soaked the sun in and the morning-cool air was a tender touch.

The south-east sector of Birrimun stretched away from me in an achingly familiar canvas, red rock punctuated with translucent purples and greens of the mulla mulla, spinifex and the odd imported cacti.

Dad had fought long and hard to keep all the flora and fauna native to the area. He won the fauna fight but lost the flora battle.

A park based on a Western theme had to have cacti, they said. The park upkeep and rates relied on the tourist dollar, and visitors wanted cacti! Just like they wanted horseshoes and bull's horns and country music when they went to bars in the Quarter.

I tethered Benny – though she didn't need it – and walked to the top of the butte. The exercise felt good, blood flowing and sweat purging me of the hospital and Moonee and Mystere.

Aquila hadn't appeared, and there were no sinister crows in sight. A giddy sense of freedom overtook me.

The vista of sand and rock made my eyes tear up for the second time in as many days.

I groaned aloud. Really, Virgin?

Benny whinnied from below, hearing my voice. I called to reassure her and headed back down. With Totes monitoring me on his shadow system, I didn't have the luxury of too much time. He would probably back me up if Bull started asking questions, but I didn't want him putting his job on the line for me.

Benny picked her own path toward Dry Gulch, leaving me free to think about Totes. We'd worked together almost eight years. He was a few years younger than me, but I would never lose the notion of him being that precocious fifteen year-old who came to work with us the year before Dad died.

Dad always said I was too hard on him, defended him against my aggravation.

But I didn't see it that way. Smart-arse geniuses weren't on my Be Tolerant With list.

The day Dad died, Totes wouldn't leave the hospital. He sat in the waiting room, cradling one of his dolls, crying. Thinking about it now choked me up again.

I tried to get a handle on my emotions. Must be fatigue, I told myself. And thinking so much about Dad.

Benny angled into Dry Gulch down a worn path. The deep, dry waterway hadn't run in two hundred years. Wind erosion had rounded off the steep edges so there were only one or two places you could get down onto the riverbed safely.

The creek stretched from a way past the butte towards Paloma station. When you climbed out the other end (which you couldn't actually do), you could see them in the distance. That end of the gulch disappeared underground – or at least had when it last ran – and popped up close to the surface again below the Paloma station well.

I'd buried the memory dot with Dad's journals about halfway along, and that's where I was headed.

Before I sent the horse upstream, I dismounted and set my phone on a rock. I didn't want Totes tracking me to the exact spot. I also didn't want to lead the Park admin straight to my illegal activity, if for some reason they confiscated Totes' shadow system and found my route.

Satisfied that I'd covered bases, I remounted and urged Benny onward.

Gulch riding was slow going, and it took over an hour to reach the site where I'd buried the journals. I'd tucked it in under an ancient tree root sticking out of the side of the riverbank.

I poked in under the root with some long-nosed pliers from my kit bag – just in case a snake or scorpion had set up home. It felt hollow, and nothing scuttled out, so I leaned over and reached my hand in. My fingertips brushed the perma-seal around the dot, but it was just out of reach.

I withdrew and sat for a moment to think. Digging it out would leave signs of soil disruption. The Park scan would flag it and it would be photographed and analysed.

When I'd put it here, I'd never envisaged retrieving it. Too painful for me to read and too personal for me to share, it seemed the right thing to do, bringing it out here. Birrimun had been his life's passion, his life's work. And, in my mind, his death. His innermost thoughts belonged out here as much as the soil and the ants and the mulla mulla.

I went back to my tool kit and took the pliers apart, wiring them together end to end, so they made a longer lever. Then I reached back in and stabbed gently at the plastic case, slowly dragging it forward.

After I bit I stopped, took the pliers out and felt with my fingers again.

Got you!

I pulled it free and sat back on my haunches, lifting my hair up off the nape of my neck to cool it. The sun had begun to bite, and sweat trickled into uncomfortable places. Packing up quickly, I mounted and took a sip or two from my canteen.

Best get back before Totes got worried and did something rash. Soon as I reached my phone, I'd message him that I was on my way.

But the trip upstream was even slower on account of the old watercourse's vagaries. Several times, I got off and led Benny over ridges so her hooves didn't crumble the edges in her efforts to climb.

She understood what I was doing and lifted her feet high on my request. We'd done this dance many times. Benny was a park horse. Preservation of the environment was as much in her DNA as mine.

Aquila landed on my shoulder at a bend in the course of the dry riverbed. I didn't feel any pressure, more like a sense of movement near my face, a breath created by her wings.

It startled me so much, I shifted in the saddle, but she took off as soon as she landed and fluttered ahead to a large boulder.

I sat up and reigned in Benny, riding as slowly to where she perched as I could.

The scars from her battle with the Mythos at Paloma were still visible, a chunk of feathers missing across her breast and a missing nail on one claw. To protect me. I still found it hard to believe, even though I'd seen it.

"What is it?" I whispered. To her. To myself.

Her gaze was solemn as always, and my pulse accelerated. I unholstered my pistol and dismounted. As quietly as I could, I crept up to the boulder. With some awkward maneuvering, I was able to peer around it without exposing too much of myself.

Two guys waited there. One had his back to me and the other was bent over, examining my phone. They wore long sleeves, jeans and hip holsters, and I wouldn't mind betting each bore the crow and circle ink under their shirts. I couldn't see any horses, so they must have tethered them up out of the gully.

I eased back and leaned against the rock, thinking. I couldn't even contact Totes to sat-scan and photograph them. But if I could get back to the stables in one piece, he should have record of their presence on his system. He might even be aware of them now but had no way of letting me know.

Aquila lifted off the rock and flew back down the way I'd just come. She landed on a tuft of spinifex that was barely clinging to the side of the bank and watched me.

I get the message.

Trouble was that this was the only way out without significantly destroying the natural contour of the bank. Not only did the idea of damage bother me, but it would leave evidence that I'd been there.

I weighed up my options and decided that a little eco-damage was still preferable to me *never* getting home. Two armed men weren't good odds.

I crept back to Benny, turned her around and tapped her cheek a couple of times. She knew to keep quiet. I'd used that signal before, though usually so as not to scare a flock of birds or a shy wallaby.

She stepped carefully and slowly, following my lead.

Aquila flew ahead of us in spurts, like a forward scout. Once out of earshot, I mounted Benny and pushed her along a bit faster. Returning home this way would take longer, but once out of Dry Gulch, I could really push the pace.

Halfway back to where I'd buried Dad's journal, Aquila left her perch ahead of me and flew up one side of the creek, disappearing from view. I stopped Benny, wondering what to do. Wait for her? Continue?

I opted for dismounting yet again and climbing the steep side to see where she'd gone. The first few feet were loose, gravelly dirt, but once past the initial scree, it packed down into heavier soil. After three of four large, awkward steps, I discovered a ledge hidden by a swathe of mulla mulla. The purple flower that thrived in the red dirt turned up in places no other flora could survive, because it preferred low water and full sun.

Beyond the ledge was a natural rock wall. I scrambled up onto the rocks and found myself back out on the plain with a clear view south. Aquila was on the ground not far away, ripping into the guts of a small dead marsupial.

I turned away, not ready to process how that could be possible, and looked back to the climb I'd just made. If I started Benny from the far side of the creek bed, she should be able to jump onto the ledge with minimum damage. Getting over the next rock wall was more difficult. Though low, she'd be jumping from a standing position.

I looked up and down the gulch. Going back toward the ambush was not an option, and the further I went west, the deeper the gully became, until it turned into the steep rock wall end I couldn't climb.

Aquila had led me to the best option I had.

I climbed back down to my horse and led her to the opposite bank.

"Come on, girl," I said, remounting. "Just a couple of leaps and we're home free."

She nickered at my cajoling tone. It usually came associated with fresh clover treats.

I straightened, loosened the reins and clipped her ribs with my heels.

With all the affront of a person slapped, she leapt across the creekbed and up the sandy scree toward the ledge.

Her front legs didn't quite make the distance, and she started to slide backward. I squeezed her sides with my calves and thighs. She responded by bunching her haunches underneath her and propelling herself forward. We dangled for a moment, but I threw my weight forward over her shoulders and she found purchase. With all four feet on the ledge, she pranced a little, ears flicking back and forth.

I glanced down. The damage behind us looked minimal, some hoof marks in the loose gravel. In a day, the wind would have changed it all again.

Now for the hard bit.

I got off and climbed up over the rocks again. Aquila was still on the ground, picking bits of fleshy somethings from her claws.

I went back to Benny and talked to her again.

"You have to trust me," I told her. "Just one jump and we're out. The other side is wide open and level."

There was no soft nicker in response this time, and as I mounted, her ears flattened. She knew what I wanted and she wasn't keen.

I gathered up the reins and put enough pressure on the bit just to let her know this wasn't optional. She tensed under my signals. Bunching up high on the saddle, I used the end of the reins to give her a light slap on her shoulder. She jumped forward stiff-legged and then baulked.

I fell onto her neck and she reared, letting out a loud whinny that echoed along the gulch.

Shit!

I waited for her to settle before employing a stern tone. "You have to jump this. They'll be coming."

Her ears flicked back and forth and she danced on the spot, backing dangerously close to the edge.

"BENNY!" I gritted my teeth and jabbed her hard in the ribs.

She baulked again but I persisted.

"Come on, girl. Come on!"

From behind me in the gully, I could hear voices. Then shouts as they sighted me.

"BENNY!"

On my final yell, she launched from standing, into the air, and cleared the rock wall with plenty to spare. Landing on the other side was a different matter. She stumbled and went down on one knee, sending me catapulting over her shoulder into the dirt.

Aquila flew into the air, screeching.

I lay there, spitting dirt from my mouth and feeling around my limbs. Everything whole. But as I rolled over, a shooting pain from the Mythos wound sucked my breath away, burning worse than fifty levels of hell.

Get up.

Aquila fluttered down near me. This close, I could see flecks of gold in her eyes and how the feathers around her eyes were dark brown and fading to grey. She looked regal and the intelligence in her gaze astounded me.

I reached out my hand to her.

She flew back a little way and turned her head sideways in the way birds do when they want to eyeball you.

"Thank you," I said, "for the warnings. But why have you come back now? What are you trying to tell me?"

Her crest rose and she shrieked, as if letting me know that now was not the time for conversation.

The voices were getting closer.

I forced myself up and into the saddle and gave Benny her head. She pointed home and went hell for leather.

TWENTY-SIX

Totes jumped out at me as I walked Benny in through the Interchange.

"Virgin, where the hell you been?"

"Just let me stable her. Then I want to see a visual history of the geographical area on my phone's GPS coordinates for the last few hours."

I stalked past him down the corridor, hiding my trembling legs and sore body in an angry gait.

Leecey was in Sombre Vol's stall and followed me down.

"You must have pushed her hard. Girl's foaming," she said.

"Had reason to," I said. "Give her some electrolytes and an augmentation top-up."

"She's not due for her booster until next month."

"Leecey."

"OK. OK. Everything alright, Virgin? Can I help?"

Leecey had a ruddy kind of complexion that glowed when she'd been working. It gave her a permanently flushed look that some people mistook for guilt.

It worried me, the amount the police were around so much right now. Detective Chance had already shown she wasn't above targeting Leecey.

"Just stay clean and away from me," I said.

Her skin flushed even deeper and she tugged at Benny's girth.

I put my hand on hers. "Look, it's just... best to keep your distance from me at the moment. You don't want to be caught up in... *whatever* it is."

"That's not just your choice, Virgin."

"Well, it's my preference."

She crossed the stirrups up over the saddle, slid it off and walked off to the tack room, humming, "You cain't always get what you want."

I wasn't sure what she meant by that, but I didn't have time to chase her and find out. Instead, I went and invaded Totes' hidey-hole.

"There were two guys in the park. They'd tracked the GPS on my phone," I said.

"Impossible!" said Totes, typing commands and tapping screens. "I have the sat scans for your route and the only person there is you. In fact, according to the tracker, you're still there."

"Had to leave my phone behind on account of guys with guns."

Totes picked up his phone.

"What're you doing?"

"Telling Bull. The police should–"

"Stop! Just show me the scan."

Lower lip pouting in disagreement, he reached for one of the dolls on his desk and petted it as he set the replay in motion for me to watch.

My GPS showed me as a moving dot on a topographical map. At the entry to Dry Gulch, it became stationary.

"I figured you'd gotten off to have a walk around. But you stayed there so long, I nearly sent the EMS out."

"I went around across the gulch and further north. My phone must have dropped out of my pocket when I crossed the creek bed. When I backtracked, looking for it, I found some guys there waiting for me," I lied.

"I'll do an infrared retrieval scan on the area around your phone. See if anything was hot."

He whispered and touched his system like it was a friend with whom he shared a secret language. I was beginning to feel like the third wheel on a date, when he finally ran some more footage on the main screen.

"My shadow system only analyses basic wavelength imaging. Let me match up the time... Wait... There..."

I watched the time meter on the bottom of the screen as an amorphous blob moved across a dark landscape.

"That's you and Benny," he said.

"How do you know?"

"You have a particular signature. See."

The horse and I separated for a few moments and then joined together and moved off again.

"That must be when you dropped your phone, when you got off. What were you looking at?"

"Just checking some damage to the sides of the Gulch," I lied again.

"But hey, then you're heading west, not north," he added.

Shit. "I went west for a bit and then north. Listen, just flip forward to the same spot an hour later. I'm in a hurry."

He did as I requested, and the evidence of me staying on a westerly course disappeared in a blur of dark pixels. He stopped it an hour along, and we watched again for a while.

"There you are again. According to the contour overlay, you're up on the bank."

"Yeah, behind a boulder. I heard something ahead of me, so I left Benny in the creek and climbed up behind a boulder to look."

"Look at what?"

Totes was right. There was no other heat signature. No other horses, no other guys with guns.

"They *have* to be there. I *saw* them," I said, distressed.

Totes held out his doll for me to cuddle. "Been a rough few days. You want some love?"

I left the stables, preoccupied and upset. I *had* seen those guys, heard their voices. They *were* real. Totally real. Not Mythos, like the crow had been.

But then, Aquila and the Mythos had looked totally real to me as well.

Maybe I was losing my grip.

I took the underground tunnel to the taxi rank on the other side, thinking I would go home, but a taxi pulled up and Sixkiller got out.

He fixed me with a narrow-eyed, pursed-lip look and let both hands rest on his holsters.

Seems he was mightily pissed.

"Hey. You sleep in?" I asked lightly.

He gestured for me to step away from the rank and the commuters in the queue.

"I've been looking for you all morning. Thet little

sidewinder Totes told me he hadn't seen you. But you've been in the Park all along."

I felt a burst of gratitude towards Totes. Maybe Dad was right about him. "It's where I think best. And I needed some time."

"Thinking get you dirty?"

I looked down at my red-dirt-stained shirt and jeans. "Took a tumble off my horse. Just going home to clean up."

"Then I'll be accompanying you. Got something you need to hear."

I sighed. "Sure." And I followed him to the back of the queue.

"Check the news feeds," he said as we waited.

"Can't. I… er... dropped my phone in the park somewhere."

"Couldn't Totes track it?"

"Must have been damaged. No GPS signal."

He stared at me suspiciously and fished a black scroll from inside his jacket and unrolled it to squint at the flexible screen.

"You been holding out on me, Marshal? Didn't think you carried a phone."

"It ain't a phone."

Our taxi turn came up and I climbed in the back, sliding across so he could fit.

He handed me his tablet, and on the drive back to Cloisters, I flipped through the local news headlines. There'd been a mass shooting last night in Mystere – fourteen tourists dead and three locals. No one had claimed responsibility and even the press didn't know who to pin it on. Some were saying it was a random attack.

"You think it's them, the crow and circle?" I asked Sixkiller.

"Fits with what the fat man said to us."

"What's the point, though? I don't get it. No political statement made. No ownership. Just a bunch of dead people no one wants to be responsible for."

He glanced at the taxi driver, then back at me, indicating he didn't wish to answer yet, so neither of us spoke again until we were in my apartment.

My fortnightly grocery delivery had been, and I was able to pour us both some fruit juice and magic up a plate of mixed nuts, some rye bread and cheese.

Sixkiller declined everything but the nuts and juice.

I skirted John Flat, who was still straddled by the coffee table, and sat down to take off my boots.

Then it hit me. Something was wrong in here.

"What is it?" he asked.

I had my boot in my hand, sock half off. "Nothing... I just..."

I got up and wandered around. It felt like someone had been in here, carefully; things were in their place but... I went to the bedroom. Everything looked undisturbed except the bedcover. It was smooth, no crinkle or hump or crease. Had I really left it like that?

I shook my head, unsure of myself, and returned to Sixkiller. "It's nothing. Just jumpy. So, what's your theory on the murders in Mystere?"

He relaxed. "Could be just a local power play. Or a low-scale terror attack. Either way, it might also be someone's way of deflecting attention."

"From what?"

"Thet's the problem. We don't know. Back in the hive, there's a bunch of analysts that do thet sort of thing all day long. They look for spikes in violent events. Then they try to work out what those events might be hiding." He waved his tablet at me. "It could be any damn thing mentioned on here. Or it might be somethin's that's barely bin reported."

"Sounds like a whole world of paranoia you got going on, Marshal."

"Welcome to international intelligence."He took some more almonds from the bowl and removed his hat, setting it on my narrow sideboard next to the Virgin doll.

Free from it, his hair fell dead straight around his face. In some people, it would have been a severe look, but on him, it softened the hard lines of his face.

"The Mythos have been finding ways to influence our world for a long time. But we believe there's a change in intensity of their desires. Their timeline, whatever it is, has accelerated," he said. "Could be this damage in Mystere is them distracting from other things that they are changing. We tend to see more activity in certain lunar cycles."

I took some time to think this over. "We believe? Or *you* believe, Marshal?"

He pressed his knuckle to his forehead. "Thought we'd gotten past this, Virgin. Thought you understood that we were dealing with something *not from here*."

"Didn't my personality profile say stubborn, Marshal?"

"Stubborn. Not stupid."

We glared at each other.

Then Aquila appeared in the air above him.

He saw the direction of my gaze and looked up. "Thank you," he said to her.

She swooped to the sideboard and perched on his hat.

I laughed outright and suddenly, all perversity drained out of me. I don't know what had happened in the park this morning, why I couldn't see the guys tracking me. But this was real. Aquila. Sixkiller. Me.

"I found some clean-skin meds in Teng's room. Caro traced them to a warehouse in Baltimore, Maryland. Does that mean anything to you?" I asked.

He stiffened. "You found traceable evidence. You should have told me."

"What, and have you send it back home to Virginia, never to be seen again? Finders keepers, Marshal. It's not like either of us was going to go to the police with it. And this way, we got the trace done quickly."

I liked to think his expression was begrudging acceptance, but it could have been closer to reignited fury.

"So, does Baltimore mean anything to you?" I asked again.

"We may have people there on our watch list."

"Then maybe you better get watching them a bit closer."

"I'll need some physical evidence as proof."

"I'll talk to Caro. As long as it doesn't implicate her or her contacts, I guess it'll be fine to share."

He made an effort to relax his mouth. "When're you going to trust me, Virgin?"

"Why *should* I trust you, Nate? I barely know you. You've been sent out here by a foreign government to spy on me because they think my father has something to do with some… supernatural conspiracy."

"Does savin' your skin count for nix?" he said in his most humble cowboy voice.

I hugged my knees to my chest and contemplated my toes. "Just give me some time. I don't take to people easily or quickly."

"That's the thing," he said. "We don't got time."

"Then we'll have to make do with what we have got."

"Which is?"

"An agreement."

"I'm listenin'…"

"Simple. We watch each other's back."

He nodded slowly. "Well, I guess that's a start. Though I thought I was doin' thet already."

"I'm going to catch some downtime in my room. You're welcome to stay out here and chill. Oh, and I have a date tonight."

"I'll escort you to it and pick you up when you're done."

"Sweet." Not.

I retrieved my tablet from the coffee table, went into my bedroom and locked the door. Drawing the blinds, I fished out Dad's journal dot from the lining of my bra, peeled off my jeans and jumped into bed.

Heart's scent on my pillows lifted my mood. He was the one good thing happening to me right now, and I didn't have time to make the most of it.

I detached the ear clip from the side of the tablet and slotted the journal dot into the tablet's port. After a copyright preamble provided by the manufacturer, Dad started to speak. His voice struck like a fist to the softest part of my stomach. I wanted to throw up.

Breathing through my nose, I settled back on my pillows.

Slow and steady. Slow and steady.

He began with the key, explaining that the journal was divided into essays and recounts and reflections.

I started with the weekly recounts that covered park business but from a personal perspective: land erosion, battles with the executive, frustration with Bull's fence-sitting on certain preservation issues. I could hear the strength of their friendship in Dad's tone, and the depth of his disappointment that his friend would not support him.

Occasionally, there was a note devoted entirely to me.

Hearing his worries about me was both humbling and distressing. At first, it focused on my lack of friends and propensity to solitude. But in the twelve months before his last entry, it switched to concerns about my safety. He seemed to be charting where I went and who I saw, flagging Caro as questionable.

I bookmarked the entries about me, then went back and listened to each journal recount immediately before them.

Sometimes he used unfamiliar, confusing acronyms, but clearly, he suspected the park was being used outside of tourist hours. He found evidence of illegals having been at Paloma station, Los Tribos and Waco Spring.

Los Tribos seemed to bother him the most.

The disturbance at Los Tribos is stronger than at Paloma and Waco. Seems whoever is using the Park has a particular interest there. The site was sacred to the Indigenous peoples in years past, but those claims were revoked when Birrimun was created. More political bastardy. I don't know if it's possible to hate these people more than I do, but for Virgin's sake, I need to rein it in. She's had no mother to soften the hard edges of my attitudes and my beliefs... As her guide, I should do better. Be more charitable...

To date, the scans show nothing. No illegals. Our young technician is good at what he does. I have no reason to doubt him. Which means they have found a way to avoid detection...

Then a few weeks before he died, the tone of the recounts changed again. His voice sounded strained. Urgent.

I think the park is being used for human trafficking. It sounds ludicrous when I say it out loud, but it's the only explanation I have. Whoever is responsible has found a way to avoid the Park security and is bringing people into the country. I'm going to take leave and do around-the-clock surveillance on Los Tribos. Maybe put a camera on the place, too.

I stopped. Dad! He'd put the recorder at Los Tribos.

I listened to every entry from then until the day he died, but he didn't mention Los Tribos or the camera again, nor did he take leave, because Bull denied it.

His monologues became more cryptic, as though he worried he was being overheard.

Still there. Every time the crow flies.

And then day before he died.

I've run a trace on my essay. It's been viewed from an address in Baltimore. Who are they? I need to make arrangements for Virgin in case.

I stopped there, sick at heart. Should have listened to these seven years ago. Here was proof that Dad felt threatened. But what would that have given me with no names, just unfounded suspicions and vague references?

I needed time to go through these journals and listen to everything. And his essays. Which one had he referred to? And the mention of Baltimore... it had to be connected in some way to Teng.

Shit! Why hadn't he shared any of this? Seven years ago, I was young but hardly a child.

Something made me glance at the bedroom door. The handle was turning.

I pulled off the ear clips. "Yes?"

"Virgin?"

"What?"

"It's after seven. When's your date?"

I checked the time. "Gimme a few minutes to change."

"You want food?"

"No."

"Right." The door handle released.

I got up, peeled the journal dot off, put it back into its slipcase and stuck it in a rusted vent in the air conditioner. Then I took a quick dunk under the shower until my mind was sufficiently in the present.

Washed and in a black dress, I emerged to find Sixkiller pacing. The inactivity must have been a drag for him, because he'd packed the plates and glasses into the dishwasher and wiped down the benches. He'd also plaited his long, straight hair so that it lay on his shoulders in neat swathes.

I raised my eyebrows. "Thanks for cleaning up."

"You're welcome," he said. "But why don't you look more rested?"

"Are you making a personal comment about my appearance, Marshal?"

"No...I just mean..." He shrugged, grunted and stalked out into the corridor to wait for me.

"Where are we going?" he asked when I came out after him.

"The Outfit. A club in the Quarter. I'm meeting Heart there."

I followed him down to the front of the Cloisters, and we caught the bus because the taxi rank was jammed. At least on the bus, I didn't feel compelled to make small talk, and clearly, neither did he.

The mutually agreed silence saw us right into the Quarter and to a bus stop a half a block's walk from the Outfit.

We walked the rest of the way and stopped between the Outfit and Dang and Darn – an upholstery booth where you could get your boots and belts embroidered while you waited. "Can you wait outside, please?" I asked.

"S'long as you promise not to hightail it out the back door," he said.

I held up my right hand. "I'd swear in a dozen different languages, if I knew them."

"So, you and Williams: is it serious?"

I gave him an incredulous look. "You honestly expect me to answer that?"

"Just looking out for you, Virgin."

"What's that supposed to mean?"

"I have family, you know, a sister and brothers. It's not outside the realm of possibility for me to feel concern for another human being."

His reply confused me. "You have a family?"

He actually smiled, and it peeled years off his face. I wondered what he was like as a younger man, before all this.

"A whole bunch of them. Youngest brother rides rodeo, oldest is a teacher. My sister's a biomedical engineer."

"Rodeo? Really?"

"Same as me until I joined the service."

"You rode rodeo professionally?" Well, that explained a lot.

"He's better than me. They're figuring him to win the NFR this year. Plan to be there to see it, too."

We've got our own National Rodeo Championships out here but nothing as grand as the NFR. The pride in his voice made Sixkiller seem far less zealous lawman and far more regular guy.

"You're avoiding my question, though, about you and the dancer," he said.

I shook my head at him in disbelief and walked right off into the Outfit without saying goodbye.

The club was half full and decked out with hay bales and pitchforks and gangsta motifs. Just one of the many mash-up theme places in the Quarter affected.

Heart stood over by the bar, talking to an attractive girl in a red shirt tied high to show her midriff. They were laughing together as she hung glasses on racks above her head. Their comfortable, carefree manner made my chest tighten. I was getting too used to having Heart around, and seeing him flirting stung.

I nearly turned right around and got out of there but he spotted me.

"Virgin!" His face lit up, salving my bruised emotions a little.

He beckoned me over and watched in an openly lewd manner as I made my way through the tables and chairs.

"Hey, you made it," he said.

I pulled a face. "Left my chaperon at the door, though. He'll be collecting me later on. Unless, of course, I have an escort home."

"In that dress, anything could happen." He leaned forward and kissed me in front of his female friend, then pulled me down onto the stool next to him. "Freya, this is Virgin… my partner."

"Welcome to the Outfit, Virgin. I'll spare you the *yeehaw*. You look like you've been around the traps."

I managed a stiff smile at her double-edged greeting. "I'm not new to the Quarter, no. Though this place is a little… young for me these days."

"We've all been dying to see who's been keeping Heart from us. You gotta know your boyfriend breaks hearts up and down the city coast."

I opened my mouth to say he wasn't my boyfriend, then shut it again. Let her think that if she wished.

Heart read my mind and seemed amused.

And that made me want to kick him.

"What'll you have to drink, honey? On the house," said Freya.

"Rum," I said, feeling it all of a sudden. "A double with a shot of ginger ale."

"Lady likes it sweet," said Freya, lifting an eyebrow.

"Virgin?"Heart frowned.

I took the glass and knocked it down, not in the mood for another lecture on looking after myself. Reading Dad's journal today had been a jolt in many ways, especially the fact that he worried about my ability to socialize. Was I really such a misfit?

"I'll have another with a lager chaser, please," I said.

Freya lifted an eyebrow and obliged. Then she moved off down the bar, leaving Heart and me alone.

"What's going on?" he said.

"I've been reading my dad's journals. Seems amongst other things that he thought his daughter was socially challenged. Hard to hear something like that from the grave," I blurted out.

He took my beer and had a few sips. "That's tough. Course, I've always found you pretty darn cool."

I polished off the second rum and took the beer back from him. "Sorry. Moment of self-indulgence has passed. But I'm really not much in the mood for this place. Maybe we can try and have a regular date some other time."

I expected him to wave me off but he surprised me with "Let's get out of here."

"Really?" I said. "You sure?"

In answer, he grabbed my hand and pulled me toward the door.

I stepped onto the street while he stopped at the coat

checker to leave a message or apology or whatever to the others.

It was busy out here. Lots of hats and boots and shouts of laughter. Most of the people walking by looked like they didn't have a care in the world.

I wanted that same feeling so badly. Two double rums and half a schooner of beer had loosened all the tight places in my body, and I decided to suggest to Heart that we go somewhere with music. But what would we do with the Marshal? That thought made me chuckle, and I looked around for my chaperon.

"Ranger! Here, Ranger!"

It wasn't Sixkiller's voice coming from the very narrow gap between the Outfit and Dang and Darn. Because I wasn't wearing my gun, I moved towards the edge of the building warily. I was safe enough out here in public, I told myself. Heart was only a shout away. And the Marshal…

"Who is it?" I called.

A face appeared from the gloom. Chains ran from his from lip to his ear and cheek and forehead. *Kadee Matari's man?*

"What do you want?" I said, sounding as shrill and shocked as I felt.

"We speak. Alone."

I glanced back at the door, willing Heart to open it and end this moment.

He flashed a knife at me. "Ranger, you must."

"You can't kill me in public."

"Don't wish to kill you. Need your help."

I couldn't help but step closer at that. "What do you mean?"

"Here, please." He vanished back into the narrow gap that was only as wide as my shoulders.

Maybe my judgment was clouded by the rum, but I followed him to the edge and peered in. The poor excuse for an alley stank of cat piss, and I couldn't see in any farther than a few feet. Face-chain guy was pressed against the wall, his face hidden in shadow.

"The Korax have taken Kadee Matari."

"What? When?"

"Today during siesta. She said if that were to happen, you must get her back."

"M-me?" I spluttered in astonishment. "Even if I knew where she was, why would I do that?"

"Because they also have the American Marshal."

I took a step into the alley so that I was up close to his face. "Not possible. He's right here."

Face-chain guy slid slowly down the wall, reached into the dark and then stood up again. He had a Stetson in his hand.

I took it and turned to the light. It was Sixkiller's.

"They took him from the pavement when you left him. Perhaps they planned to take you as well but luck was on your side."

"How do you know? What were you doing here?"

"Following you, waiting for a chance to speak. You're our best hope."

"Why? I know as much about these people as you do. Maybe less. I have no idea where to find them, where to start."

"Until you came to visit, we had no trouble. Now the Korax seek to claim our place."

"They've made a move on you? I thought you were

working *with* them."

His chains tinkled as his face worked in agitation. "She works alone. *We* work alone."

The man handed me a phone, then pushed past me, causing me to flatten against the wall. "There is one number in here. Call me when you have found her."

When I stepped back onto the street, he had gone but Heart was standing at the door of The Outfit looking panicked.

He saw me and ran over. "What are you doing down there? With everything that's…"

"Give me your phone," I interrupted him.

"What? Why?"

"I don't have one. At least, not one I can use. Please. Quickly."

He handed it over and watched me as I thumbed in Totes' number.

"Who is this?" asked the Park tech.

"Virgin. Do you have any kind of locator on the Marshal?"

Silence for a moment. "Why?"

"Just answer the question."

"I told you. He found the bug in his apartment and he doesn't have a phone. I'm not secret service, Virgin. I don't plant things on people."

"So you don't know where he is right now?"

"Nope. Is something up?"

"Call Bull and tell him I'm coming into the office. I need to see him right away."

"Virgin?"

"Please, Totes. Just do it."

"OK. But where are you calling fr–"

I hung up and gave Heart back his phone. "Sorry. I have to go."

"Wow!" He grabbed my arm. "You can't just bail without an explanation."

I took his hand off my sleeve and squeezed it. "The Marshal's been taken."

TWENTY-SEVEN

"T-taken? Like abducted?" said Heart.

"Yeah, just like they tried to do with me the other night."

"But how do you know? Who told you?" He glanced up and down the street.

"I have to go. I'm sorry. I'd say I'll see you later tonight, but that might not pan out. You understand?"

He raised both hands in a helpless gesture. "Sure, Virgin, but let me at least escort you to work."

I didn't want to be *escorted*, but it seemed churlish to reject his courtesy. "Sure."

We grabbed a priority taxi from a red-coded rank across the road. The PTs ran on a different grid system to the rest of the traffic, but you paid for it accordingly. I figured Parks Southern wouldn't baulk at the cost it in this instance.

Heart asked me a few questions about who, and where, and what I would do, but I wasn't good for questions I had no answers to.

And I was having a hard time believing the Marshal'd been taken. Sixkiller seemed so untouchable, I half expected him to be waiting in Bull's office for me, looking smug or a trifle disdainful.

"Call me?" said Heart as we parted in the foyer of Parks Southern.

"When I get a new phone."

He dropped a kiss on my cheek. "You make my heart ache, Virgin. Be careful."

I frowned, not sure what he meant. "Always."

"Let me know if I can help," he added.

"Unlikely. But if you hear anything… you know… rumours."

"I'll head back to work now and ask the girls. They hear all sorts of things. The Marshal must have been taken close to the club. Someone might have seen something."

"Thanks, I appreciate it."

I left him there and ran past security to the lift. It took an age for it to ping open at Bull's floor.

"Where is he?" I asked Jethro, his assistant, as I burst in the door.

"He won't be a moment, Virgin; he's on a VIP call."

"Fuck that!" I marched past him and went straight on in.

"Virgin?" Bull quickly tapped his desk, and the screen he was staring at went to black.

I caught a glimpse of a woman's face but it was no one I knew.

"Can't you ever do as you're asked?" he barked.

"The Marshal's gone. We don't really have time for you to be politicking."

"I know. I was in a conference about it. One you rudely interrupted."

"How do you know?"

"He has a locator on him, which sent a distress signal, then stopped. Tell me what you know and what you think."

I sat on the other side of the desk and went through it, explaining the visit from Kadee Matari's man. I finished with "Maybe we should contact Detective Chance."

"I think this beyond Aus-Police, Virgin. Now I have your full report, I'll be bringing in some outside help. You need to just sit tight and wait until they arrive."

"When will that be?"

"Tomorrow, maybe."

"Tomorrow, *maybe?* Jeez, Bull, he could be dead by then."

"If you want to look at it that way, he could be dead by now. But you don't steal people off the street to kill them. They're making a point or will make a demand. The Marshal is smart. He'll know how to survive in this situation."

"What situation, Bull? It's not you out there. What if they're torturing him? He's killed one of them already."

"Look, I appreciate your emotional investment in this, but we need experts figuring it. Be available for a briefing tomorrow when they arrive. In the meantime, stay at home and keep this to yourself."

I glared at him, speechless. *Emotional investment?* What happened to plain human decency and loyalty?

I got up and headed for the door.

"And, Virgin, Totes will drop a new phone off to you at home. Stay in touch."

"Yes, boss." No, boss.

He stood up and crossed his arms to press the fact that he meant what he said. "Security will take you back to Cloisters."

No point in going head to head with him on that. I had my own plan, which meant getting back to my apartment as soon as possible anyway.

"Tomorrow, then," I said.

I left him and was told by Jethro that security would meet me in the lobby. His tone and manner were offhand and I didn't blame him for it. Most assistants took the task of protecting their boss very seriously. They didn't like being brushed off.

But even though I didn't blame him, I also didn't care.

Security brought a sleek company limo around to the front door and drove me home in the PT lane. I was sitting on my couch with a beer and strip of beef jerky exactly twenty-three minutes later.

I didn't ask, but I expected at least one of them stayed on outside my door or down at the front entrance. It would be an annoyance later when I wanted to leave, but Caro would play her part.

A knock meant I had to drag my butt off the couch to look through the sec-cam. It was Totes, waving a phone under the camera.

I let him in and went back to my posse on the couch.

He stood near the door, doing the awkward foot-to-foot shuffle. He looked kinda oily, like he hadn't washed in a while.

"What's going on with the Marshal?" he asked.

"Ask Bull. I'm on a gag order."

His eyes widened. "Things aren't right, Virgin. I've been checking the coding on the Park-scan systems. I keep finding anomalies."

"What kind?"

"Just small things. The system is meant to self-repair and alert me when it does. But it's like it's running a second layer of code that I can't see, and that's causing bubbles."

"Have you told Bull?"

"Not until I know what it is. Don't mention it, please."

"That might explain why we couldn't see those guys waiting to ambush me. How long till you figure it out?" I said.

"I haven't slept in a couple of days."

I held out my hand for the phone. "Do you have my new number?"

He gave me a coy look.

"Right. Thanks for dropping it in."

He waved at the Virgin doll on the sideboard and let himself out.

I got busy transferring my contacts list from my tablet to my new phone, then sent Caro an urgent text.

She arrived with pizza as I was getting through my third beer.

"I'll take that," she said, snaffling my longneck.

I relieved her of the pizza carton and sat down again. "How did you know I was hungry?"

"You message me close to midnight. Of course you're hungry."

Pepperoni, olive and pineapple with stringy cheese hanging from the crust. I folded the cheese around my finger and popped it in my mouth. Heaven.

"So, wassup?" she said, slouched in my armchair, sipping the beer. Despite the dark rings, her eyes were bright. Sharp.

"Your friend Hamish. I might need to contact him."

"Oh?" She sat up straight.

"Nate's been taken off the street down near the Outfit in the Quarter."

"How do you know?"

I told her what had happened and about my visit from Kadee's right-hand guy. "I've been to Bull. He doesn't want to involve the police. Says he's got some specialists coming tomorrow. The Marshal's a pain in my arse, Caro, but he doesn't deserve to have to wait till Bull has all his T's crossed for someone to start looking for him."

"What do you need from me?"

"Matari's guy says the Crow and Circle have taken them, and I think Dad's essays might have clues about who or where they are. I need you to help me read them now, tonight."

"Essays?"

"Yeah, he kept journals, but I haven't been able to bring myself to look at them until yesterday. See, Nate told me Dad had something to do with this. That's why he is out here. They think that maybe I'm connected by default."

"Was your dad an activist?"

"Certainly about the environment. But he had strong opinions on everything, you know. A few of his essays were published online. Could be that he got himself targeted because of it. But it's going to take a while to check through them. I need another set of eyes."

"Let's get started, then." You didn't have to join the dots with Caro. She was usually on the page ahead.

I got the journal from its hidey-hole in the air con and file-shared the essays to her tablet. We sat then, reading and eating and drinking until I could see fingers of daylight stretching across the floor through the bedroom window.

I'd dozed a couple of times and woke myself up falling sideways. Caro, though, never raised her head from the screen.

"This could be something," she said, rousing me from my current trance. "Make some coffee."

I got up and boiled the jug, dropping some bread in the toaster as well. When I carried it over and set it on the coffee table, she looked up and blinked.

"How can you concentrate like that? All night?" I asked.

"Practice," she said, munching. "You know I don't sleep much."

That was true. Her insomnia was one of the reasons we'd met at the psychiatrist's.

"What have you got?"

"Your dad missed his calling in life. Some of this is damn fine work."

I nodded. "Like I said… always an opinion."

"Not just opinion. Ideas that should be heard. This essay is about a common world mythology. Your dad sees it as an untapped power. He claims that working toward a common mythology is the only way to contain terrorism, anarchical acts and crime."

"Think I've heard him talk about that before. But a common world mythology, come on, Caro. Like that's ever going to happen. People kill each other over shoes."

She looked thoughtful. "He's not suggesting it's an overnight revolution. It's something that you do slowly, methodically."

"Do what, though?"

"Change belief systems. Like Stockholm Syndrome, except on a worldwide stage."

I shook my head. "Great theory, but I can't see any practical way of achieving it."

She shrugged. "Maybe you're right. But I've been thinking about the crow-and-circle tattoo a lot. In the Indigenous culture, the crow is a culture hero."

"What's that mean?"

"It's a legendary creature thought to have stolen fire for them. Having the crow inside a circle could be a symbol of containing or controlling the iconic crow, controlling the mythology. That's why your dad's essay resonated with me. It made sense."

I massaged my temples, trying to get my brain to process where she was going with this. "You think these people are here to take over our Indigenous culture."

"Well, as I said, it's a symbol. Essentially, yes, but it might extend to all Australian culture. As your dad says, control the mythology and you control the people. When you think about it, the media have been working that angle for years using communication saturation and manipulation. But what your dad's talking about is even more insidious."

It seemed a far-fetched concept, but I had too much respect for Caro to dismiss it out of hand. "How do you think this will help with locating Nate?"

"What did Kadee Matari say the talisman meant?"

"She didn't really say a lot other than it was a warning that different fringe factions had lent their mark to."

She tapped her tablet so that a note page opened. "Which factions?"

"Rastafarians, Indigenes, Coastal Romani, Vodun, Druze, Yoruba and Akan," I said, listing them off on my fingers.

"The guy you took it from… did you recognize him, his style, the clothes he wore…?"

I thought about it. "If I had to pick one of those groups, I'd say Romani."

"What about the guy you spoke with in Mystere?"

"Papa Brisé? He wasn't involved in signing the talisman."

"Interesting," she said. "Clearly, he's not seen as significant."

"He's a direct competitor for business and territory. They wouldn't spit on each other, he and Kadee Matari. So what are you suggesting?"

"Let's suppose that the factions whose signatures are on the talisman are *all* at risk from the Crow and Circle."

"Bull says they're called the Korax."

"Bull?"

"Long story."

She nodded, reining in her curiosity. "As I was saying… The Korax… It stands to reason that the Korax will be watching them. If we watch them too–"

"Stake out the stake-out?"

"Bad cop analogy, but yeah."

"It will take time."

"You got any better ideas?"

"Bull might."

"Or he might not."

I ate the last of my bread crust and put the plate down. "Let's get started, then."

"What do you know about the fringe groups marked on the talisman?"

"Less than you, I expect, but I do know someone with ties to the Coastal Romani."

"I wrote an article on the changing face of Rasta, so I've still got some contacts there," she said.

"That's only two."

"Hamish will help."

"Not until you tell me who he is, Caro. I mean, he ran over that guy like he was roadkill. Didn't even blink."

"Fine. I met him in East Africa– Burundi. He helped me out of a tight spot and I'm repaying the favour. He needed somewhere to lay low for a while."

"He's a mercenary?"

"Hamish believes in PE," she said. "Private Enterprise."

"Well, that's splitting hairs."

"As you do when you must. Hamish will watch Africans. It's a bit of a specialty of his."

"You mean he's already doing that anyway?"

"Let's just say he won't have to crane his neck." She tucked her tablet into her bag and stood to stretch.

"I'll text you if I find out anything," I said.

"Right." She headed for the door.

"And, Caro…"

She waved without turning back. "I know… *thanks.*"

"Actually, I need you to help me get past my bodyguards."

"The one in the corridor. That's easy. Wait ten minutes and go down the stairs."

The thought of going down the stairs in my current state of exhaustion was akin to being asked to climb *up* a mountain. "Thanks."

"See? I knew you had some gratitude tucked away in there." She laughed and shut the door behind her.

A soon as she left, I jumped in the shower to revive myself. Then into a grey shirt and jeans. Boots. Hair pulled back. The mirror reflected eyes that would have done a three-day-binge hangover proud, and some unattractively blotchy skin.

Find Sixkiller, I told myself, and you can get some sleep.

I called Leecey.

"'Lo?" She sounded sleepy.

"Did I wake you? You going to work?"

"Not today. Reduced hours, seeing as the park's shut."

"Great. Meet me at the Strellis Café on Parkway in a half hour."

"What f–"

I hung up. If nothing else, curiosity would get here there.

I slammed a cap down over my head, grabbed my kit and peered out the door. True to Caro's word, the coast was clear. I took the stairs and left by the laundry pickup exit.

Leecey was waiting for me at a table out on the street. Strellis Café was a tiny Toast and Tart café that struggled to compete with the large Beverage Club franchise down the road. I frequented it because it was close to the South sector tunnel entrance and because I had a thing for supporting indies. The owner, Bijou, had paid last year's rent on the proceeds of my regular hollandaise eggs, cheese muffin and Russian tea breakfasts.

It meant I always got quick service and an extra-large smile. For the months after Dad died, that smile was the best thing in my life.

"The usual, Virgin?"

"Two, please," I said, nodding at Leecey. "Breakfast's on me."

"That sounds ominous. What's up?" she said.

"Who runs the Coastal Romani?"

She frowned and picked up the salt shaker, suddenly finding it riveting. "Why do you want to know that?"

"Why I want to know would take me most of the day to explain. I don't need to meet them. I just need to watch them for a bit."

"Watch them?"

"Like a stake-out. Just see who comes and goes."

"They don't like to be followed."

"They won't know."

"I don't think that it's—"

"You said you wanted to help me, Leecey."

"And you told me to stay away."

I leaned back, hands wide. "Things change."

She turned the shaker a few more times, then set it down. "I owe you more than I can ever repay, Virgin, so of course I'll help you. But you gotta know, if they see us—"

"If they see *me*. Once you've shown me who, you're out of the picture."

Her lips pursed stubbornly. "I don't think so."

I saw her determination and sighed. "Fine. But we have to do this right away."

"Don't you mean after breakfast?"

I leaned back to let Bijou place a plate in front of me. The smell of the bacon sent a rush of saliva into my mouth. "Definitely after breakfast!"

She talked about the Park murder investigation and Detective Chance as we killed time on the Coast bus trip.

"She's gunning for you, Virgin," she said. "Been sniffing around Johnnie."

"She's been up to DreamWorks?"

Leecey nodded. "He won't say nothing to her, but he's not clean. It won't help the picture she's painting. And if he got busted…"

"Shit!"I closed my eyes. My brother tested every shred of patience I ever had and then some. But love was a funny thing. Forgiveness seemed to have no limits until it did.

"I've talked to him, Virgin. He knows what's going on. Hey – here's our stop."

I nodded, trying to shelve that worry for the moment.

We got off the bus and left the terminal to walk out onto a boulevard of restaurants, sarong booths and the ocean. A tin-pan band tinged and clanged on the boulevard, and balloon animals bobbed on sticks in the breeze. The sun was bright and I felt an unbidden rush of pleasure to see the water and inhale the salt in the air.

She hailed a taxi, which drove us down the boulevard a few klicks until we reached a huge water silo.

"We'll have to shanks it the rest of the way," said Leecey.

I paid the cabbie. "Show me."

After a couple of blocks on foot, we left the Esplanade to travel west, and I felt a pang of regret at losing sight of the water.

Within a couple more blocks, the retailers had dwindled off and the standard of rental housing had degraded to salt-bleached weatherboard cottages and dank, low salmon bricks.

Another two, and Leecey led me back toward the direction of the beach. Out here, washing was on lines, not in dryers, and gardens were tiny pockets of bead weed.

To the north of us lay a long strip of salt marsh, and in front, a tufts-of-brown-grass motor park.

"They live there?" I nodded at the box-shaped chalets in the Park.

"When they're not on the road," she said. "Been spending summer here for as long as I can remember."

"Who am I looking at?"

"Vandlo and Sabina Heron. Herons are old Rom. Came from England a hundred years ago. Good people but mistrustful and private."

"Nothing wrong with that," I said.

"I'll go and pay respects to the Herons and then visit with my stepmother. That'll give you time to see what you need."

"Keep an eye on your messages in case shit happens."

She gave me a thoughtful look and glanced at the bulge in my jacket. "Don't shoot any of my people, Virgin."

"Not my plan, Leecey."

She nodded. "See you in a coupla hours."

She left the cover of the salmon brick low-sets and hiked toward the front of the motor park, taking a dirt boundary road around to the front boom gate. Two young Romani males came out to greet her.

After a friendly exchange, I watched her thread her way between chalets to the centre of the park. Greyhound-thin dogs leapt up at her as she approached a cabin with a large annex. I couldn't see who spoke to her from underneath it, but she disappeared inside.

That gave me time to study the landscape around the park. It was almost midday now, and the sun bit its way through the sea breeze. The salt marsh baked beneath it, giving up glints of shifting water from time to time.

There was little cover among the low, succulent bush, so I turned my attention to the rows of residentials on the other two sides. No one was about on the streets. Cars sat parked in driveways like hot metal slugs, and noise was reduced to the flap of washing, the hum of air cons and some distant TV noise. Across in the motor park, though, there were shouts and the buzz of power drills.

I took binoculars from my backpack and scanned each and every house for anything unusual. One my first pass, I saw nothing but shoes left to shed sand on porches and towels hung across railings.

Where would they watch from, I wondered?

I scanned again and again until my arms began to ache and my eyes burned from squinting against the glass. I didn't dare get up and walk along, for fear of being recognized. If the Korax were here, they would likely know me.

I sank back onto my heels and called Caro.

She answered on the first ring. "Anything?"

"Not yet," I said. "You?"

"Rastas don't get up before 3pm. Couldn't be more dull. Where are you?"

"South of Cheyenne Beach."

"The salt marshes? Nice." Always one for sarcasm. "But listen. You have any problems, Hamish is just west of you. Call him. I'll send you his number. Remember to delete it when we're done."

"Sure," I said. "I'll check back in a while."

I hung up and got back onto my heels to do another scope.

Leecey had just emerged from the annex with a backward wave and walked down a row toward a smaller, pale blue van with yellow awning. A man called to her from across the way, and I held the glass on him for a moment. He looked like the guy in the alley, but I couldn't be sure. If Sixkiller were here, I could ask him...

A woman a few houses away left her front door, carrying canvas shopping bags.

I swung the glass to her as she climbed into her car and reversed from the driveway, disappearing up the street with the *zizz* of an electric motor. Pretty most all suburbans had their food home-delivered, but there was still the odd pilgrim ready to battle traffic and crowds for the retail experience.

Her real-time shopping trip left a clear view through to the driveway of the next house and a hunched figure hiding inside a child's plastic fort.

I rested the glass against the corner of the salmon brick and ratcheted up my magnification. It was definitely an adult male, not a child, wearing a singlet and shorts.

Now to get closer.

I counted the houses. Seven along. I ducked back down the side of the one I was at and skirted along the back. When I came to the correct house, I squatted down behind the vine growing along the back fence and thought what to do next.

I needed help for this, and it wasn't something I wanted to involve Leecey in. With only a faint sense of misgiving, I called Hamish's number.

"Yes." His voice was curt like I remembered it.

"It's Virgin. I need your help."

"You've made a sighting?"

"Yes."

Pause. "I've got a fix on you. Be there in thirty minutes."

"But how will–"

He hung up.

I spent twenty-five of those minutes maneuvering into a position to see the Korax guy better. That wasn't easy to manage considering the swing set, the pile of grass clippings and an upturned wheelbarrow that impaired my line of sight. I climbed the back fence and half buried myself in the grass. From there, I could see his back through the porthole in the kindy gym. Half of his tattoo showed along the singlet line.

"Better hope you don't suffer allergies," said a voice from behind me.

Hamish was crouched back at the fence, dressed in jeans and a dark shirt.

"Only way to keep an eye on him," I said, scratching my arms.

"We should get him moving. Go wait in my car." He pointed back down the lane. "Blue sedan. I figure the bike halfway along the next block is his. We'll follow when he runs."

"What do you mean, *when he runs*?"

He gave an odd smile that didn't connect with his eyes. "Just wait in the car."

I didn't much like being told what to do, but I *had* asked for his help, so I crawled out of the glass clippings and joined him behind the fence.

"Dust off first, though," he said, handing me the keys.

"He's in the child's cubby near the front driveway," I said.

He nodded. "Saw him on my first pass."

His first pass? I took the keys and headed off down the lane, shaking grass from my clothes.

By the time I'd climbed into the front seat, Hamish had disappeared. The inside was rental-car clean, although something told me this hadn't been hired through regular channels.

Curious, I opened the glove compartment to see if he'd left any identifying documents, but other than the car's spec chip, it was empty.

Hamish ripped the door open and was in the driver's seat before I could close it.

"What are you doing?" he said in a voice that froze me.

"Umm… just looking for… There!"

A figure jumped a fence in front of us and ran away from us.

He jumped in and pressed the ignition. The car eased quietly along the lane toward the intersecting street. Seconds later, a motorbike buzzed past, and Hamish accelerated with practised ease.

I remembered how he drove back to the Park Sector from the Million Mile – competent and fast. We hadn't spoken a word on the way home that night, and I found it hard to think of anything to say now.

He kept checking the rectangular unit attached to his steering wheel as we followed the bike at a distance.

"You put a tracker on his bike?"

He didn't answer. I realized then that Hamish wasn't one for restating the obvious, so I settled back and kept my mouth shut.

The bike's route took us directly back to the city and eventually onto the Ringway. I'd expected to be heading south towards Mystere or northeast to DreamWorks, not back into the heart of the Southern Sector business district.

We passed by Cloisters and the Parks Southern offices, heading further east to the light industrial area. Finally, Hamish pulled into a loading zone in front of a lighting warehouse.

"Here?" I asked.

He shook his head and nodded across the road. "According to this, he went right in there," he said, pointing to the security roller door in front of the undercroft parking.

"It's called Roscoes," I said, looking at the signage. I got out my phone and searched for them, but Hamish was ahead of me.

"Rigging company," he said, head bent over his tracking unit.

I glanced at him. "Does that thing make coffee, too?"

"New generation multipurpose defence mobile." He flicked his fingers across the screen a few more times.

While I was still waiting for my phone to download data, he gave a low whistle at what he'd read from his screen.

"What?"

"They contract exclusively to ComTel."

A cold feeling crept through my body. "But ComTel's our *national* communications company."

"Criminals come in all shades, Ranger, from all kinds of backgrounds."

"How... Where... The Marshal... How will we...?" I couldn't organize my thoughts to speak properly.

"I'd say you've got problems."

"I need to speak to Caro."

He nodded. "Agreed."

TWENTY-EIGHT

While Caro and I shared custard pie and strong coffee at her apartment, Hamish pored over his magic box.

Caro only had two chairs, so he sat on the floor, legs crossed, back ramrod-straight against the wall. I offered him food but he didn't seem to hear me.

"Hamish doesn't eat when he's thinking," said Caro. "Wish I was the same."

Seemingly unaware of our conversation, he stretched his neck from side to side and sprang to his feet. "I'll be back in a while."

"Hamish?" asked Caro.

He looked at me not her. "Wash that grass off and get some sleep. I'll be back to get you from your place."

"Pardon?"

"You want your guy out? Then I have to do some reconnaissance. I'll be back soon after dark."

"How do you know where t–"

But he'd gone.

Caro sighed and cut us both another piece of pie. "Don't ask me to explain him. I can't. But I do know I would have died in Burundi if he hadn't pulled me out of the crossfire."

"What happened?"

"You can imagine it. Lines change all the time in conflict. What's safe in the morning might be overtaken by your enemy in the afternoon. I made a mistake. He was in the area on 'other business' and caught my shortwave call. Next thing, I was being ridden out of the war zone on a two-stroke with no brakes and a flat tyre." She gave a little shudder. "Never been so terrified before, but Hamish–"

"He makes me nervous."

"When Hamish takes on a job, he finishes it. He's obsessive about closure."

"And Nate?"

"Finding Nate's his current job. Maybe you better go home and get some rest like he said."

I yawned. Last night's lack of sleep had caught up like a wall of falling bricks. "Can't think."

Caro put out a hand and pulled me up. "I'll walk you to the rank."

I ran the cabby's name and number on my SafeTravel app before I got in. He checked out, so I waved Caro goodbye, jumped into the back seat and closed my eyes.

He woke me to pay the fare, and I let him beep my One Card. The lift seemed to take a lifetime to get to my floor, and I was grateful that Heart wasn't there when I got to my apartment.

I fell on the bed fully clothed and flaked out like I'd been drugged. At some stage, I woke and saw Aquila on the bed's end. But then, it may have just been a dream.

Full clarity and a dry mouth came some time later. I rolled over and opened my eyes when the air conditioner made a *thunk*.

Hamish, not Aquila, was standing at the foot of my bed with the air con's remote in his hand. He wore black fatigues with deep pockets and a dark long-sleeved jersey.

"Crap!" I said, plucking at the sheet, even though I was dressed. "What are you doing in here?"

"Knocked a few times but you didn't hear. Had to let myself in."

I got up and grabbed my boots, walking past him into the living room. "What did you find?"

"Marshal's not there. But the guy we followed told me this."

I swallowed. "He t-told you? Just like that?"

"He knew it was the right thing to do," he said with a disturbing smile.

This man had a serious personality disorder. "A-and?"

"He didn't know where the Marshal was, only that he was being shifted out when the others arrived."

"Others arrived? What's that mean? And he didn't happen to say when that was, did he?"

That smile deepened as he reached into one of his pockets, pulled out his next-gen coffee maker/defence mobile and showed me a message on the screen. "Wrote it down to be sure."

I read the two words on the page.

Wet moon.

Some things clunked into place. The guy who'd been murdered in the park had said that. The Korax must be gaining illegal entry into the country through the park somehow, and I thought that I'd heard that. I grabbed my tablet from the coffee table and checked the lunar calendar online.

"The wet moon is tonight. We have to get to the park," I said.

His eyes narrowed. "What? Out in the open?"

I stared at him. "You're agoraphobic?"

"I deal in cities," he said. "Not open spaces."

I wanted to laugh but thought better of it. "Can you ride a horse?"

"If I have to," he said.

"Great. I'll explain my theory on the way."

"Uh-uh. No spaces."

"I… Oh…"

He put the next-gen away and retreated to the door. "Later."

"But, Hamish–"

The door shut before I could finish. I stood there confused and overwhelmed by apprehension. I was now on my own.

I could call Bull but I had no idea what he would do with the information, or if he'd even act upon it. Then there was Detective Chance, who was less likely to give credence to what I had to say and more inclined to use it as an excuse to me lock me up.

That left me with Caro and maybe Heart, neither of whom I was prepared to put in a risky situation.

The only solution I could think of had its own risks. But it was better than going after Sixkiller alone.

I did a contact search on my new phone and put a call through to Juno's Cantina in Mystere. "I need to get a message to Papa Brisé. Ask him to call Virgin Jackson on this number right away."

The guy on the other end sounded doubtful, but he took the message.

I went to the kitchen and opened a sachet of red beans and mixed some eggs. With a decent dollop of chilli, I turned it into a spicy omelette. A packet of crispbreads and a bottle of water completed the quick meal while I sat to wait and figure shit out.

I was seeing a story that went like this. The Korax – a fringe gang – had found an illegal way into the country through the park. If Sixkiller was right, then once here, they were using violent acts to distract from their real agenda – whatever that was. At a guess, they seemed to be making a move on the black market here. They didn't want Sixkiller or me interfering in that plan, and short of making me vanish, they'd taken him.

If the wet moon was the time they'd set for their next drop of people, then it was likely they might ship him and Kadee Matari out on that exchange. *If they haven't killed them already.* Sixkiller had already put a bullet in one of their own. What use would they have for keeping him alive?

I didn't have an answer to that, but I refused to believe that the Marshal was dead. I needed him to tell me more about Dad.

And I owed him.

My theory didn't allow any room for the whole Mythos and disincarnate side of the puzzle –other than Sixkiller's earlier observation that the lunar phase affected their opportunity to be here. But I couldn't go any further with that idea right now. It was simpler to deal in concretes.

My phone buzzed, so I put down the empty omelette plate and answered.

"Caro?"

"I just picked up something on the police band. They've matched your DNA on the park guy's body. They're sending a car to pick you up."

"This is such bullshit. Of course my DNA's on him. I touched him."

"I don't know the details, but you need to lay low. Is Hamish with you?"

"No."

"That's strange. Thought he'd taken a liking to you."

I raised my eyebrows, even though she couldn't see them. "That's terrifying."

"What do you want to do?"

I flipped through my options and made my decision quickly. "I can't let them take me into custody tonight. It might be my only chance to find Nate."

"How much time do you need?"

"A few hours."

"Meet me at Horners. I know a place you can wait."

Of course she did.

"And Ginny, hurry. There was a unit in your area when they called it through."

I ran to my bedroom, got my full kit bag with flashlight, knife and spare pistol, and pulled the journal dot from inside the air con vent in case the police decided to break in here and search.

A quick look outside my door revealed an empty corridor. Park security had obviously been pulled off me. I was surprised Bull hadn't called, demanding to know my whereabouts. Something else might have caught his attention.

I took the stairs through the laundry exit and walked two blocks south to a different taxi rank. Wait time in the queue look good, but I changed my mind, worrying they had an alert out on my One Card.

Where Caro wanted to meet me was only five blocks away, so I decided to take my chances and walk. Head down, I kept to the busier streets, trying to look as preoccupied and distant as everyone else going about their business.

A set of beat cops surprised me near the corner of Parkway and Palomino Street. I ducked into a chocolatier and stood trembling in front of the candied fruit until they passed.

Caro was waiting for me in a back booth at Hoofs and Horners. She got up straight away and gestured for me to follow her out the back. We left the bar through the kitchen restrooms, climbed some fire stairs and walked across a corrugated landing into an adjoining building. She pressed a sequence on the coded lock of a filthy wooden door and let us into a dark corridor and another landing. This building stank of fried onions.

Some more stairs and she opened a door in a dark corner near an industrial-strength air conditioning unit.

Inside the windowless room, there were some plastic chairs, a single portable bed, a sink and a cupboard. The wall above the sink was speckled with mould, and the room temperature was set at freezing.

I raised my eyebrows.

"Welcome to the glamour of a safe house."

"You still surprise me," I said.

"Sometimes, I have to give sources a place to stay while I'm interviewing them. Being next to the air con unit makes it hard to eavesdrop on."

I glanced around looking for signs of an inhabitant. "Hamish?"

"Hamish is somewhere else."

"You have more than one of these?"

She shrugged and ran her fingers through her blonde curls. Even in jeans, street boots and a canvas jacket, she looked sweet as angel pie.

"Best you don't know," she said.

On impulse, I hugged her.

She peered up at me from the embrace. Her head only reached my shoulder. "Ginny?"

"I'm OK. Just thanking you properly."

She grinned. "Noted."

My phone buzzed and I answered it.

"What you fuckeen want, Ranger?"

"Papa Brisé?"

Caro's eyes widened and I walked away from her to the sink.

"I have the answers to some of your questions, but I need your help tonight," I said.

"Why should I fuckeen help you?"

"I know where Kadee Matari is. You help me get her and the Marshal, and she's all yours. You can use the leverage however you want."

He breathed heavily into the receiver, digesting what I said. "The Crow and Circle have the Stoned Witch? I heard the fuckeen rumours she's been taken, but–"

"Yes. And I think they're shifting her out of the country tonight while they're bringing more people in. You've got a chance to get her and maybe take back control of your place."

He only paused for a breath or two. "What do you want?"

"You and a few of your people."

"Where?"

"The tunnel under 1029 Parkway entrance just after on dark. I'll meet you there."

"Parkway? In the city?"

"You know how to get here?" I asked.

"Don't get fuckeen cute, Ranger. It doesn't work for you."

He clicked off.

I turned to Caro and she stabbed her finger at the chairs.

"Take a load off. It's going to be another long night," she said.

We perched on the plastic chairs and she pulled two bottles of ginger ale and some flatbread from her backpack. The sugary drink settled my nerves, and the bread softened the knot in my stomach.

"So you really think ComTel is trafficking people in through the park?"

I shrugged. "Maybe not trafficking; maybe just allowing illegals in. ComTel operates the EM canopy above the park that prevents anyone gaining aerial entry."

"But if ComTel controls it…"

"Park Southern's technical department monitors it, but if their guardian programme was somehow compromised, then ComTel or someone in ComTel could do as they please. It would just mean paying off someone in Air Traffic Control to turn a blind eye."

"Seems risky."

"Maybe. But since the asylum seekers war, the government's poured so much money into border security along the coast, it's impossible to land illegally that way." I thought about Totes' complaint about anomalies in his system. "Anyway, I guess I'll find out tonight."

"Will this Papa Brisé come?"

"I don't know. Yes, I expect. Having Kadee Matari in his debt will be too tempting not to. They're locked in a turf war, and I think the Korax are agitating, making things worse."

"Ginny, maybe you should contact your boss."

"Bull?" I looked at her with surprise. "Why?"

"Hamish is AWOL and you're teaming up with some dead-set criminals to walk into a questionable situation. What if you're outnumbered? What if your allies decide to turn on you? How can you trust a man from Mystere called *Papa Brisé*?"

"I can trust him as much as the next person." Or as little – which was more my mantra. Caro shook her head. "There're too many unknowns. I don't like it."

"I appreciate the concern, but there must have been some unknowns in Burundi, Caro. It didn't stop you."

"I had Hamish," she said. "You don't."

There was a soft click and we both turned toward the door.

Hamish was standing there. "That would be incorrect."

TWENTY-NINE

"H-Haim? How did you f-find this place?" Caro stuttered.

"Followed the Ranger."

"How did you get in?" I asked.

"Now, that would be telling," he said, but he didn't look at me when he spoke.

He was dressed all in a dusty grey, the kind of colour that made you blend into a crowd. The long pack on his shoulders was strained into an odd shape that made me wonder what he had in there.

I glanced at the time on my phone. Totes should have gone home, and the stables would be unmanned. "I need to go."

Caro got up and collected the cans. "Look after her, Hamish."

He kept his gaze on her. "You might want a good alibi for the next few hours."

She nodded and gave me a hug. Twice in one day was some kind of record for us."If in doubt, bail! Hamish will get you out."

"I'll be fine."

She slapped Hamish on the shoulder as she left. "Wipe the keypad when you leave."

That left us alone and awkward.

I picked up my own pack and slung it around my shoulders. "Thought you didn't like open spaces," I said. "And horses."

He went to the door, ran a keycard scrubber through it, then wiped it down meticulously with a swab he pulled from a flat pack in one of his pockets.

"I don't," he said. "Let's go."

We walked to the Park Southern tunnel entrance. At least, I walked. Hamish was somewhere close by but I couldn't see him in the dinner time crowds.

When I reached the stairs down to the tunnel, I touched my security card to the gate. It slid open on silent rollers.

Hamish appeared from the shadows of the stairwell and strolled on through. I call it a stroll, but really, he was light on his feet and cautious.

After spending time with the Marshal, I'd become accustomed to a confident stride that reminded me of a ship cutting through waves. Hamish was more a cat on a hot tin roof.

He peered ahead into the tunnel and turned to me. "Now?"

"We wait for Papa Brisé."

"Who?"

"When I thought you weren't coming, I called in some help."

He nodded. "You wait. I'll look around."

"No... but... you won't be able to..."

He'd already gone, sprinting off.

I sighed and threw my hands in the air. What had Caro done, fixing me up with this guy? I checked my watch. The Wet Moon would rise in little over an hour, and I had no idea where in the park this exchange would occur. Dad had felt that Los Tribos was a focal spot, so I planned to go to the top of the butte and watch in that direction for changes in the skyline.

"Ranger?"

I glanced up from my troubled musings and saw Papa Brisé and the three guys that Sixkiller and I had encountered in Mystere with him. They were all wearing long coats despite the warm evening and glowering expressions.

"Do you... Have you...?" I faltered on asking outright if they were armed.

He nodded at his men and they opened their coats. Each one had a semiauto and belts of ammo strapped around their torsos.

I swallowed nervously. The sight of the hardware made my own pistols and knife feel kinda ridiculous. Had I lost my mind, bringing these men here? "Did you travel on the bus like that?"

Papa Brisé bared his teeth. "Express delivery. Like a pizza."

"We have to get out in the park and get a vantage point so we can spot the exchange."

Papa Brisé rolled his eyes. He was already sweating heavily. "How we gonna do that?"

"Horseback," I said.

"Fo' real?"

I nodded.

"You better deliver tonight, Ranger. Or I slit your fuckeen insides open for making me get on the back of a fuckeen live animal."

"They're well trained," I said. "They'll follow my horse's lead."

He licked his lips and gave me a lizardlike stare.

"There's one other thing," I said. "Someone else's helping me… us. He's dressed in grey, medium height, medium colouring and he'll appear from nowhere. Don't, you know, shoot him."

"I'm thinking you're going to be the only one I'm going to be fuckeen shooting tonight. But that's *after* I gut you."

I squared my shoulders against the ugly threat. "Come on, then. This way."

Every step we took along the tunnel and up the stairs into the stables entrance, I regretted what I'd done. I should have called the police. I should have called Bull. The Marshal wasn't my responsibility. Someone else could have dealt with it.

But no one else would have believed me.

No one.

I used my security card on the door and signalled for Papa Brisé to wait while I ran down the corridors and checked that the offices were empty. In Tote's hidey-hole, a thousand lights were blinking, but aside from the row of glassy-eyed dolls, I was the only one there to see them.

"Come in," I called back to my posse. "Pull the door shut. It'll lock behind you."

They made a strange procession along the corridors of the stables.

I planted them by the Interchange door while I saddled up five horses. It took some time, made worse by my sweat-slick fingers.

When I was done, I led Benny out first and stood her in front of the door. The others would follow her lead once we were outside, so I brought them up behind her.

The whole mounting and quick explanation of how to sit and hold reins went more smoothly than I expected. Papa Brisé had clearly ridden before, despite his surliness, and his three men weren't the kind to get nervous about much.

I had them assembled in front of the door, ready to mount, when Hamish did his usual appearing-from-nowhere trick.

Papa Brisé and his men all reached inside their coats and I jumped in front of Hamish, hands spread.

"Whoa. Steady. He's with us."

Their hands dropped away but their expressions remained suspicious.

I turned to Hamish and scooped up a set of reins to hand to him. The mare I'd kept for him was the most placid of the stable horses.

He gave me a strange look then took them from me and vaulted into the saddle.

"But I thought you…"

He silenced me with a look that suggested that he'd ridden before but something bad had happened along the way. His posture, hands and feet were all right, but his face was whiter than the fluorescent lights above us.

Sombre Vol whinnied to us, unhappy about being left behind. On impulse, I grabbed a bridle and brought him from the stall. The Marshal might need him.

He pranced around, disturbing the others as I mounted Benny. Sooner we were in the open, the better! I used my phone code to open the Interchange doors and led the not-even-a-little-bit-merry band into the park.

We grouped around the water trough, giving our eyes time to adapt to the moonlit darkness, setting up our headlamps.

"We're going to ride out past the windmill and up to the butte and watch the skyline from there. I'm guessing the exchange will be an aerial drop, and we'll have the best view from there. Once we starting riding up, it's best to stay in single file. I'm going to set the GPS on each mount to the same coordinates. They'll know where to go, so you just have to stay on board. Keep quiet on the ride. OK?"

If grunts were affirmations, I got four of them. Hamish said nothing.

I used my phone to set each horse's destination. We struck out then, bunched together for the first part of the journey across the plain.

Exhilaration beat my anxiety down for a bit. The air was rich with the scent of the old man banksia that grew along the Park walls and cooling desert sand. And the feel of the light breeze on my skin and Benny's familiar gait beneath me were a blessed meditation.

Sombre Vol nudged against her from time to time, upsetting my balance but not my brief return of equilibrium. His GPS chip had been removed in readiness to send him back to the trader, so I had to juggle his reins and keep him alongside me.

The trail ride up the side of the butte in the near dark was slow, and I heard Papa Brisé swearing under his breath. I glanced back constantly, counting the silhouettes and wondering how Hamish was faring at the back.

My phone started buzzing before we reached the top, but I couldn't risk taking it out to read it until we reached the summit.

Benny knew this path well and she paced herself on the steeper sections, giving a little whinny of satisfaction when we reached the top.

Papa Brisé and his men dismounted around me, and we stood on the plateau, gazing up at the night sky. I took their silent, solemn gazes to mean they were impressed and a little awed. That's how I felt looking out at the stars right now: humbled but scared and angry that it was being violated.

That anger came from my core, fuelled not just by my beliefs but by my dad's and the fact that it had somehow cost him his life.

My phone beeped a reminder that I had to check my messages. It was from Caro.

Bull has search parties out for you. Something's going on. Ditch your phone. Cops been here too.

"Crap!"

Hamish appeared next to me. "Cold feet, Ranger?"

"The Park agency is tracking my phone. And the cops are out looking to arrest me for murder," I whispered.

"Popular," he said.

"That's one word for it."

"Why did you jump in front of me back there in stables?" he asked.

"They were twitchy," I said, inclining my head toward the others. "Didn't want them... you know... shooting you."

He nodded slowly. "Don't ever do that again, you understand. I can take care of myself."

"You're welcome. Message received."

I turned my back on him and spoke to Papa Brisé and his men. "I'm going to have to lose my phone, which means I won't be able to set destinations for the horses. You're actually going to have to ride them."

The four of them glared back at me like they might be happy to end all my problems right now with a bullet or ten, so I tried for reassurance. "Look, they'll follow my horse out of habit, so just stay calm and it will be fine."

Papa Brisé spat on the ground. "Fuckeen women. Always changing the fuckeen story."

I cleared my throat and moved away a few steps before I said something I regretted.

"That went well," said Hamish in my ear again.

"Look, all I care about is getting the Marshal back."

"Sounds... intimate." he said.

I threw him a hostile stare. "No. But I owe him. And... he means well."

To my astonishment, Hamish chuckled. "Well, I wouldn't be wishing for that as a eulogy on my tombstone."

"I don't intend it to be on his, either."

"Well," said Hamish, his head tilted upward, "it looks like you're up."

I saw the flash as well, like a small burst of lightning high in the north-west sky. I got a compass bearing and ran it through the Park map on my phone. It was on a direct trajectory toward Los Tribos.

Dad was right.

A gust of wind brushed my face, and Aquila fluttered past to land on the ground between Hamish and me. Her grey and brown colouring rendered her almost a shadow in the moonlit dark, but her eyes had an eerie buttery glow.

"What are you staring at?" said Hamish.

I lifted my gaze from her and raised my voice. "That's it, fellahs… over to the west. Time to ride."

I reset the horses' GPS for the last time.

"Once we're on the flat, we'll have to move at speed. Try and relax in the saddle," I added.

"Fuck you," said Papa Brisé.

I took that as an affirmative, threw my new phone over the edge and sent Benny down the slope.

By the time Hamish, the last in line, hit flat ground, my stomach had begun to churn.

"Put out your lights and stay close," I said, urging Benny into a canter.

Our small posse rode into the west, the horses' hooves silenced by soft sand and the whip of the breeze. On instinct, the animals stayed bunched together under the moonlight, and I kept Sombre Vol to my right, away from the others. He pranced and pulled, anxious to be free of me, but I held tight to the reins and spoke soothingly to him.

As we rode closer towards Los Tribos, the darkness and the dip of the dunes were our cover. The sliver of lighting we'd seen high in the sky had transformed into a large gyro-drone with hooded landing lights.

We reined in and watched from a distance. The fingers of Los Tribos stood silhouetted against the lights, as if they were poised to cup the aircraft.

"Looks like army shit," said Papa Brisé.

"Not army," said Hamish, squinting through a night scope he'd produced from his bulky kit.

"What would you fuckeen know? And who the fuck are you, anyway?"

Hamish didn't reply, but he dismounted. "No markings on it, Ranger. We should walk the rest of the way."

He was right. Any closer and we risked being caught in the gyro's landing lights.

Left untethered, Benny and the others would stay together. Sombre Vol was my only concern. The horse was half wild still, but I couldn't tie him to Benny and risk them hurting each other if they got spooked.

I dismounted and let go of both sets of reins. The others followed my lead.

Benny sloped off a short distance, then settled into a resting pose, one foot lifted. The others gravitated towards her, but Vol gave a triumphant buck and galloped off in the direction we'd come.

"Damn." I went to pick up Benny's reins to remount.

"Leave the horse!" said Hamish in a quiet voice. "We stay behind that one," he said, pointing to the index finger of Los Tribos. "It's got the widest base. With no comms, we need to stay together."

I nodded. "OK. Fine."

Hamish unzipped his pack and in several quick, practiced movements, slotted together a small rifle of a kind I'd never seen. At least, I think that's what it was. Though it had the basic rifle shape, there didn't appear to be a trigger, only a switch, and the nozzle was wide like a miniature satellite dish.

His action attracted the attention of the Mystere guys. They watched intently as Hamish fitted a bulky, square battery onto the top of the weapon and slung the whole thing across his back.

He then produced a second rifle, similar to their own, but with a belt of tiny, caseless cartridges, which he wound around the butt. He positioned that across his back as well, then hit the ground and started crawling.

Something changed in the MY3 guys' attitude. Without bidding, Papa Brisé and the others slung their semiautos the same way.

I shifted my holster around to the small of my back as well and hit the sand next to Papa Brisé. "What're those rifles he's got?"

He turned his sweaty, sandy, tense face towards me. "Just do what the fuckeen man says, Ranger."

The man? Shit.

I squirrelled across gravelly sand after the others toward the solid rock protrusion. My pistols bumped against the small of my back, and sand got in my mouth and eyes.

I was the last to the rock. Hamish was already at one edge, with his scope glued to his eye. Papa Brisé had taken the other side, and his men sat in the middle with their backs to the rock, carefully blowing sand from their weapons.

Hamish beckoned me to his vantage point.

I had to lean in close to him to see, and he smelt of gun lube and particularly musky cologne.

"One gyro-drone, one cushion-bus, twelve bodies, five armed."

I cleared my throat over a dry spot. "A hover-bus?"

He handed me the scope. "See for yourself."

I took it and adjusted the lens until the people and objects sharpened into view. There seemed to be an exchange going on, alright: people transferring from the gyro to the bus. Well-dressed, everyday kind of people who would look comfortable in a suit. No gang tattoos, no singlets, no hardware. Not what I expected.

"It's one of our tourist buses doing the pickup. Can't see who's driving it, though."

The doors on the bus opened and two figures emerged. Kadee Matari was the first out, falling onto her knees in the sand.

I heard Papa Brisé swear under his breath.

The second figure stumbled but did not fall. I'd have known him without the scope, and a huge surge of relief flowed through me – Sixkiller was alive.

"He's there," I said.

With them off the bus, the dozen who'd been on the gyro climbed into the bus. "They're bussing them out now," I said. "I don't want a shoot-out. I just want the Marshal and Kadee Matari safe."

"Who?"

"There's a woman with him. She's… important." I inclined my head towards Papa Brisé.

Hamish made an impatient noise. "You never mentioned her before."

"I wasn't sure that she'd even be here."

"What did I tell you about fuckeen women?" muttered Papa Brisé.

I handed Hamish back the glass. "We should move in after the bus has left but before the gyro takes off."

"Not much margin for error," he said.

"The Marshal'll find a way to delay the drone if he has to. You call it. Leave it as long as you can so the bus is on its way. That will take two guards out of the equation." I looked across at Papa Brisé and the others. "You got that? Hamish calls it."

Quick curt nods.

"But the Stoned Witch is ours," said Papa Brisé.

"Yes," I said. "And the Marshal stays with me."

"Agreed."

I crawled across to where Papa Brisé crouched and handed him the spare phone in my pocket. "There's one number in here. It will get you Kadee Matari's people. They're waiting for the call."

He raised his eyebrows as he took it.

"Let's go," said Hamish.

We all got to our feet, ready to move.

Hamish kept the scope to his eyes, hand steady.

I couldn't see Aquila but she was close. I could feel her.

"Now!" whispered Hamish.

We emerged from behind the rock finger at a run. Or as close to as we could in the soft sand.

Sixkiller saw us first, because he shoved Kadee Matari in the back so she fell again. His action distracted the guards, and Hamish dropped one of them with a single shot. His partner fired twice; one zinged close by me, the other took one of Papa Brisé's men in the shoulder.

The MY3 gangster lordlet out a roar of fury and sprayed the shooter and the drone with semiauto fire.

The gyro lifted almost immediately and set off a volley of return shots from auto-cannons mounted above the skids.

We all dove facefirst into the sand, except Hamish, who fell and rolled.

As the gyro hurtled toward us, nose dipped, cannons set to obliteration, he clicked the battery into a locking position and pressed the switch.

The gyro's rotors slowed, all the lights dimmed and it sank like a stone.

The impact made a *whoof* sound like a huge wave crashing on the beach, and sand pelted us with the sting of thousands of tiny bullets.

When I dared to look up, I saw a crater had formed in front of us with the gyro half buried at the bottom.

Papa Brisé and his men were all alive, bodies caked in sand like me. But Hamish was upright and already advancing, having switched to carrying his assault rifle.

He climbed aboard the gyro and disappeared inside.

I saw Aquila then as well, on the tip of one of the skids, preening her feathers in an unconcerned manner.

Thanks for the warning, I thought at her with heavy sarcasm.

But her head never lifted from her delicate task.

"Virgin," called a hoarse voice.

The Marshal was kneeling on the opposite bank of the sand crater with his hand pressed to Kadee Matari's side. She looked small and fragile beside him, and she wasn't moving.

"Is she alright?" I called back.

"Gunshot. Needs medical."

I glanced at Papa Brisé. "I'll find the horses and get my kit. Best we get out of here, in case the noise registered with the Park surveillance – or the people on the bus."

"What is this Godforsaken fuckeen place? Sand and shit and more fuckeen sand," he groaned, dusting himself down. He signalled his two uninjured men. "Bring the Stoned Witch."

"What about medical help?"

"We use our own people."

I remembered the mute girl and nodded. "Fine. Just make sure you let her people know you've got her. I want them off my back."

"Don' you fuckeen worry, Ranger" – he patted the phone in his pocket – "I will."

He got up and watched his men struggle across the crater, past the disabled gyro, toward the collapsed body.

I motioned Sixkiller to let them take her, and I started back past the rock finger toward where we'd left the horses.

They hadn't strayed far, despite the gunshots, and Benny came on my whistle. The others ambled after her, and I collected all their reins.

I petted her and hugged her nose. "Clever girl."

As I led them back, Sixkiller met me near the base of the rock finger we'd hidden behind.

"You figured it out," he said quietly.

"Some of it. Enough to work out they were trafficking through the park. But that was more thanks to my dad's journal."

I think he smiled at me, but it was darker in the shadow of the rock and hard to tell.

"Thank you for coming."

No mistaking the emotion in his voice, though.

"I think I owed you," I said awkwardly. "Are you… whole?"

"Hungry, pissed, but whole. I won't forget you did this, Virgin. Though I was expecting the cavalry."

"Bull had a plan. But mine was quicker."

He glanced back in the direction of the fallen gyro. "Pretty glad about that."

"Do you know where they were taking you?"

"No. But I recognized the driver."

"Oh?"

"He was talking to your friend Corah at the reopening of the restaurant."

"Corah?"

He drew in a breath that sounded like a disappointed sigh. "Yeah."

"I think we've got some probably got some more sharing to do, Marshal, when we get a moment."

A nod and no protest.

I handed him Benny's lead and lowered my voice. "There was nothing supernatural going on, though. Just some criminals breaking the law."

His gaze strayed to the sky and the horizon. "Right."

"You'll have to double with me on the ride back. I brought Vol for you, but he bolted when I had to leave them untethered."

"Figures. Who took out the gyro with the pulse rifle?"

"You'll meet him soon." I glanced around and then back at the horses. I was one mount short – the mare that Hamish had been riding. "Or not."

"Not easy to come by. Illegal in most places because they wreak havoc."

"That sounds like him."

"Ranger!" called Papa Brisé. "Come and stop this bitch from fuckeen bleeding all over me."

I grabbed my kit bag off Benny. "Come on. Let's get moving."

I sprayed glue on Kadee Matari's wound and it sealed almost immediately. She didn't regain consciousness, though, as we passed her up to Papa Brisé on his horse. He held her slight body surprisingly gently while he waited for us to mount.

I ministered quickly to his injured man's wound as well and stuck him with a pain-quill. Hard to say how serious it was, being the shoulder. I wasn't sure where the bullet had lodged, only that it was hurting the guy like hell.

He nodded gratefully as the pain-quill took effect and I held his horse's head for him and gave him my knee to get up.

I hit the saddle next. Then Sixkiller. His long body cupped around mine, his legs dangling, toes kicking at my heels. I hadn't doubled with anyone on a horse since I was a kid. It wasn't much the same as my memory.

We struck out toward the south on my dead reckoning, using the distant outline of the butte and the lay of Los Tribos as my bearings.

The silence was only broken by the snuffle of the horses and the occasional moans from Papa Brisé's injured man.

Sixkiller's body was warm and sticky against mine, but he didn't bother me with questions or conversation. Both of us were too exhausted. At one stage, he sagged heavily against me, his head knocking on my shoulder.

I lifted my elbow into his ribs to wake him up, and it didn't happen again.

Aquila seemed to have vanished once more, and I pondered her apparent indifference at the events that had just unfolded. It was as if she had turned up to sightsee, not to warn me.

When the dunes finally intersected a clay-packed road, I knew we were only about ten kays from the Interchange. I heaved a silent sigh of relief as Benny's feet contacted harder ground. She lifted her head, knowing home was close. Even with her augmentations, Sixkiller and I were a heavy load.

Dawn was nearly on us too, and I could see better. The windmill and pump house came into sight first. Then the ring of palm tree silhouettes. I turned Benny and did a loop of our posse.

Still no sign of Hamish.

I wasn't sure whether that was a problem or not but decided to deal with immediate issues.

"Soon as we get to the Interchange, you get out of here, get her fixed up. I'll have to stable the horses first. You know the way out," I said, trotting up alongside Papa Brisé, who cradled Kadee Matari in his arms. She looked asleep, not unconscious.

"Hope you got remembered the fuckeen door key, Ranger?"

"Opens with a movement sensor," I said.

"Not gonna have to ask me twice," he said through tight lips. "Godforsaken fuckeen place."

I nudged Benny back to the lead. She could smell the water trough on the other side of the palms, and her gait quickened.

As we drew even with the windmill and pump house, the weight on my chest lifted. *Made it!*

Then Sixkiller leaned close and whispered in my ear. "In the palms. Ten o'clock."

In the grainy dawn, my senses seemed sharpened. I saw a huge, shaggy bison standing there, head raised as if sniffing the air.

Ohitika. Shit.

Then Aquila soared down from the sky, squealing at me without warning.

"I think we'd better–" I began but never finished.

A volley of shots from the palms near the bison took one of the MY3 guys clean off his horse.

Sixkiller slid straight down off Benny's back, pulling me with him.

"Fuckeen fuckeen fuck!" shouted Papa Brisé as he flopped to the ground with Kadee Matari tucked under his arm.

We all scrambled for the cover of the windmill's pump house. Papa Brisé's men dragged their fallen friend with them. I couldn't see if he was alive, because I'd already stretched out flat around one side and begun firing.

Return fire came from different spots west along the tree line, a half dozen of them at least.

Where had they come from? The bus entry, I guessed.

Papa Brisé and his men peeled off some rounds, which peppered the palms but only caused the attack on us to intensify.

"We have to get to the Interchange or we're dead," said Sixkiller as he crawled alongside me. "And then there's that," he said, looking up.

I followed his upward glance. The sun had burst over the horizon, and the daylight revealed a swooping figure that spiked my adrenalin even higher. The crow from the station house.

"It's coming for us," I said.

"And so are they," he said.

A cloud of movement lifted from the palm trees, and a murder of smaller crows streamed in our direction.

My throat closed over and my guts liquefied.

I just kept firing at the trees and watching the birds approach.

"Virgin," said Sixkiller. "Something you should know…"

Not now, Nate.

"I'm–"

But I never heard him, or he didn't say it.

Another ear-splitting squeal from Aquila drew my attention back to the sky. She was flying straight at the giant Mythos.

No. NO!

A moment later, she crashed violently into its side, knocking it off its trajectory toward us. The impact sent her plummeting to the ground in a shriek of pain. The Mythos fell away too, descending with more control but slowly, like it was injured.

I started to get up, but the Marshal hauled me down again. "You can't help her."

He rolled on top of me then, pressing me down into the dirt as the crows swarmed us.

"Get off!" I shouted, fighting to get out from under him.

But he clamped his hands on my shoulders even harder. "Stay still," he hissed. "They won't hurt me as much."

I lay rigid and helpless as he writhed under the assault of their beaks and claws. Aquila was on the ground a short distance away, lifeless. The Mythos had landed not far from her, fluttering but able to fly, as though its wing was damaged.

"Fuckeen go!" I heard Papa Brisé shout.

Where? I tried to raise my head a fraction.

Papa Brisé was up and running toward the gap in the palm trees, carrying Kadee Matari over his shoulder. His men scrambled after him, two of them carrying the third between them. When they didn't fall before a hail of bullets, I realized that the gunfire had changed direction.

I scanned both ways and spotted Hamish farther west but in a line with us, causing a heavily armed distraction from behind some kind of inflatable, projectile-proof barrier.

"Nate! We have to go now! Look!"

"Can't," he groaned.

He began to spasm from the buffeting, and he rolled off me a little, leaving my right arm exposed.

The crows pecked and tore at it, and I snatched it back underneath my body and whistled for Benny.

"Vir… gin…" Sixkiller whispered.

His blood was all over me, my neck, my cheek. Slippery and pungent and warm.

"You said they wouldn't hurt you badly," I cried.

"Too… many… of… them," he said.

Then his body went limp.

"Benny!" I roared. "Come!"

She galloped up, eyes wild.

I twisted and shoved Sixkiller off me. Then I grabbed his arm. "Get up! Get up!"

The crows swarmed me and I batted and slammed at them while trying to get him up into the saddle.

My eyes blurred over with blood that might have been his or mine. Deep, knifelike stabs pierced my body, and I began to feel weak. I formed a picture of Sixkiller's disincarnate in my mind.

Ohitika! Help him! Please!

An enraged bellow rang in my ears. Thundering hooves shook the ground.

The stinging stabs and slicing claws stopped abruptly as, in one cawing unison, the crows left us and converged on the shaggy bison charging our way.

"Now!" I said, pushing. "Get up!"

He flopped awkwardly across the saddle, and I grabbed the pommel to help me mount, but I didn't have the strength.

Instead, I leaned on her neck and whispered, "Home" in her ears.

She snorted and half reared but took off when I slapped her rump.

I managed to stay standing long enough to watch her make it through the gap. Then everything seemed to fade.

A dim awareness stayed with me, the kind you have when you're just waking or just falling asleep.

The gunfire seemed to reach a crescendo and then a lull.

A voice penetrated my haze. "Fuck, what happened to you?"

I blinked a few times and concentrated hard. Hamish's face snapped into focus.

"I... In the–"

"Save it!" he said. "Take this."

He pushed something under my tongue, and instant life poured into my veins. I sat up and looked around. We were still behind the pump house. The gunfire had stopped, and I heard shouts in the distance.

"Can you ride?" he asked.

"Yes. I don't know. If I have to."

"Good girl."

He helped me to my feet. Daylight had arrived properly, and beyond the windmill, near the gap in the palm trees, I saw a bunch of figures in vests holding weapons.

"Who are they?" I whispered.

"Feds," he said. "Someone made a call."

"Who?"

"I don't know, but it was timely. I couldn't have held them off much longer. You must have someone watching over you."

"How did you... Where did you... that shield... ?"Questions piled up on my tongue and got stuck.

"Another time," he said. "You're a mess. I'm going to put you up on this nag and send you in their direction. It's safe enough now they've taken your ambushers into custody."

"But you–"

"I'm heading elsewhere. Been interesting knowing you, Ranger. Go get patched up."

With that, he gave me a leg up onto the back of a horse that pranced and gave a small buck, nearly unseating me straight away.

Vol! "Where did you find him?"

"He found me. Even the wild ones come home in the end," said Hamish with a meaningful wink. He put three fingers to his forehead in a brief salute and let go of the bridle.

The horse didn't wait for my signal; he just leapt straight ahead toward the Interchange. I managed one glance back over my shoulder and saw Hamish on the mare, heading out into the park again.

Where he was going, I had no idea, but Hamish could look after himself. The park was still likely in breach. If there was a way out that he wouldn't be seen, he'd find it. Or maybe he'd lay low until things had settled. No doubt his kit bag contained survival food as well.

I looked ahead and concentrated on staying on Sombre Vol as she galloped towards the palms.

Armed men challenged us from all directions as we reached the gap, but the horse wasn't stopping. It charged right on up to the water trough with me clinging to the pommel and his mane.

When he stopped and sank his nose into the water, I slipped to the ground, legs trembling.

The point of a rifle pressed into my neck. I looked up and saw a ring of Feds around me in bulky, dark uniforms and combat helmets.

One of them hauled me upright and stripped me of my knife and my empty pistol.

"Throw her in with the rest," ordered the guy with the gun against my flesh.

The way parted for us and I saw some vehicles. One was a distance away, over toward the tourist entry – it was the air-bus that had been at Los Tribos. Two others were parked closer to the Interchange door: a medics' van with Benny standing hoof up right next to it, and the other a large military paddy wagon full of the illegal immigrant detainees.

That's where we seemed to be headed. I was about to be put in a tiny space with the people who'd been trying to kill me.

"No!" I shouted. "Let go me. I'm the Park ranger!"

Their grip tightened as I started to wriggle, and I panicked. I kicked one of them high and hard in the stomach and ripped my arm from his fingers. I swung my fist at the other one and connected with his visor. My fingers cracked, sending an electrifying pain up my arm.

As I recoiled, the visor guard grabbed me by both shoulders, and the guy I'd kicked came back at me with a stomach punch that sent me doubling over.

The taste of something hot washed the back of my throat and I threw up on both of them.

"Crap. Toss her in the bin!" one said to the other.

But as they thrust me towards the paddy wagon, someone behind us yelled, "Stop!"

They both snapped to attention, their grips loosening.

"Yes, sir," they said in unison.

"Let her go." The voice was firm and commanding and shockingly familiar.

They did as he bid and I fell in a heap and lay there, grateful just to be still. My fingers throbbed and my skin felt like a war zone.

"Ranger?" said the same voice – this time softer and closer.

I lifted my face, aware that I was coated in blood and vomit.

The man who knelt in front of me wore civvies – jeans and shirt – but a badge hung around his neck, and he had a pistol holstered on his waist. Sweat stood out on his forehead, which I found odd, because I was feeling so cold.

"For chrissakes," I whispered with feeling. "Heart?"

THIRTY

My lover – the Federal agent – helped me up.

"You're–"

"Undercover," he said. "Now walk."

With his help, I limped slowly to the medics' van. It took a painstaking effort to reach the open door and the waiting medic who helped me onto a stretcher. The bed's pneumatics hissed and it lifted and slid in alongside another body. Sixkiller.

"Take care of her," said Heart. "I'll be back soon."

The door shut on us and I turned my head. The Marshal was a mess of bloody cuts, and his clothes hung from him in strips. He appeared to be asleep.

"Is he alright?" I asked.

"Sedated," said the medic as she hooked me up to a drip. "What happened to you two? Looks like someone shoved you in a shredder."

"Knife attacks. There were a… lot of them."

"Strange-shaped knives," she commented as she peeled away my shirt.

"Strange people," I said. "Foreigners."

It was the best I could come up with.

She sprayed my skin first with antiseptic and

anaesthetic, then pasted some glue on the deeper cuts.
Then she put an inflatable glove on my hand to support
my cracked fingers.

I watched the drip flowing into my veins while she
worked and felt the cold sensation at the entry point
on my wrist. The bleeding eased with her attentions
and, probably, thanks to me still being full of Sixkiller's
blood. I wondered if my transfusion had left him
vulnerable in this attack.

"You'll live. But the scarring might be bad and the
hand will hurt for a while," she said as she produced a
patient's tunic. "You sure it was a knife that cut you? It
looks more like… I don't know, but the cuts are jagged.
Little rips."

"Maybe the knives were serrated?"

"So many of them. Like torture."

"That's how it felt." I grimaced as I slipped my arms
through the sleeves. Though the anaesthetic had dulled
the pain to bearable when I was still, when I moved, it
was a whole different matter.

There was a knock on the door.

"That'll be the agent," she said. "I'll be outside
checking the horse."

"Her name is Benny. And thanks."

She smiled and climbed out, leaving Heart to take
her spot.

He pulled the door closed again for privacy.

"He sedated?" he asked of Sixkiller.

"Yeah. But she thinks he'll be fine." The medic had
wiped my face clean of vomit and blood, but I could
smell it all over me.

Unexpectedly, Heart leaned forward and kissed me.

"Well, shit," I said as he drew back. "You've got some explaining to do."

His expression turned sheepish. "And you don't?"

"Feds first," I said.

He flushed. "I've been undercover for a few years. I can't disclose the details of the case, but more recently, it involved you."

"So you've been sleeping with me as part of your job?" I wasn't angry as much as stunned.

He hesitated. "I won't insult you by saying that it started out that way and I fell in love. But the truth is that... I really do like you, Virgin, and it seemed... useful."

"*Useful?*" I exclaimed. "Jeez, flatter a girl to death, why don't you, you ignorant arse?"

Now I was angry.

He seemed to take the insult in stride. If I'd been in decent shape, I would probably have punched him in the teeth.

"We're going to need to interview you properly as soon as you're recovered. We found some saddled horses running free. Were there other people with you out there? What happened?" he asked.

I stared blankly at him, not prepared to give up a damn thing to a Fed. "Just me. I got a lead that the park's Canopy had been compromised after the Marshal was kidnapped, so I came to check it out."

"By yourself?"

"That's my style."

"I suppose it is," he said thoughtfully.

"I brought an extra horse for Nate."

"And?"

"Saw a flash-bang over at a place called Los Tribos. Went to look and saw a gyro landing there and offloading a bunch of people. It got messy; I got the Marshal out while they were arguing amongst themselves. By the time we made it back here, we rode into an ambush."

"Sounds like you're making it up as you go, Virgin."

"The story… no… My life… yeah, pretty much."

That answer irritated him. "Who tipped you off?"

"Tell me who told you to come looking for me here and I'll tell you my source."

He vacillated a moment, then said, "Totes had put a recorder in the eyes of the Virgin doll."

"Totes works for you?"

"Let's just say he's on loan."

"I'll give him fucking lo–"

The door flung open right then and Detective Indira Chance stood before us in the opening, hands on hips. She was flanked by two officers; both had their service pistols drawn.

"Virgin Jackson, you're under arrest for the murder of–"

"But–" I started to say.

"She's under our jurisdiction," interceded Heart holding his badge out. "You can't arrest her. Federal takes precedence."

"Not over a murder charge, Agent. Now please get out of our way."

"But–" I started again.

"Stand down, Detective!" said Heart. He got out and stood next to her, his expression bullish as hers. "We'll clear this up with you through the correct channels, but the Ranger is mine."

"You could be wrong there, *Agent*," said another voice from behind them both.

Bull Hunt shouldered his way past Chance's coppers to stand between Heart and her.

He showed both of them a card. "Call your superiors now and authenticate it."

Heart swore softly and Detective Chance looked plain pissed. The pair of them turned away from Bull to make their calls. Heart had an earpiece in, but Chance had to pull out her phone and dial up.

Bull took the opportunity to look me up and down. "Blazing bluebells, Virgin. You been chewed up and spat out by a piranha?"

"Not so much as him," I said, inclining my head toward the sedated Marshal.

Bull stared at Sixkiller, speechless for a moment.

"He saved me from a... knife attack. But he'll be OK," I said.

"He'd better be or so help me, I'll–"

Chance hung up and turned back to us with a hard look. "I'm leaving your case file open, Ranger. I'll get you for this one way or the other." With that, she jerked her head for her constables to follow her, and she strode away.

That left Heart. His expression when he faced us was deeply troubled. "I'll be seeing you, Virgin."

"I don't think so," I said.

He looked at Bull. "Please watch out for her, sir."

Hunt grunted. "Virgin can look after herself."

I stared at Bull in amazement.

Heart hesitated, then walked away from us.

"I never liked him," said Bull.

"You never met him before. Did you have him checked out like you said you would?"

"Still waiting for the report to land in my inbox."

"Well," I said. "You can probably delete it now."

Bull laughed.

I watched Heart disappear into a group of police, and a few moments later, he was obscured by the air-bus passing us with an armed escort.

I thought for a second that I saw Hamish on board, but then it was gone, and I figured I was wrong.

My boss held out his hand. "Can you walk?"

"Slowly," I said.

"It's not too far."

"What isn't?" I asked.

"This." He helped me down and we walked around the side of the van past Benny, who whinnied and nuzzled my hand.

I kissed her cheek and followed Bull to the rear, where a military-grade tip-jet sat, giving off a low humming sound.

"What the hell is that? Sounds like it's going to explode," I asked.

"Protection field," he explained. "Wait."

We stood there as a battle-ready soldier approached us. He stopped a few arm's-lengths away and spoke into a pickup on the side of his helmet. The humming stopped and he beckoned us forward.

As soon as we'd stepped over the invisible threshold, the humming started up again. I felt my body hair stand on end.

"Bull! Are you going to tell me what's going on?"

He offered me his arm to climb onto the tip-jet's skid

and into the open doorway. "Actually, Virgin, I'm not coming. And I just want you to know... I would have told you before, but I promised him."

He gave me a gentle push, which gained momentum because the soldier pulled me.

Inside, was a suite of seats facing each other as cosy as someone's lounge room. When the door slid shut, all other sound cancelled out. I'd been in gyros before but never a tip-jet that was soundproof.

An older woman sat in one of the seats, her legs and arms crossed.

"Hello, Ms Jackson. Please call me Oceane," the woman said in a North American accent.

The soldier helped me into a seat opposite her.

"Ranger Jackson, meet Commander Oceane Orlean of the GJIC," he said. Then he added, "The Global Joint Intelligence Community."

I took that in. And her. She was in her fifties at least, maybe older, and there was energy in her strong face. I'd heard of GJIC, or *Gee-Jic* in the vernacular, via the odd news item or policy document, but mainly from Caro's reverent whispers about who had sway in today's world.

Gee-Jic, according to Caro, was the real deal in global power.

"Oceane," I said suddenly. "That's an unusual name. I've only heard it once before, and that was..." I tapered off.

"Yes, Virgin," she said finally, watching me with keen eyes. "I'm your mother."

THIRTY-ONE

"My mother doesn't exist."

It sounded crazy when I said it, but that's how I'd always figured it. Dad had never said she was dead, but he'd never said she wasn't. He just said things didn't work out very early on and that they'd made the decision that I would be best off with him.

If I ever thought about it, I imagined her as a restless entertainer on the club scene. Someone in counterpoint to him. Someone who found his loner ways and deep convictions attractive but hard to live with forever.

It'd never seemed relevant to ask him for details. I didn't miss what I'd never had. Most of my friends came from fractured or single-parent families; it was no big deal.

But this. *This!*

She blanched a little at my reply and recovered herself. "I didn't expect to meet you under these circumstances, and I don't have much time. So, if you could afford me your patience while I explain some things, I'll let you get back to your life."

I was so dumbstruck by how cool she was that I nodded mutely.

As she began to talk, I felt the rush as the tip-jet lifted into the air.

"Please don't be alarmed. We are taking you home. But before we land, I'd like you to know some things."

"That would be a change," I said.

She allowed a tight, small smile, then went on. "For some time, my organisation has been aware that there is a well-planned takeover being orchestrated on many fringe religious groups by an extremely dangerous criminal cluster."

I waited.

"In the past few years, this group has broadened their MO to subvert different professions as well. From an early assessment of our arrests here today, the group that you discovered arriving illegally through the park were intended to infiltrate the highest levels of politics and industry. You are to be commended for your efforts in catching them at it. You are also to be chastised for turning a God-given opportunity into a shitstorm."

I blinked, feeling like a child being told off by her... *mother.* "This group is the Korax?"

"That's where our conversation becomes delicate." She nodded to the soldier, who walked down the short aisle and disappeared into what I assumed was the cockpit.

"Has the Marshal spoken to you about the Mythos?" *Really?* "A little."

"The concept is unbelievable, I know. But I'm here to tell you, Virgin, that they exist. You know that. Look at you. I myself have been a victim."

She pulled her shirt free from her waistband and showed me a scar almost identical to the one on my shoulder, though silvered with age.

"The Mythos have a plan and they are executing it," she said. "In as little as a decade, we could lose our world to them."

Her pause felt heavy as she chose her next words carefully.

"Your father had a theory, among many, that if someone was able to unify human mythology, get everyone to believe the same stories, drink from the same cup, if you will, then they would have the ultimate tool of manipulation. He always said that the media had been blundering about in a similar scenario for years but that they were neither cohesive nor cognitive enough to truly achieve it."

"I've read his essay."

"Your father was a clever, clever man, Virgin, but he was limited by his dogmas. Unfortunately, his essay found its way to the wrong people, and now, we fear, the Mythos are now trying to accomplish the very thing he predicted."

"The Mythos are aliens?"

Another smile, this one wearily patronising. "Aliens we could deal with. No, the Mythos are something else."

"You can't explain it better than that?"

"You've seen them, Virgin. How would you describe them?"

I couldn't, so I asked another question. "Why am I here?"

"The Marshal has identified you as someone who can help us to manage our impending situation."

"He's working for you?"

"Yes."

"And now you're recruiting me?"

"Yes. That's why the police are no longer going to arrest you for various crimes."

"But I didn't kill the guy in the park."

"It looks like you did. If I withdraw my protection from you, you will likely go to jail. So what do you say?"

I stared out the windows. Though they were tinted, I saw the familiar outline of the Cloisters and felt the thump as the tip-jet made contact with the top of the building.

"I'd like to go home."

I thought she might protest or blackmail me some more, but she just nodded. "We'll be in touch."

The soldier reappeared and opened the drone's sliding door.

I climbed out onto the terrace and left my mother, her bodyguard and her billion-dollar aircraft without a backward glance.

THIRTY-TWO

Caro was waiting outside my door, engrossed in her phone screen. She glanced up when the lift pinged open, and her mouth dropped open.

Hi,' I said.

"Hey, I got a call from the Feds saying you needed me. They didn't say I should bring a plastic surgeon."

The Feds? On this day, nothing would surprise me. I opened up the door with my good hand.

Caro followed me in.

I went straight to the Virgin doll on the sideboard, pinched the eyes out of it and dropped them and the doll down the laundry chute. When I returned, she was sitting cross-legged on the couch, staring down at John Flat.

"I'm growing fond of him," she said.

I got a six-pack of beers from the fridge, carefully broke a couple of longnecks out of the cardboard holder and passed one to her.

We both took long, belch-inducing swigs.

"Well?" she said.

I took a breath. "Here's the thing: I could be mistaken for a bowl of chow mein and the Marshal's in hospital looking worse than me, it turns out my stripper boyfriend's a federal agent, my technician's a narc, the cops have dropped the murder charges for the time being – but only if I work for my bastardly mother who I just met and happens to be the Commander of the GJIC.

"On the bright side," I added, "Hamish is a complete legend."

Her eyes went wide for a moment, then she lifted her beer.

"I knew I could smell a story, Ginny," she said.

I raised my beer as well and clinked hers. "Well, Caro, I'll drink to that!"

ACKNOWLEDGMENTS

Thanks to Tara Wynne for accepting whichever direction I take in my writing, and making it work for me.

To the Escape Club crew – almost three years together and still going strong.

Amy Parker, my English daughter, for the first read.

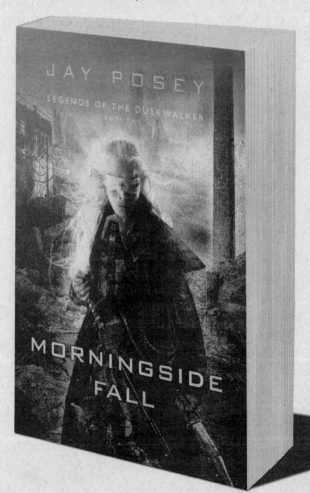

JAY POSEY

LEGENDS OF THE DUSKWALKER
BOOK TWO

MORNINGSIDE FALL

The ultimate divine comedy.

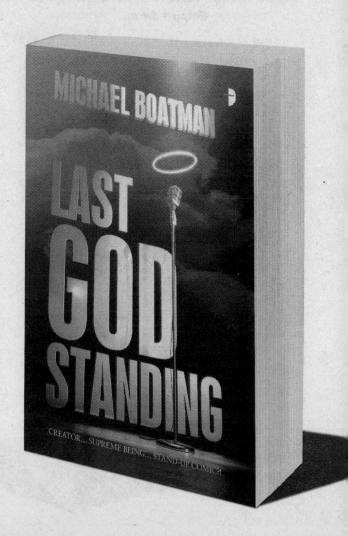

MICHAEL BOATMAN

LAST GOD STANDING

CREATOR… SUPREME BEING… STAND-UP COMIC?!

Gods and monsters roam the streets in this superior urban fantasy from the author of *Empire State*.

HANG WIRE

ADAM CHRISTOPHER

AN URBAN FANTASY FROM THE AUTHOR OF

EMPIRE STATE | SEVEN WONDERS | THE AGE ATOMIC

BUY STUFF, LOOK COOL, BE HAPPY

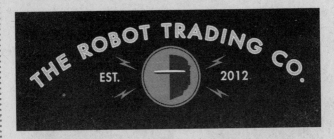

Never miss an Angry Robot or Strange Chemistry title again. Simply go to our website, and sign up for an **Ebook Subscription**. Every month we'll beam our latest books directly into your cerebral cortex* for you to enjoy. Hell, yeah!

READER'S VOICE: *Gee, that sure is swell. I wish other publishers were that cool.*

SHADOWY ANGRY ROBOT SPOKESTHING: *So do we, my friend, so do we.*

Go here: | **robottradingcompany.com** |

* or your Inbox, if that is more convenient for your puny human needs.